Lady Suspicious

A Series of Senseless Complications
Book Six

Kate Archer

DRAGONBLADE PUBLISHING, INC.

ARE YOU SIGNED UP FOR DRAGONBLADE'S BLOG?

You'll get the latest news and information on exclusive giveaways, exclusive excerpts, coming releases, sales, free books, cover reveals and more.

Check out our complete list of authors, too!

No spam, no junk. That's a promise!

Sign Up Here

www.dragonbladepublishing.com

Dearest Reader;

Thank you for your support of a small press. At Dragonblade Publishing, we strive to bring you the highest quality Historical Romance from some of the best authors in the business. Without your support, there is no 'us', so we sincerely hope you adore these stories and find some new favorite authors along the way.

Happy Reading!

CEO, Dragonblade Publishing

Additional Dragonblade books by Author Kate Archer

A Series of Senseless Complications
Lady Ferocity (Book 1)
Lady Graceless (Book 2)
Lady Impatience (Book 3)
Lady Dramatic (Book 4)
Lady Liar (Book 5)
Lady Suspicious (Book 6)

A Very Fine Muddle
Romance Me, Viscount (Book 1)
Be Daring, Duke (Book 2)
Stand With Me, Earl (Book 3)
Sweep Me Up, Baron (Book 4)
Write for Me, Marquess (Book 5)
Convince Me, Viscount (Book 6)

A Series of Worthy Young Ladies
The Meddler (Book 1)
The Sprinter (Book 2)
The Undaunted (Book 3)
The Champion (Book 4)
The Jilter (Book 5)
The Regal (Book 6)

The Dukes' Pact Series
The Viscount's Sinful Bargain (Book 1)
The Marquess' Daring Wager (Book 2)
The Lord's Desperate Pledge (Book 3)
The Baron's Dangerous Contract (Book 4)
The Peer's Roguish Word (Book 5)
The Earl's Iron Warrant (Book 6)

PROLOGUE

ROLAND NICOLET, THE Duke of Pelham, had so far done what most men would only despair of accomplishing. He'd launched five daughters out of the house to be settled creditably. He still had two more to go but he felt his dream of an empty house really was in reach these days.

He was rather amazed that his hair had not fallen out from the adventure. His girls were all comely and came well-funded, but that did not stop them from complicating every likely match and turning every season into a heart-stopping ride. At times he had felt himself a coachman wrestling an out-of-control team of horses and just trying to keep his carriage out of a ditch.

Last season had been the usual corker. The queen herself had even had to step into it, as his dear Verity had set London tongues wagging. She had proposed the preposterous notion that she was a lady scientist studying the eyesight of fish when they were out of water. The duke supposed that if there were a fish finding itself on land and needing to see anything past its fate as somebody's dinner, it might be interesting to know what it saw. Fortunately, Lord Wembly had not been put off by Verity's unique style of nonsense.

Now it was Winsome's turn and the duke was ready to brace himself for whatever she'd come up with. He was certain it would be something, as his girl was of a suspicious nature and saw a conspiracy around every corner. His youngest, Valor, even added to the problem with her pervasive fear of murderers and rogues. It was likely to take a stalwart and persistent gentleman to convince Winsome of the veracity of his intentions.

If there was one bright spot, it was that he was just now ginning himself up for another entertaining contretemps with his sister, Lady Marchfield. She would, he was certain, send another butler into his house in her endless effort to impose regularity. He might have put his foot down and stopped the habit years ago, but it was too entertaining to give up. His housekeeper, Mrs. Right, drove out the incoming interlopers in the most amusing manners possible.

The only thing to disturb him, if he chose to dwell on it, was that he'd not yet received the letter that came every year, informing him of this new butler. That must be considered strange, as Lady Marchfield always did send the communication in good time.

But then, he held out hope that news of her latest effort had just been lost in the post.

CHAPTER ONE

A Remote Estate in the Dales, 1808

Winsome Nicolet viewed the upcoming season with narrowed eyes and a wary mind. On the one hand, she had watched her older sisters go through it and come out the other end happily settled. But on the other, she had been deeply affected by Mrs. Right's oft-mentioned idea that London was full of rogues. The lady had always said so, and Winsome trusted Mrs. Right to know what was what. In further evidence, she had overheard things over the years that she probably was not meant to hear, and she'd read of an untold amount of ghastly situations. All of it added up to what must be the truth—rogues were not as uncommon as people might think and a lady must skirt around dangerous and unseen perils to avoid disaster.

There was Lady Elspeth, who'd run off to Gretna Green with Mr. Windaker. He was to be a viscount someday and so perhaps the match would not have been opposed, at least not on its face. Of course, once the lady's father looked more closely, it would have fallen apart. Mr. Windaker knew it well enough and he convinced Lady Elspeth of the romance of racing to Scotland to declare their love over an anvil. It was only later that she would discover that Mr. Windaker was deep in debt and getting deeper every day from his gambling habit. Rogue.

Then there was Miss Welder, the ward of an elderly baroness who had perhaps not supervised her charge as well as she should have. Winsome had only heard very quiet and vague whispers about poor Miss Welder. As far as she could put it together, the whispers hinted that the lady had been compromised and then discarded. By a rogue.

And of course the situation regarding poor Lady Jacinda was well understood. She'd wed a marquess who'd made himself agreeable in the courting, got her with child, and then shipped her off to his estate, never to be seen again. It was said that if one wrote the lady a letter it would go unanswered, as the household staff confiscated her correspondence. The marquess did not care for his lady to be writing friends and relations about his treatment. Another rogue.

Those were the real-life cases she knew about. She also knew of all sorts of ways a lady might be tricked by a rogue that she'd read about in books. She favored gothic novels and found the perfidy of the villain, who was almost always a man unless it was a ghost, positively hair-raising. She'd begun with it when she'd read *The Mysteries of Udolpho* and had hardly slept for weeks.

At first, she'd read those frightening stories because they were thrilling and sent ice down the back of her neck. There was something wonderful about reading by candlelight when she was meant to be sleeping, listening to the distant creaks of the house as she read of horrors around every corner. Over time, though, she began to read them for the information, so she would not get tricked.

Unfortunately, what nobody, not in books or in life, seemed to be clear on was how to spot a rogue. They were masters of disguise, so how was a person to avoid being taken in by one until it was too late? Had her sisters all just got lucky? That might be the case. Any one of her brothers-in-law might have been a rogue; it was perhaps happenstance that they were not.

It chilled Winsome's heart that she might be fooled. She might wed a rogue and then only discover it when it was too late to do anything about it. She might commit herself and then rue her decision forevermore. After all, was that not what had happened to the women she'd heard whispers about? Had that not happened to all the many ladies she'd read about in her collection of novels? It was true that in her books, the lady usually escaped real harm in the end, but that was just because the author knew that readers would prefer it.

And anyway, where did the writers of those novels get their ideas? Winsome must believe that they got them from real situations they knew about.

Once a lady was tricked, what could she do about it? She had no power and was dependent on the men in her sphere. She must depend upon them to be honorable and not have secrets or terrible plans. Of all her sisters, Winsome was the most aware that they'd been raised in a rather idyllic setting—remote in the Dales with an indulgent father. The outside world was likely to be far different.

She would be on her guard at all times to prevent being taken in by a less-than-honorable man.

They would leave for Town on the morrow. The easy ways of the Dales would be left behind. Her guard would go up and stay up until she was assured she dealt with an honest man, whoever he might turn out to be.

That idea shifted Winsome's thoughts, as it had often done over the past months, to the Marquess of Manderbey. That lord had attended Verity's wedding to Lord Wembly. Winsome had been struck by his handsome face and smooth and sophisticated manners. He was so urbane! As well, he was great friends with Lord Wembly, who had already proved himself reliable, so there was every chance Lord Manderbey was not a rogue. It would have to be proved, but at least there was a chance.

Of course, she reminded herself that he would not have taken much notice of her. She'd only been the younger sister and not even out. For all she knew, he was married by now. Still, he was lovely to think about.

Her father came into the drawing room with the post. Winsome said, "Did she write?"

Of course, they both knew the *she* in question was Lady Marchfield and the letter that was expected was the insult-laden letter pointing out the duke's faults and outlining some details about the latest butler who'd been installed in her father's house on Grosvenor Square.

The duke shook his head.

"This is very mysterious, Papa," Winsome said. "Our aunt always writes. She always sends the letters with plenty of time to spare. You know how organized she is, she would never wait until the last minute to write. Do you suppose she's given up on the idea? Or maybe she could not find anybody? Perhaps too many butlers have heard…what goes on."

"I hope she's not given up, not at all like my sister to do it," the duke said. "I count on her persevering with the thing. Mrs. Right's machinations in getting one of those fellows out the door is always a high point to the season. In any case, if word *has* gone round that a butler residing in the house will not last long, then I suppose it will be noted that every last one of those fellows landed squarely on his feet whether they deserved to or not."

Winsome snorted. Last year had been the odd American.

"Even Mr. Klonsume," the duke went on, "who regularly writes to your aunt from New York. He's gone on to style himself as Sir Morus of the Order of Owen and made himself a coat of arms. I understand he does very well with it." The duke laughed. "She's told him to stop writing but he never does. I expect he makes a great show of sending off a letter to an English countess—American ingenuity, he'd call it."

Valor came into the room with her pug, Sir Galahad, in her arms. "Papa," she said, "Thomas has been hinting that there might not be room in the luggage carriages for Sir Galahad's bed. Our dear dog cannot be expected to travel without his bed."

"They'll get it in one way or another, Val," the duke said. "Heaven forbid a dog with a smashed-in face and bulging eyes does not have his own four poster to lie around in."

Valor ignored these insults thrown at her little pug. Really, Winsome was not certain they even were insults. They were closer to statements of fact. As for the bed in question, Lord

Wembly had given Sir Galahad a miniature four poster with a liberally stuffed mattress and draped in silks to soothe Valor over Verity leaving the house.

Winsome did have some grave concerns over how Valor would comport herself this season, as she would be the last sister to go before Valor herself, which would not be for some years yet. If Winsome were to wed, Valor would be left alone.

Last season, Valor had gone so far as to send a letter to Lord Wembly, pretending to be Verity and breaking off the engagement. Lord Wembly had seen through it, fortunately, but it was a rather bold thing to even try.

"Thomas says there's no room in the luggage carriages because Winsome's court dress is so enormous," Valor said with a snort. "Winny, can you believe you have to wear that big, round thing? If you put icing on your head, you'd look like a cake."

Winsome *could* believe she had to wear it, she just wasn't happy she had to wear it. The queen had informed her papa, in no uncertain terms, that he was not to send another letter excusing one of his daughters from making her curtsy. From now on, they must turn up. Sadly for Winsome, the *they* in question was only her and Valor.

"I would not laugh so hard, Val," she said. "After I wear it, it will be put away for your turn. We are nearly the same size, only the hem will need to be taken up, and maybe not even that, as you might grow taller."

"I won't have a turn. I don't have to go to court because I'm not going to go running around looking for a gentleman to sleep in the same room with me, like you will do. Like all my sisters have, even though we know Mr. Stratton stares at Felicity when she sleeps. They probably all do that! How do my sisters not die to know it? I'm to stay with Papa forever. Oh, and Papa, you will be glad to know that all my new hostessing clothes are packed in trunks," Valor said.

Winsome sighed. That was another idea Valor had clung to. She claimed she would never leave the duke and she would act as his hostess forever. She had insisted that poor Madame LaFray, who had arrived to design Winsome's wardrobe, also design Valor's "hostessing" wardrobe.

Winsome had not seen the results as Valor kept them a closely guarded secret, but Madame LaFray had mentioned that Winsome's youngest sister had insisted on heavy fabrics that were really better suited to an older matron, and an array of fussy lace fichus. The fabrics, as Madame LaFray had no idea about the hostessing clothes before she arrived, had all been bought at a local haberdasher some miles away. The materials were out of fashion, as London changed its mind on the regular and it took time for the news to reach more far-off places. Valor was not put off by that.

Madame LaFray had even gone to the duke about it, as she did not wish to be on the hook for what she deemed, "Des vêtements malheureusement démodés."

"Excellent news," the duke said to the information that the hostessing clothes were packed. Or the idea that Valor would stay with him forever. Though, Winsome did not believe he found either to be excellent news. The duke really was a sympathetic father and would not for the world throw water on Valor's current hopes and ideas. At least, not yet. Winsome suspected he would not actually allow his youngest daughter to throw her life away in such a pointless manner.

It *would* be pointless, too. Valor would like her own household someday, Winsome was sure of it. Just as all her sisters had and Winsome herself longed for. As soon as she assured herself that she did not connect herself to a rogue.

There was something that happened to a person when they got older. She had once been in firm agreement with Valor over the horror of a man being in one's own room all night and possibly looking at one when one slept. When Felicity had her season, the idea had seemed positively bizarre. Had their sister gone mad, that she would leave the congeniality of their household for *that*?

Now, the whole idea did not seem terrible, but more interesting than anything else. Very interesting, actually. She was certain the same would happen to Valor. She could hardly say how or when it happened to her, it just had.

"You will be so proud of what I've had Madame LaFray make for me, Papa," Valor said. "I will look very grown. You will not even believe it."

Winsome guessed that the only veracity in that statement was: "You will not even believe it."

"Tremendous," the duke said. "Now, it is our last dinner in the Dales for a while. And a cold dinner at that, as Cook is already on his way to Grosvenor Square. Let us go in and discover what Charlie and Thomas have managed to scrape together. We leave for Town first thing on the morrow."

"With Sir Galahad's bed," Valor said.

"With Sir Galahad's bed," the duke said resignedly to his youngest, currently the ruling tyrant of the Nicolet household.

LELAND DUNMORE, MARQUESS of Manderbey, only son of the Duke of Albany, finally finished off his pile of correspondence. It was really incredible how a person could have so many cousins in need of money. Some were near his own age and got themselves into trouble gambling, which he found enormously irritating. Some were dowagers and limped along on modest portions, which he sympathized with.

He'd just finished the last two letters. The first, to Viscount St. John which was of such a scathing nature that he supposed it would burst into flames in the fellow's hands. On top of the general embarrassment of St. John's profligacy, the man was being considered for the next ambassadorship to Portugal. If he went on the way he'd been doing, he would not only embarrass the family, but the English Crown too.

There would be no further requests to be bailed out from that quarter, as Leland had made clear. St. John did not have the funds to go carelessly throwing away what he did have at a dice table. The next time he did, Leland would let him sink.

He was all but certain that St. John lobbied for the ambassadorship as he imagined there might be money to be made there. St. John had made mention of the court currently being housed in Rio de Janeiro to hide from Napoleon and how there were several opportunities there for a fellow to make his fortune. Leland had pointed out that if he withdrew monetary support and St. John kept gambling, it would be obvious to anybody looking. The Crown would not risk appointing a gentleman to represent England who could not even manage his own finances.

The second was to the Dowager Viscountess St. John. As her irascible son was not supporting her as he should, Leland would supplement her income. He'd hired a steward of sorts for the dower house. He was a local gentleman who managed his own businesses and would be well able to handle the dowager's rather straightforward accounts. The steward was to hold the purse and supply Lady St. John with whatever she needed while keeping her son's grubby hands off of it. St. John would be outraged, and Leland was glad of it.

He sat back and sipped his brandy. It was a gift from fate to be so well-supplied with money himself, but it was an ongoing burden to support all sorts of people across England. He would take on the burden, but he would not fund St. John's stupid gambling habit, nor any of his other relations who took up the practice. Helping was one thing, but throwing away money was quite another. If those fellows wished to risk their estates in a gambling hell, then *they* could pay the price for their stupidity, not him.

The brandy soothed him. His cleared desk soothed him. His thoughts began to turn to more pleasant subjects. The season was set to begin.

He always did enjoy it, there was no end of people he would

not see otherwise. Last season had been capped off by Wembly's very interesting wedding. Of all his friends, the baron would have been the last person he'd thought to have the queen in attendance at his nuptials. But then, it seemed his bride, Lady Verity, had captured Her Majesty's notice.

Someone else entirely had captured his own notice that day. Lady Winsome Nicolet, one of the duke's vast array of daughters. She would be out this season and he did not suppose he'd ever set eyes on a more spectacular lady. She had piles of blonde hair that had the palest tinge of copper to it, sparkling blue eyes, a generous mouth, and a light sprinkling of freckles across her nose. It was those freckles that had done him in.

He had a weakness for a sprinkling of freckles. He supposed it went back to his early infatuation with a shopkeeper's daughter. In those early days, he was forever inventing reasons to go to the village in hopes of encountering her. As she was ten years his senior, he did not have much of sense to say when he did encounter her. She'd married a grocer and blessedly put him out of his youthful misery.

But here was a fine lady with a dusting of freckles. She was lovely. And then, her conversation had held a note of seriousness to it that one might not expect to find in a lady not yet even out. Perhaps it was self-assuredness? There was a certain manner in her that he'd liked. She seemed direct, he supposed.

In any case, he was looking forward to seeing her. Perhaps he ought to send Wembly a note and suggest a dinner inviting himself and the Nicolets? He did not suppose Wembly's aunt, Lady Pegatha, would mind it. It was her house, but Wembly regularly stayed there during the season.

Yes, certainly he ought to. He'd seen Lady Winsome, but the rest of the *ton* had not. When they did, he presumed the invitations would come flying to her door. He ought to ensure that an invitation involving himself got there first.

He reached for his stationery, but before he could begin the thing, his dowager duchess barreled her way into his library. The lady had the dower house down the lane but though she'd ostensibly moved into it, she made free with the main house. As far as his grandmother was concerned, no room was off limits. She'd push her way into his bedchamber if she grew tired of waiting for him to come out of it.

He had, on occasion, mentioned that the dower house at the family's seat in Sussex was far larger and well appointed. It was meant to house a dowager duchess. The cottage she currently occupied nearby his house in Torquay was not at all grand. Among the selling points to going home to Sussex that he did not mention was that it happened to be far away, and he could use a reprieve from his grandmother just now.

However, the dowager was too used to ruling the roost in Sussex as the reigning duchess, and found it irritating to find herself pushed out and a newly minted duchess rearranging things.

"There you are," the dowager said. She was a sprightly and small lady with bright eyes. She was of undetermined years, as her reports of her alleged age varied widely depending on her purpose. She was very old if she wished to engender sympathy and she was improbably young when she had no need of it. She looked round the room and peered behind a chair. "No sign of them yet."

One might think, from that sort of display, that his grandmother was going senile. Leland knew very well that was not the case though.

"No sign of what, pray?" he asked, tenting his fingers.

"Grandchildren. What else?"

Leland had been afraid that was what this performance was about. She'd been relentless on the subject for two years already. The last gambit had involved clutching at her heart and pretending she was on the verge of expiring and lamenting that she'd not lived to see grandchildren.

When Leland had pointed out there was nothing he could do about it in her last moments on earth, she'd stalked off. He imagined she came up with these ridiculous hints in league with her lady's maid. His grandmother and the pert Miss Wilson were thick as thieves.

"That's it, then," his grandmother said in her usual opaque manner. As he did not answer, she said, "I'm coming with you."

"Coming with me where?" he asked. He had no invitations for the next week and then he would be off to Town.

"London. It will do me good and more importantly, it will do you good. I'll dig up someone for you to wed so I can have grandchildren in the house before I die."

Leland had been leaning back in his chair. He steadied himself. "What do you mean, you will go to Town? You never go to Town."

"And now I do. Do I really have the energy to play matchmaker at this late date in my history? Who knows, but I've got to try. I'm going to Town. Arrange it all, Manderbey."

With that, the dowager stalked off to harass somebody else. Leland supposed when she said, "Arrange it all," she meant trunks pulled from the attics, carriages hired, her rooms in Hanover Square readied, cards ordered, the news sent out that she would be available for invitations, and who knew what else. His secretary would have to consult with Miss Wilson for a list and the discovery of precisely how many trunks she would bring.

None of that was the worrying part, though. She was intent on playing matchmaker. Unfortunately, when his grandmother was intent on a thing there was not much hope of stopping her. He was almost certain she would cause him trouble. She'd go poking around for willing ladies and she would find them, too. He did not flatter himself in any personal way, but he was well aware that his future wife would someday be a duchess. There were those ambitious ladies, and even more ambitious mamas, haunting the town who would be all too willing.

He did not necessarily condemn those ladies' ambitions, he just did not wish it for himself. His parents' marriage was a good one and had not been based on a transaction. He very much wished for the same.

Leland very briefly thought about refusing to take the dowager to Town. It was a very brief thought though. If she were left behind against her wishes she'd do something diabolical about it. Last year, he'd attempted to refuse to bring her along to a local horse race. She had countered by claiming that she would take out an advertisement in the newspaper outlining how her only grandson had abandoned her. As the son of a duke, he must at least keep his family's name out of the newspapers.

She would go and she would make trouble. It did not even sound as if the dowager would be concerned with his personal happiness or be at all discerning in her hunt. She'd claimed she would "dig somebody up." He thought he ought to be offended by that. He was not so unpleasant that a lady would have to be *dug up*.

The dowager suddenly poked her head back in the door. "I'll need more money than I've got. I'll need a whole new wardrobe—I've got to keep up with the times!"

Of course she needed more money. It seemed everybody in the world always needed more money, and they needed it from him.

CHAPTER TWO

As THE NICOLETS made their way to Town, they were now a much smaller party than they had been. Winsome recalled when it had at one time required two carriages to accommodate all of the duke's daughters. Now, one carriage was sufficient for herself, Valor, and Mrs. Right. At least, it would have been more than sufficient, but for Sir Galahad's four poster miniature bed and Sir Galahad himself being in there too. The bed had been dismantled to fit and most of it was under their feet.

Nevertheless, the trip had held its amusements. The year before, their dear Papa had found that all his usual jests did not work anymore. He'd been in the habit of ordering something that did not exist, like brocabbage pie or Grassingdon Hambac, and feigning outrage by claiming it was a Yorkshire staple. After the innkeeper scrambled to discover what it was, the duke would jovially inform everybody that he'd made the whole thing up. His outlook had been that sort of jest was fun for everybody, despite some of the everybodys not appearing particularly amused. But then that gambit had been tried too many times and last year the duke had been roundly defeated at inn after inn.

Their father was nothing if not inventive though. This year, at each inn they stopped at, he claimed it was Captain James Cook Day. Cook was a Yorkshire man, so it was almost plausible. The associated ritual, however, was not at all plausible.

The duke would stand at precisely nine o'clock in the evening, claiming it was the very moment the captain had been struck down, with only his bones returned to England. Then, he would put hand over heart and recite a poem of his own invention while the staff of the various inn's looked on, not entirely certain of whether they ought to appear reverential.

He sailed the oceans for king and queen; He kept sailing until he was no longer seen. At the Sandwich Islands he met with a lance; He should have turned back when he had the chance.

Then the duke would ask for a moment of silence, which did not go on very long as he could not help himself from laughing and revealing he'd made the whole thing up.

Winsome had not known that a party could actually be barred from returning to an inn. It seemed to be the case though. That particular innkeeper, seeming to lose all reason, said the duke would not be allowed through the doors again and he would personally write to the queen to inform her of it. Apparently, there was not enough money in the world to induce him to put up with it.

At another inn, the woman who ran the kitchens and who had previously proved herself entirely immune to any respect for the duke's rank, came into the dining room with a butcher's knife still in her hand and said: "I'll Captain Cook you all the way back to the Dales."

The duke took it all as being the height of amusement, but Winsome began to wonder if one of these trips would entail them all sleeping in the carriages, as nobody would allow them inside.

They had arrived to their last overnight stop before pressing on to London. Winsome had gently suggested to her papa to forgo the Captain Cook Day poem, but he'd only laughed and said he'd take it under advisement.

Winsome, Valor, and Mrs. Right all stayed together in one room, an extra bed having been dragged in. Mrs. Right fussed with Winsome's hair while Valor was lounging on her bed with Sir Galahad. She'd already explained to the little dog, again, that his special bed could not be brought in because it was just now in pieces.

"Do you suppose Papa will heed my advice and give up on Captain Cook Day?" Winsome asked.

Mrs. Right considered it. "Probably not. He does like a jest and he spent ages composing the poem."

"I hope he doesn't," Valor said. "It's so funny. They get mad like Lady Marchfield does all the time. Maybe Papa will read her the poem too."

"But that's the point, Valor," Winsome said. "They do get mad. We've already been barred from one of the inns. As well, that cook at the other, she might really come after us with a knife one of these days."

"Papa would be very cross about it and make her stop," Valor said. "And Sir Galahad would protect me. I believe he would be very brave on my account. If he really had to."

Winsome noticed there was no mention of Sir Galahad racing to her own rescue. She supposed that was just as well, as the little dog was unlikely to save anybody from anything. Sir Galahad's primary skill appeared to be lounging.

"Come now, girls," Mrs. Right said, "your father will already be in the private dining room waiting for us. You know what happens when he's left alone for too long a time and there's a bottle in front of him."

Valor scooped up Sir Galahad. "Our poor Papa does not like to drink alone because he drinks too much when he doesn't have anybody to talk to."

"Let us go talk to him, then," Mrs. Right said.

They made their way down the stairs. In the front hall of the inn, a rather outraged gentleman was having words with the innkeeper.

"My good man," the gentleman said sounding almost panicked, "you cannot expect me to dine out here? In public view? Out here?"

Winsome thought he said "out here" as if they were the two most preposterous words ever spoken. He was a comely gentleman, but his rather high and panicked voice took away from his appearance.

"My lord," the innkeeper said, "the private dining room has already been reserved. I cannot invent a second room that does not exist. Would you, perhaps, care to dine in your bedchamber?"

"In my *room?*" the lord said, indicating more preposterous words had been spoken.

Mrs. Right took Winsome and Valor by the arms and steered them around the unhappy lord. He noticed them going by, and then he noticed them heading to the private dining room.

"Ladies! My good ladies!" he called after them.

Mrs. Right turned and said, "I am in charge of these girls and they will not be conversing with strangers at an inn. Good day to you."

The lord did look crestfallen to hear it. Just then, the dining room doors opened and the duke came through them. "What is all the ruckus out here?"

"Nothing, nothing at all," the innkeeper said, twisting his hands together.

"Nothing!" the lord said. He hurried to the duke. "My lord, this inn is only in possession of one private dining room, and this deranged innkeeper suggests I remain out here, to dine with the hoi polloi. If you can imagine such an outrage."

"It's Your Grace," the duke said. "Duke of Pelham."

The lord looked very much put on the back foot. "I see!" He looked toward the innkeeper and said accusingly, "I had not known. Nobody mentioned you were a duke, my apologies." He bowed. "Your Grace, allow me to introduce myself. Earl of Landry, at your service."

"Yes, yes, well as you seem to be having some sort of mental collapse over the idea of dining in view of the hoi polloi, as you term it, you'd best come in."

"You are everything gracious, Your Grace. Your condescension will live in my thoughts forevermore!"

"No need to get hysterical over it," the duke said drily.

They proceeded into the dining room with the previously unknown gentleman, now known as the Earl of Landry. Earl or not, Mrs. Right looked suspiciously at him and directed Winsome and Valor to the other side of the table. The Earl would be safely tucked between the duke and Mrs. Right.

The waiters brought wine around, and lemonade for Valor. "Well, Landry, you might as well be introduced to the last of this brood of mine. That's Lady Winsome, and my youngest, Lady Valor. And this is Mrs. Right. There's five of them not here, as I've launched them out of the house, one after the next."

"Ladies. An honor," Lord Landry said, looking wide-eyed to hear of daughters launched out of a house.

Valor eyed the earl. "Are you always so nervous?" she asked. "About the hoi polloi watching you eat?"

Now the earl appeared even more startled, which did not surprise Winsome. Valor generally was startling. "Well I simply could not countenance dining in such close quarters with them," he said. "There seemed to be some rough fellows hanging about."

"Do you suppose any of them are murderers?" Valor asked.

Lord Landry set down his wine with a shaking hand. "I hadn't done. Do *you* think any of them are murderers?"

"Possibly," Valor said matter-of-factly. "Because you never do know, do you?"

Winsome nodded. "A murderer would not wear a sign, would he? He will do everything to make it seem as if he's not a murderer. The more innocent he looks, the higher the chance he's up to no good."

Lord Landry paled just a bit. "Gad, I hadn't thought, but that could be right. A wolf in sheep's clothing, as it were. And then, at an inn where everybody is so transient? Would that not be the perfect place to be a murderer? Why had that never occurred to me?"

Valor nodded gravely. "I'm going to sleep next to my dog so murderers cannot get me." She peered down at Sir Galahad on her lap. The little pug yawned in response to being named the sole member of her personal guard.

"I will be alone," Lord Landry said softly. "Why didn't I bring one of my dogs?"

Winsome felt as if none of them would get much sleep this night, now that murderers had been speculated on. It really was true, there might be one just outside the dining room doors and how would they know it? She had often thought that murderers were masters at hiding their true nature, else how would they get close enough to anybody to murder them?

As for rogues, they were even more plentiful. In all likelihood, there were several in the vicinity, mulling over their devious plans.

Only the duke appeared unaffected by the idea of murderers lurking nearby. He laughed and said, "Perhaps enough macabre talk for one evening. Landry, I suppose you are aware that it is Captain James Cook Day?"

"No, I had not known," Lord Landry said. "Captain James Cook Day. Is it widely celebrated?"

Winsome bit her lip. Any hope that the duke would skip the Captain Cook Day gambit had gone up in smoke.

"Captain Cook was a Yorkshire man, so we take it very seriously up there," the duke said.

"Yes, I imagine you would," Lord Landry said.

"Courageous fellow, must be honored," the duke said.

Valor was snorting to herself. Then she shouted, "Wait until nine o'clock, you'll see!"

"See? What will I see?" Lord Landry asked, concern drifting over his features.

"Never mind it, Lord Landry," Mrs. Right said.

He nodded in the housekeeper's direction. "Yes, of course, if that is what you would advise. Naturally I will if you think it best."

Gracious, he was such an overly agreeable man, as if he were afraid of ever crossing anybody. He was a veritable wet noodle.

"By the by, Mrs. Right," he said, "I did not catch your connection to the family."

"I'm the housekeeper," she said, looking as if she were daring the gentleman to make comment on it.

Winsome did not imagine Lord Landry would challenge that idea or any other idea.

"Oh I see! Yes, of course," he said. "Yes, I did imagine so. That is, not to say you might not have been a cousin…yes, why not a cousin…is what I say…"

The duke seemed to perceive that the wet noodle was covering himself in uncomfortable sauce and cut him off before he could drown in it any further. "I presume you are on your way to Town for the season, Landry?"

Lord Landry shook his head sadly. "I am afraid so, Your Grace."

"You're afraid of Town too?" Valor asked. "Is it the hoi polloi again?"

"I'm afraid of what must happen in the town," Lord Landry said.

Valor leaned forward. "What? What's to happen?"

Lord Landry colored. "I ought not say, I ought not have mentioned it."

"But now you have so you'd better spell it out for us," the duke said. The waiters had brought in the soup. The duke paused to say to the senior of them, "Tell all your people to gather here at precisely nine o'clock. It's Captain James Cook Day and we will honor that courageous gentleman with all the respect that he deserves."

Winsome thought the waiters had a deal of trouble keeping the surprise from their expressions. Or perhaps it was resentment. It was hard to tell.

The doors shut and the duke said, "Well? What's to happen to you in Town? Afraid the hoi polloi will be in your drawing room?"

Valor laughed hysterically. "Papa, you are so funny. How could they even get there so fast when he just saw them out there, right outside?"

Lord Landry dabbed at his eyes with a napkin. He did seem quite overcome and Winsome was beginning to be afraid of what he was afraid of, though she did not know what it was yet.

"I've been pressured from all sides!" he cried. "The whole extended family is against me. They say I must wed and if I do not and there is no heir I will go down in the flames of infamy forevermore! They despise my cousin, you see, and he or one of his sons would take the title. He is very profligate, and they do not care for it."

The duke appeared a bit confused by the explanation, as was Winsome herself. The duke said, "Come now, man. Everybody has got to do his duty."

"That's what *they* say!"

"It's not as if you're still wet behind the ears. How old are you, anyway?"

"Twenty-seven," the lord whispered.

"No wonder they want you to get on with it," the duke said. "Have you got a decent house and a fair amount of funds?"

"Big house and piles and piles of money, I'm afraid." He shook his head, looking very much in despair, and muttered, "Nothing ever goes my way."

"I do not see why a fellow would be afraid of being well set. I also do not see that you should encounter any difficulties securing a lady," the duke said.

Winsome was not so certain. The poor man appeared frightened of his own shadow.

It occurred to her that since he was a lord of the right generation, he might know Lord Manderbey. That might be a deal more interesting than the lord's problems with his family. "Lord Landry, do you have a circle in Town? Our Verity wed Lord Wembly last season and we found him very pleasant. As well, we found his friend, Lord Manderbey, very pleasant. Are you acquainted with those gentlemen?"

She did not suppose the inquiry was done very subtly, especially considering her father held a napkin to his lips to cover his laughter.

"Yes, yes," Lord Landry said. "I know them both from school. I know Manderbey a bit better as he's just in the next county over from me. He's a funny fellow—always complaining that people are dunning him for money."

Winsome sat back. Lord Manderbey was being dunned for money? She would have never guessed he was in financial straits.

She suppressed a sigh. That was the problem with gentlemen—you never really knew. She supposed if he did not hide the idea then he could not be roguish. Having problems of the money variety was no shame and could happen for no end of reasons.

But if he did hide it from the wider world, specifically from any ladies he might encounter, well that *would* make him a rogue. If he hid it, the cause was likely gambling and the reason would probably be to secure a large dowry before anybody knew he had need of it. She'd seen it a dozen times in her novels. She'd even heard of it once in real life.

The problem with that was the lady would not be loved, she would just be necessary. And she also supposed the why of it mattered too. If it were something like gambling, where he threw it all away, that was something to know about a person. That person was careless and would likely be careless of a wife.

How was she to find it out? If she asked him, would he admit to being in financial straits? Or would he fail to mention that he was dunned? Could she ask him? How did one bring up such a thing?

Winsome reminded herself that it was unlikely she would have the opportunity to have that conversation. Then she remembered something else that might make the question moot.

"Lord Landry, I suppose Lord Manderbey is married by now?"

"Is he?" the lord said with surprise. "I had not even heard of an engagement."

"Oh, perhaps I am mistaken," Winsome said, feeling very

pleased with his response. She should not feel as pleased as she did, as a very large question had been posed. She felt she should be very on her guard with Lord Manderbey, even though he was unlikely to give her a second look. She had really felt he *had* given her a second look at Verity's wedding breakfast, but her rational mind reminded her that he was likely only being kind to a younger sister.

The servants of the inn, and the innkeeper himself, filed into the room. Winsome presumed it must be nine o'clock.

The duke rose, and Lord Landry followed suit. "Hand over heart," the duke said.

Everyone did as directed, though Valor was heaving in silent laughter into Sir Galahad's fur.

In a very grave tone, her father said, "He sailed the oceans for king and queen; He kept sailing until he was no longer seen. At the Sandwich Islands he met with a lance; He should have turned back when he had the chance. Oh Bering Sea blocking the way with ice, sending him back to Sandwich was not very nice."

Good heavens, he'd even added to it. There had been no mention of the Bering Sea until now.

Lord Landry nodded. "God bless Captain Cook. Very moving, Your Grace. Very moving, indeed."

"Was it?" the duke asked. "Hah! I made the whole thing up! The whole thing, even the Captain Cook Day! I don't know how everybody falls for it—he was not even killed with a lance."

Lord Landry sank down into his seat. The innkeeper turned on his heel and stalked out. One of the waiters unceremoniously dropped a tray onto a sideboard with a crash and followed the innkeeper out the door. The rest of them just shook their heads. Later, when the duke wished for port to be brought in, he had to go out and find somebody. Winsome suspected this was yet another inn that would bar the doors against the Nicolets.

CHAPTER THREE

THE TRIP TO London was not quite as comfortable as it could have been. Leland was confounded that he'd ended up trapped in a carriage with his grandmother when he'd imagined he'd taken every precaution against it. He'd arranged for the lady to have her own carriage, but Miss Wilson currently occupied that vehicle quite alone. Once he'd seen the dowager climb into his own carriage, he'd declared he would ride his horse. That idea sank like a stone after various clutchings of the heart and wonderings if she was to die alone, unaccompanied and ignored.

His grandmother claimed they needed to ride together in the same carriage so they could, as she said, "put their heads together." This had seemed to translate to she would talk and he would listen.

"To my mind," the dowager said, "you require a lady who is comely so you do not lose interest—there can be no grandchildren if you lose interest. I presume you know how that all works. Then, of course, she must be tolerably intelligent, I have no patience for a dullard. She must play the pianoforte, or a harp if that's all we can dig up. Do not present me with a lady strumming on a guitar! I like to listen to music, except a guitar, and my own fingers are too arthritic for it these days. And do not bring me a picky eater! Nothing more tedious than an over-delicate type turning her nose up at wholesome country dishes. She must have a tolerable seat on a horse. It is pleasant to view a lady rider.

Then of course, I presume you will have some of your own requirements."

Leland did not answer this long and considered opinion regarding who could be *dug up*. He was mystified as to why she was so against a guitar, though that and everything else on her list was irrelevant.

"We'll start with Almack's and see the lay of the land there," the dowager prattled on. "Though, I will not confine myself to it! There will be plenty of suitable young ladies who do not attend, for one reason or another."

"I have not purchased a voucher for Almack's," Leland pointed out. He generally avoided it as he had little use for the formality of the place, the rules, the drinks, the food, and a few of the patronesses. There was something inherently unpleasant about people who'd taken on the mantle of being arbiters of taste and rulers of society. It put his back up.

"Fear not," the dowager said. "I've arranged it. Remember? I told you I needed money?"

"You said that was for clothes," Leland said.

The dowager shrugged. "Some of it was and some of it wasn't. Oh, and guess what else? Gracious I forgot we have another appointment before Almack's. You know I have long known the queen."

Leland waited for her to expound on the point of mentioning the queen. "And?"

"And I've wrangled us invitations to the reception after the next drawing room. You see? We do not even bring anyone for a curtsy to the queen, but we will go. It is rather ingenious, we will get a bird's eye view of all the Lady So-and-So's who come to bend their knee. We'll be ahead of the pack, as it were, in having a look at them all. In any case, it's tomorrow."

"Grandmama," Leland said, "I really cannot have you interfering in my personal life just because you've decided you want grandchildren. I will marry when I choose to marry to who I choose to marry and that is the end of it. Maybe my future marchioness plays the guitar and maybe she does not. Do not attempt to arrange my calendar or carry on in this highhanded manner."

He'd made some version of that speech a dozen times before with no effect. He really needed her to take it in though. He would not be pushed to the altar.

The dowager dramatically whipped out a handkerchief and wept into it with surprising gusto.

"Do not even bother with that," Leland said.

She promptly dropped her handkerchief to reveal entirely dry eyes. "All I will say at this moment, is that we have an invitation to St. James and vouchers and tickets for the opening ball at Almack's. I pray you will escort me, as if you do not I will be forced to advertise far and wide that I, a weak and decrepit old lady, limped to those places all alone. My grandson, who I had thought had a care for me, was too busy to bother with it. And then, who knows what sort of trouble I might stir up were I to go marauding through St. James and Almack's entirely unsupervised?"

Leland folded his arms. That was a nice bit of blackmail, and unfortunately true. He was grateful to note that they'd entered the environs of London. It would not be too long before he could escape the carriage. He would repair immediately to his room and she would have no luck attempting to follow him in there. The Hanover Square staff had been instructed to install a hefty lock on his door so his grandmother could not barge into it.

Or perhaps he ought to just turn the carriage around and go home. This season might prove to be far more trouble than it was worth.

But on the other hand, he was looking forward to meeting with Lady Winsome Nicolet again, now that she was to be properly out. He wondered if she would attend the queen's drawing room. He also wondered how he could steer his grandmother well clear of her, as he would not appreciate any meddling in that direction.

MRS. RIGHT HID her trepidation as the carriages approached Grosvenor Square. Winsome and Valor were already in a state and Sir Galahad had picked up on it and was panting heavily.

Nobody knew what they were to find when they arrived. Lady Marchfield had been religiously dependable about sending a letter ahead of time informing them that she'd hired another butler for the house. She often sent information *about* the fellow she'd hired that had been helpful to Mrs. Right's plans to get him out. This year, she had been ominously silent.

Silent. Lady Marchfield was never, ever, silent.

Had she given it up? Mrs. Right would like to think so. But she also knew that Lady Marchfield was crafty and that she would not like to admit defeat. Especially after last year's debacle. Last season, they had arrived and found her jubilantly standing outside the front doors so she might witness their surprise at being inflicted with Mr. Klonsume, the American.

Mrs. Right peered out the windows. There was no sign of the lady. Was that good or bad?

"What if she did something scary?" Valor whispered.

"Do not you fret about it, love," Mrs. Right said. "If there is not a butler waiting for us, that is good news. If there is, I will make short work of him, as I always do."

She soothed Valor with the idea, though she was not certain she had soothed herself. She had an unaccountable sense of foreboding. Her instincts were like embroidery needles pricking at her from all directions.

Their carriage had stopped just behind the duke's own. He and his valet, Reynolds, were already on the pavement. Charlie hurried to open their door, peering at Mrs. Right as if he might divine something from her expression.

"Let us proceed," she said, with all the confidence she could muster.

They entered the house and all was quiet. Mrs. Right sent Thomas and Charlie downstairs to see if Cook had heard any word of a butler or seen any sign of Lady Marchfield. As Winsome and Valor raced up the stairs to claim their bedchambers and the duke poured himself a brandy in the drawing room, Mrs. Right peered around for any sign that a butler had been there.

Nothing was out of place. Maybe Lady Marchfield had really given it up. If she had, she would not write the duke about it. After all, the countess was a proud woman. She'd just drop the matter and pretend she'd never had anything to do with it.

Thomas and Charlie ran back up the stairs from the kitchens. "Cook says he's not seen hide nor hair of a butler," Thomas said breathlessly. "But, he's convinced there is something awry."

"Awry?" Mrs. Right asked. She did not like the sound of *awry*.

"A few days ago," Charlie said, "he began to suspect that someone was in the house. He'd hear a sound but could not determine where it was coming from. He'd look around and there was nobody."

"He began to doubt the amounts of food he had in the kitchens, as if somebody was taking things," Thomas said. "All the doors and windows were secured so he could not work it out. He was beginning to imagine he was going mad."

"Then last night, before he retired, he measured the length of the loaf of bread on the counter." Charlie took in a deep breath. "This morning, the loaf was shorter."

Mrs. Right felt a chill down her spine. They all gazed round as if the mystery was somewhere waiting to be discovered nearby. "Have you checked the men's quarters?" she asked.

"Cook says there is no sign of anybody having been there," Charlie said.

"He says he's checked everywhere," Thomas said. "Now, I don't like to say, but could it be...a ghost?"

"A ghost who steals bread?" Mrs. Right asked. "Now, if there *is* someone in the house, they cannot stay hidden forever. I reckon it is some poor street urchin who has slipped in for warmth and food and will slip out again now that the house is full."

This seemed to greatly relieve the footmen, though Mrs. Right was not nearly as confident in the idea as she sounded.

She hurried down the stairs to the servants' hall, determined to speak with Cook directly. Perhaps the fellow *was* going mad? It could not be a rational idea to go round measuring loaves of bread, after all.

"Did they tell you, Mrs. Right?" the cook said, twisting his hands together. "Did they tell you that something is awry in this house?"

"They did," Mrs. Right said. "But you are sure? You are sure that someone is—"

"In the house? As sure as the nose on my face. Why are they here, though? Who is it? Why is someone here, somewhere, hiding away and chilling my blood? I've hardly slept in days, what with worryin' over being murdered in my bed."

"Now as I told the boys, if there is somebody here, it could very well be a street urchin slipped in for warmth and food," she said, not any more convinced than she had been when she said it the first time.

"An urchin," Cook said thoughtfully. "I suppose it could be. Where is the rascal hiding though?"

Mrs. Right and the Cook both looked round the kitchens.

"And then, there is also the smallest possibility that you've been greatly affected by coming here alone," Mrs. Right said. "In other years, some of the grooms have come ahead too. Perhaps I ought to have sent your kitchen maids, but then they are two young girls and to send them with no matronly supervision, well it would not have been seemly."

"You hint that I may have imagined it all?"

"It is only a possibility. This house does creak, which could prompt ideas."

"But the bread, Mrs. Right. I was very careful about measuring the bread."

"Ah, yes, the bread."

They both gazed round the kitchens, wondering about the bread.

WINSOME EXAMINED HER dress. She would be inclined to think that there had never in all the world been such a monstrosity made, had not Madame LaFray mentioned that she'd constructed more than a few of them in her time.

It was the dreaded court dress.

Valor had spent the past quarter hour rolling on Winsome's bed and laughing hysterically. Now that Mrs. Right had, with a great deal of trouble, got Winsome into the dress, Valor cried, "It looks like a pile of curtains fell on you."

Winsome would very much like to throw something at Valor, despite the fact that she was not wrong. It did look like a pile of curtains had fallen on her.

"Now," Mrs. Right said soothingly, "it is not an attractive dress, there is no getting round it. However, it's only to be worn once. It's my understanding that Lady Marchfield will take you in, you will curtsy, spend a few minutes at a reception, and then come home and take the thing off, never to be put on again."

"That's the other thing," Winsome said. "Our aunt. We have not seen her yet. We don't know if she will send a butler yet. Her silence is a bit nerve-wracking. She's not forgotten about us, as she sent for the court invitation and secured my voucher and tickets to Almack's, but what is she thinking?"

Winsome well understood that because the queen was involved and Lady Marchfield had been informed that Winsome must make her curtsy, her aunt had written to the Lord Chamberlain and received the invitation. A lady must take her into the queen, though Winsome dearly wished it could have been her father. She had not been so sure her aunt would arrange Almack's, but she had. The voucher had been delivered this morning.

It was not as if her father could not arrange things with Almack's, he just never got around to it. He said it would put him in a bad frame of mind to ask those patronesses for anything, considering how little they bothered to give him at their famously lackluster suppers.

"Mrs. Right, Thomas says there was someone in the house when we got here," Valor said. "And they never found him. He thinks they might still be here! Our aunt might have sent a murderer into the house, she was that mad at Papa."

"Aye, don't I know the boys keep talking about somebody being in the house every time you kick me awake at night," Mrs. Right said. "I've told them, it's all nonsense."

Valor had refused to sleep alone in her room and Mrs. Right had all but moved into it on account of the idea that someone, a stranger, might have been in the house.

"I have to be safe!" Valor pointed out, hugging Sir Galahad.

"I really do not see why Sir Galahad has to be in the bed with us, though," Mrs. Right said. "He snores something terrible."

Valor shrugged, as was her usual response to either her or her pug causing anybody trouble.

"All right now, love," Mrs. Right said to Winsome, "let's get you down the stairs. I think you'll need some help, I should not like you to take a tumble."

As Winsome prepared herself for the embarrassing hours to come, Valor fell back into hysterical laughter. "But if you fall, Winsome, you won't even get hurt because you're so wrapped up!"

Again, Valor was right, but that did not stop Winsome wishing to pick up a scent bottle and fling it at her sister's head. The dress could not be called anything but a monstrosity and Winsome really did not understand why the queen preferred the silhouette. The fabric was a white satin and there was so, so, much of it. The bodice was form-fitting, but then it sprung out in all directions. It was decorated with lace and bits and bobs in an awful fashion that their dressmaker had insisted was the style de rigueur. The hoops and the number of crinolines required to hold up the volume of the skirt was both astonishing and appalling. When Madame LaFray had begun fitting the skirt on her, one layer after the next, Winsome had at first thought she was joking.

She had also thought the madame was joking when she explained that only pearls and diamonds should be worn. There was no explanation as to why.

And then, of course, there was the final humiliation—the three ostrich feathers atop her head that waved when she moved. As far as she was concerned, the feathers made her appear a rooster strutting around a barnyard.

Winsome's only consolation was that she would not be alone in being preposterously outfitted. Every other lady making her curtsy would be in the same condition.

As Mrs. Right helped her down the stairs, the housekeeper said quietly, "If you can do it, try to find out what Lady Marchfield is thinking on the butler front. I did not like to say within Valor's hearing, as the footmen have still got her frightened that somebody is in the house."

"*Is* somebody in the house?" Winsome asked.

"Oh, I cannot think so. At least, it does not seem likely."

Winsome was surprised that Mrs. Right did not sound as certain of it as she'd thought. She had, of course, heard of the idea on the day they'd arrived to Grosvenor Square. However, the house had been searched all the way up to the attics. Nobody was found and she'd thought the consensus was that Cook had got nervous staying in the house alone.

The duke awaited them in the great hall. "Papa," Winsome said, "do not tease me or I will fall into a heap."

"No intention of it," the duke said. "Though I believe you can now comprehend why I tried to keep all you girls as far away from this absurdity as possible."

Charlie and Thomas were keeping watch out the windows. Charlie shot toward the doors and said, "She is here."

As they all understood the "she" to be Lady Marchfield, the duke said, "Let us go out to meet the carriage. No point in drawing out this particular day."

Winsome nodded. "The sooner it's over, the better."

It was no small feat to get Winsome into the carriage once she got there. After pushing hoops this way and that, she was finally crammed into it while the duke climbed in after her.

"Well Lady Misery, here we are again. I see you've given up the butler gambit—I'm disappointed, it was a very good game," the duke said.

Rather than at all acknowledge the duke, Lady Marchfield patted Winsome's hand. "You look lovely, my dear. At least as lovely as one can do in a court dress."

"You *have* given it up, is that right?" the duke asked, his tone faintly tinged with concern.

Again, Lady Marchfield pretended she did not hear the duke. To Winsome, she said, "I do not suppose anybody has outlined what you are to do today. I will walk you in front of Her Majesty. When I stop, you take a few steps forward and curtsy as low as you can manage. Her Majesty may say a few words, or not. If she does, be nothing more than grateful and demure. Do not attempt cleverness, she does not like it. After you are dismissed, we will both walk out backwards. Do not show your back to the throne!"

Winsome was grateful for the information. She'd understood the general idea but nobody had mentioned walking backward to get out of the place.

"Come now, Misery," the duke said. "Admit it, you've given up on the butler game."

"Have I?" Lady Marchfield said mysteriously.

"Haven't you?"

Lady Marchfield only looked out the carriage window by way of answer.

As St. James was not far, they passed through the gates sooner than Winsome would have wished. Happily, there was a long line of carriages ahead of them. Or unhappily. She really did not know. On the one hand, she wished to never arrive. On the other, she wished to hurry and be done with it.

"Come now," the duke said to his sister. "Let us have it done between us. It was amusing for me but perhaps less so for you. I am willing to give it up."

"Good to know," Lady Marchfield said.

"Have we given it up?"

"Roland, I understand that you would be pleased to know what I think and what I might have done. I am simply not inclined to inform you."

What she might have done. What had she done? Did it have anything to do with the idea that there had been someone in the house?

The duke looked discomfited, and her aunt looked pleased. That was probably not a good state of affairs.

The carriage lurched forward. They were nearly there. Winsome put the butler battle between her father and aunt aside. In moments, she was to attempt getting out of the carriage wearing a monstrous skirt. She had not got into it with any grace but she must somehow manage getting out without making a fool of herself.

CHAPTER FOUR

L ELAND HAD BEEN all but forced to accompany his grandmother to the palace for the queen's drawing room. As he did not have sisters, he'd never had cause to attend one. Though, he'd heard tell of the preposterous gowns the ladies being presented would be forced to wear, mostly to do with the complaints over the backbreaking cost of them.

Now, they were in a reception room while the ladies who would make their curtsies and the matrons who accompanied them were elsewhere. Apparently, after each made their successful curtsy, they would be escorted here to be congratulated.

The room was filled with pacing fathers and older brothers, they all looked as if they'd sent their young lady off to a campaign of war.

"Why are they all so nervous looking?" he asked the dowager. "What could possibly go wrong?"

"The girl could fall, that's what. She's got to curtsy very low, practically to a kneel. Then she has to back out. As she is doing all that, she is encased in a hot air balloon of a dress. It's everybody's nightmare, a girl would never live it down. I expect the queen insists on that ridiculous court dress for the excitement of it. Will she or will she not fall over."

He nodded. The whole thing sounded ghastly.

"Come, take me to a sideboard," the dowager said. "I expect

the palace has come up with something worth having. Then, we'll stand there with a good view of the doors and you can see who comes through it that you like. Ignore what they're wearing!"

Leland held out his arm. He had no intention of following his grandmother's directives, but a glass of claret might go some way toward smoothing this experience. In any case, the whole point of why he'd come was to keep an eye on the dowager and ensure she did not commit him to a wedding of her choosing. And, if he were to be entirely honest, he understood that Lady Winsome would be presented.

As they approached the sideboard, Leland spotted Lord Landry. He'd not seen the fellow in an age, as he did not ever come to Town. What in the world was he doing in the palace for the queen's drawing room? He had no sister to be presented.

"Landry," he said, as the dowager plowed ahead to the sideboard. "What brings you here?"

Landry, who looked very downcast, said, "Forced to come. Family's idea. My cousin, Lady Lisbeth, is doing her curtsy."

"Oh I see," Leland said, though he really did not. He had several cousins who had made their curtsy and he'd never been dragged here for it. "I'm here only to keep a tight rein on my grandmother."

Very suddenly, Landry grabbed his coat sleeve. "I'm supposed to be introduced to ladies. They want to get me married! Ganged up on me about it. The family."

"Ah," Leland said, "well, certainly, it might be thought to be the right time?"

"That's what they say. But women, Manderbey, do not you find them…a little bit frightening? With all their…ways?"

"Um perhaps only my dowager," Leland said, not entirely sure what Landry was getting at.

The Lord Chamberlain had flung open the doors and the first lady to get through her curtsy was announced. There would be a regular stream from now on, Leland supposed.

The dowager approached with a piece of cheese in one hand and a glass of Canary in the other. Leland stared at the cheese. "Good God, did they not offer a plate and linen?"

"Can't be bothered with it," the dowager said. "Who's going to scold an old and infirm lady over it? I'll claim I'm senile if they do."

"I see. Dowager, I believe you have met Lord Landry, a viscount from the next county over."

"I remember. What's brought you here?"

Lord Landry looked a bit panicked over the question and Leland supposed he was attempting to decide if he should point to his cousin being presented or that the family wanted to marry him off.

The Lord Chamberlain announced, "Lady Winsome Nicolet, daughter of the Duke of Pelham, accompanied by the Countess of Marchfield."

Leland turned. There she was. From the bodice up, she was spectacular. Not even the absurd ostrich feathers could take away from her piles of blonde waves and the copper strands running through it, picking up the light. She was in high color, her cheeks suffused pink and her pretty blue eyes sparkling.

Of course, below the bodice the dress was absolutely preposterous. Leland began to think that if too many more ladies thusly attired entered the reception room, there would not be much space to maneuver through it.

Her father, the duke, collected her and they were heads together. Then he nodded and led her to the sideboard. Oddly, Lady Marchfield had not come very far inside the doors and now she turned around and walked out, much to the Lord Chamberlain's surprise.

Leland had not been paying the least attention to the conversation between the dowager and Landry. Now, he walked off without so much as a by your leave.

"Your Grace, Lady Winsome," he said, as the duke poured his daughter a glass of champagne.

"Lord Manderbey," Lady Winsome said. "I pray you do not expect a curtsy while I'm in this dress. One was all I can manage."

"Manderbey," the duke said jovially. "Last saw you at my daughter Verity's wedding. What brings you here?"

"No particular reason, I'm afraid," Leland said. "My dowager insisted on coming and insisted I attend her."

The duke's eyes scanned the room. "Hah! The Duchess of Ralston. She was a corker in her younger years."

"She still is, I regret to report."

"Ah, look there Winny, the dowager talks to Landry." To Leland, he said, "We met him on the road, at an inn. He dined with us."

"Oh I see," Leland said. Landry had said nothing about that. Of course, he did not suppose there would have been reason to mention it. Though, Leland found he did not particularly like the idea of dining together in an inn. Those places were so much more relaxed in their standards. Anything might go on at an inn. Had Lady Winsome and Landry sat next to each other? How close?

He stopped his thoughts from the very stupid gymnastics they were just now engaged in.

"There was only one dining room," Lady Winsome said. "Lord Landry had feared he would be left to dine with, what did he say, Papa?"

"The hoi polloi," the duke said with a snort. "Never saw a man so hysterical over such a thing."

That did sound like Landry and Leland found himself very satisfied with it. He was perhaps less satisfied that the dowager was barreling toward him just now. Please God stop her from saying anything embarrassing.

"Duke, I have not seen you in an age," the dowager said. "Not since you set Lady Vanderwake's curtains afire. Goodness, those were jolly times."

"Duchess," the duke said. "I've since set Lady Jellerbey's curtains on fire too, sorry you missed it."

"The same old rascal, I see."

"May I present Lady Winsome, one of my far-too-numerous daughters."

"Do not curtsy, Lady Winsome," the dowager said. "I should not wish to cause a fall-over."

"That is very kind, Your Grace."

"Well now, as we have not encountered each other in years, I suppose I ought to host a dinner," the duke said. "Bring Manderbey along with you. How is Thursday?"

"We would be delighted," the dowager said.

Leland was surprised nobody had bothered to inquire into *his* calendar. But he was not sorry over the idea that there would be a dinner.

"Now what about Almack's?" the dowager asked the duke. "I intend to drag my grandson to that bastion of boredom."

The duke laughed. "We will attend. Here is a hint—I bring a flask of brandy, it makes the boredom less boring."

"Hah! I might do just the same. I'll bring a flask of Canary. Let them try to stop me!"

"That's the spirit," the duke said.

"Now, Duke, I do not suppose you will mind if my grandson lends an arm to Lady Winsome. She must wish to take a turn round the room after her ordeal and will need support in that ludicrous get-up she's been forced into."

"I do not mind it," the duke said.

The duke and the dowager both stared at Leland. The two of them were outrageous. "Lady Winsome," he said, putting out his arm.

She laid her hand gently on his arm. He said, "There is not much room to actually take a turn."

"In this dress, I think you mean?"

"Yes. Perhaps we might shoot for getting through to the windows and admiring the view."

Lady Winsome nodded. "I am a regular sailing ship leaving a harbor."

He laughed at the unexpected description. She really had a particular wit about her.

After they were out of earshot of the duke and the dowager, he said, "I will apologize for my dowager's various outrages, both now and in future."

"Is she rather dependable on that front?"

"As regular as a well-maintained clock."

"Some people find my father outrageous," Lady Winsome said.

"Yes, I understand some do. Was your dinner at the inn with Lord Landry pleasant?" It was a stupid thing to ask, and apropos of nothing, but he really did wish to know it. Landry was a regular drooping daisy of a fellow, but there was no accounting for what a woman might approve of.

"Pleasant enough," Lady Winsome said. She paused, then said, "Lord Landry mentioned you. He said he'd known you for a long time and…you complained a lot over being dunned for money."

"Did he?"

"Yes, I do not know why he should have mentioned it."

"Nor I," Leland said. Why on earth should Landry have spoken of his irritation over relatives coming out of the woodwork, looking for money? He probably had one of his nervous attacks, which generally sent him into a babble.

"It is just that, my father is never dunned," Lady Winsome said.

Leland laughed. "Nobody gets themselves in deep with cards, then?"

Lady Winsome's eyes widened. "It's cards, is it?"

"Usually," he said. She seemed surprised. He supposed the duke did not have the sort of needy and foolhardy relations that he had.

"Oh I see," she said pensively.

He could not at first work out why the idea seemed to strike hard, but then he remembered she'd been raised somewhere remote in the Dales. She would not have been exposed to profligate young men looking round them to discover where they could locate more funds to throw away. The idea must be found shocking.

Leland turned the conversation to more usual subjects and discovered she'd brought her horse with her to Town. A Dales pony. As far as he could gather, all of the Nicolet daughters were expert horsewomen, but for the youngest, who would only walk her horse. At least, he must suppose so, as Lady Winsome described galloping across fields and jumping farmers' stone walls.

He also found out Lady Winsome favored gothic novels. He had not read any himself, but understood they were very popular with ladies. He was not precisely sure why, though, after she described the one she'd just finished reading. A Spanish ghost who'd been unjustly killed during the Inquisition got transported to England via a haunted vase and was so enraged that it attempted to drive the inhabitants of a castle mad? The prince and his betrothed were particularly hard hit, as the ghost kept trying to make the princess jump off a balcony, while the prince kept getting the urge to throw himself into a fire. Apparently, it all ended well enough, though he was not at all clear on what happened to the vase, or the ghost.

"So your father mentioned you will attend Almack's?" he asked, though the idea had already been confirmed.

"Yes, of course I will, it seems a duty as all my sisters have gone. You will attend, I think?"

"Yes, yes," he said. She really was the loveliest creature he'd ever set eyes on.

"There you are, Winny," the duke said. "Time to scarper like housebreakers at dawn. We've done our duty, no need to be excessive about it. Landry is going to take us, since your aunt has done a runner. Manderbey, the dowager and I have got it all worked out. We will see you Wednesday at Almack's and Thursday to dine."

Leland bowed and the duke took his daughter away. He watched them head toward the doors, the duke gently pushing people to the side to make way for Lady Winsome. She really was so pretty, and there was to be a dinner.

All he need concern himself about was that his grandmother did not read too much into it and decide to involve herself in some way. And why Landry should be taking them home.

THOUGH IT WAS still early morning, Winsome had donned her pelisse and hurried two doors down to Lord Thorpe's house to find her sister, Serenity.

She must talk to a sister, and Valor was not the right sister. The day before, Valor had been satisfied enough to hear that the curtsy to the queen had been a dreadful experience. Winsome had not mentioned she had encountered Lord Manderbey in the reception room.

Winsome really was very glad that the curtsy was over. There had been something nerve-wracking about standing in a line of other ladies, waiting to be called, while her aunt stood stone-faced by her side. At times she'd wished to hurry, or slow down, or disappear altogether. She sometimes had a strong urge to pick up her stupid skirt and run away. After all, what could they do to her if she did?

Other of the older relations who acted as escorts were patting their girl's hand or whispering comforting things to them. All Lady Marchfield had to say was curtsy to the ground, be demure, back away, and don't fall over.

Then, her time had come. She did as her aunt had advised and curtsied very low. The queen instructed her to rise. Just when Winsome had been hoping to make her escape, Her Majesty said, "Another Nicolet, I see?"

Winsome had prayed she would not be talked to. As it was,

she said, "Yes, Your Majesty."

"Lady Winsome, do you intend on causing as much mayhem as your most recent sister?"

Of course, Verity *had* made a societal ruckus, even causing the queen to step into it. But how was one to know the future? Nevertheless, she suspected the correct answer and gave it. "No, Your Majesty."

"I suppose we will see," Queen Charlotte said. "You may retreat."

Winsome backed away as carefully as she could. It was so awkward to not be able to see where one was going. She hoped there was not a stool behind her that she'd failed to note.

But finally, she was out of it. She'd curtsied low and backed out without falling over anything. She had, until this moment, been the smallest bit resentful that she and not her older sisters had been forced to go through it. Now, though, as she reflected on the experience, she realized what a blessing it was.

Felicity would have been in a temper over it. Grace would have never got out of it without rolling across the carpet. Patience would have toe-tapped through it, letting all and sundry know she found the slow-moving ceremony tedious. Serenity surely would have wept. And Verity, one could only speculate on what nonsense she might have posed to the queen. Her Majesty had eventually found out about Verity's nonsense through other means, but it would not have gone over as well at a presentation. In the end, Winsome must satisfy herself that she was the only sister suited to come through the whole preposterous afternoon unscathed.

Once she *had* come through it, her aunt had led her to the reception room and handed her over to the duke. Then, Lady Marchfield had left. She'd just said, "Good day," turned, and left.

Her aunt had left them there without their own carriage. What in the world was Lady Marchfield up to? It was all so strange. Winsome had prayed they were not to walk home. It was not too far, but the dress…

And then, much to her great surprise, she'd encountered both Lord Manderbey and Lord Landry. Not only to her surprise, though. To her trepidation, too.

She'd been determined to discover if what Lord Landry had said was true. He'd hinted that Lord Manderbey was in some sort of financial straits. He was dunned on account of it. Had he admitted it or had he not? He made some offhand comment about cards. But he'd really not revealed if he were in straits from foolish gambles. He seemed to laugh it off. Was it nothing, or was he hiding a secret?

Gentlemen were so cagey!

But then, he was so handsome. So sophisticated. Really, such an elegantly manly sort of man. He was tall and his features were finely composed—deep-set dark eyes, prominent cheekbones, dark hair. When they'd stood at the windows she'd detected the scent of bergamot soap. His clothes were immaculate and he was not overdecorated, just wearing a gold signet ring. Everything about him spoke of a quiet ingrained confidence.

During the years her sisters had gone before her, she'd given much thought to what her type of gentleman must be. She'd never come to a conclusion until she'd set eyes on Lord Manderbey at Verity's wedding. She'd been thinking of him ever since.

Was that wise, though? After all, there were several things running against it. He'd not expressed any particular interest. She'd felt something between them, some sort of initial spark, but that could very well be her wishful imaginings. And then, even if he did express interest, what sort of man was he really, underneath the urbane mien?

Could he be an inveterate gambler, always sinking under debt? If he were, and he expressed an interest in her, how could she know it was not her dowry that attracted his notice? She would not mind so much living in straightened circumstances as she would mind knowing she'd just been a ticket to more money to gamble away. As well, she must not forget all the lessons she'd learned from her novels. The villain did not advertise himself. He could often be mistaken for an honorable man…until it was too late. At least, almost too late, as the case usually was in stories.

It was a brisk morning and Winsome pulled her cloak tight around her as she hurried to Serenity's house two doors down. Lord Thorpe's butler answered the door, looking surprised to see her. She supposed he would be, as it was not yet nine o'clock.

"Lady Winsome," he said, "Lord Thorpe has gone out to exercise his horse in the park and Lady Thorpe is still abed with her breakfast."

"Oh she will not mind if I barge in," Winsome said, handing over her pelisse. "I know where it is."

She took the stairs two at a time and made her way to Lord and Lady Thorpe's suite of rooms. After a quick knock, she let herself in. At no surprise to Winsome whatsoever, she found Serenity teary-eyed with a cup of tea on the window bench. Havoc and Nelson, Lord Thorpe's great beast and Serenity's beloved three-legged dog, lounged on a sunny spot of carpet. They both wagged their tails but did not bother to get up.

"Winny! You've been out already. What a morning! Did you note the dew sparkling in the sunshine—it is sublime."

Of course, Winsome had not at all noticed the sublime dew. "Spectacular, I'm sure," she said, giving Nelson and Havoc some head scratches. "I've come to tell you everything about yesterday to hear your thoughts."

"Gracious, the curtsy. How did you get on? I'm sure I would have wept."

Winsome had no doubt of it. Though Serenity was grateful not to have been put through it, as all her sisters would be, she was eager to hear every last detail. She rang for a second pot of tea and an extra cup and Winsome told it to her.

CHAPTER FIVE

"So you see my trepidation," Winsome said when she'd finished recounting to Serenity everything she knew, or suspected, about Lord Manderbey.

Serenity nodded. "You worry that Lord Manderbey is not as he seems. Goodness, that is always a problem with gentlemen. At least, it seems so. Of course, I had not the smallest doubt of Thorpe being anything other than what he is, which is perfect. But then, everybody knows how sensitive to other people I am."

"Yes, he's perfect," Winsome said, in a bid to close the subject of Lord Thorpe's perfection. "But other gentlemen…how can we be certain?"

"That is true. Goodness, just yesterday we heard that Sir Tristan has gone to the continent to escape his debts. We had no idea he was in so deep."

"Yes, that is it exactly! You see the problem. And Serenity, I would not even mind discovering I was to be poor, at least not mind very much, I do not think. But I could not bear to discover that I'd only been pursued for my dowry. That I really could not bear."

Serenity set her teacup down. "Do you say things have progressed so quickly?"

Winsome could feel her cheeks get hot. "No, they really have not progressed at all. I might be a bit silly there. He has not indicated any direct interest. At the palace, his grandmother forced him to take me round the room. Then Papa is forcing him to come to dine. For all I know, he is set on another lady or nobody at all. But then you know how I am, I cannot help but to play out every eventuality in my mind and anticipate every outcome."

"Papa's dinner though," Serenity said. "We will wish to play Fact or Fib afterward. Perhaps we might gain some information there?"

"Yes, we might," Winsome said thoughtfully.

"I am assuming we will all be invited to it, of course."

"Yes, I am sure of it. You know how Papa misses everybody even though he claims he does not. Especially now that it's just me and Val." She paused, an idea just coming to her. "I suppose the dinner will be our introduction to Valor's hostessing clothes too. Madame LaFray says they're dreadful."

Serenity laughed over the idea. Winsome did not view it with the same mirth. Whatever Valor was to clothe herself in, it was bound to be embarrassing. Madame LaFray was never wrong. And then, Valor had got into the habit of making a speech too, which their father indulged her in as he found it amusing. It would be a lot for a stranger to the family to take in. And then, even before that, there was Almack's.

"You will attend Almack's on Wednesday to support me?" Winsome asked.

"Oh yes, we will all be there—the whole Nicolet clan."

At least that was a relief.

Serenity gazed out the window. "Winny, do you realize this is the very spot Thorpe sat in when he saw me out the window, for the first time, as I was glorying in the snow under the street-lamps?"

Winsome had not in fact realized that, but in true Serenity fashion, she was given a minute-by-minute description of that remarkable event, replete with the accompanying glories of nature and what was her current understanding of Thorpe's feelings in that moment. Apparently, he'd been enchanted.

As a general thing, Mrs. Right was not inclined to feel jumpy or uncertain or nervous. Sadly, she felt all of those things at the moment. As much as she'd tried to convince the staff that there was nobody in the house, evidence kept disputing that hopeful idea.

In truth, it had begun to feel as if they were being toyed with in some manner. Food continued to be taken from the kitchens and whoever was doing it was getting bolder by the minute. This morning, a plate and a half-eaten roll had been left on the servants' hall table. Very deliberately, she thought.

She'd had some hope that it was one of the boys doing it as a joke, but the fear in their eyes said otherwise.

Who was doing it? Why was it being done? Where were they hiding?

Winsome had told her that Lady Marchfield had acted exceedingly odd at the queen's drawing room. In the carriage, she'd refused to answer the duke's questions about being finished with sending butlers. Then, she'd left them at court with no arrangements to be taken home.

Lady Marchfield had to be at the bottom of this! Was this some sort of twisted revenge? Perhaps they'd gone too far with the lady. Perhaps she'd sunk into madness over it. Who knew what the lady might do?

Thomas, Charlie, and Cook stared morosely at the half-eaten roll that had been discovered. Mrs. Right was their leader, she had to act.

"All right. I will call a locksmith and have the locks to the servants' entrance changed. We have searched the house thoroughly so if someone is helping themselves to our pantry they are coming from the outside. Somehow, somebody has got hold of a key. As a further precaution, we will set up a watch between us. If there is anybody in the house, we will catch them and eject them. I will not stand for this nonsense.

"A watch, Mrs. Right?" Thomas asked. "You mean one of us will be down here alone?"

Mrs. Right could see Thomas's point. And she now considered how tired everybody would be if their sleep were interrupted by watch duty. "Very well, we will start with the locks and then see where we are." Thinking to raise their spirits, she said, "I reckon that will be the end of it."

At least, she dearly hoped so. These days, she went through the house feeling as if she were watched from every corner.

ALVIN BEETSON, EARL of Landry, felt pressured from all sides. How had time flown by so fast? He had once been so happy in his little corner of England, farming and trotting his horse around his estate in blessed peace. Then last year the extended family had come together like a foreign army. They wished him to wed. They turned up unexpectedly and stayed for days, pressuring him to wed. He never knew when they'd turn up next.

Of course, he'd always wished to wed. Though, he had thought that some magical thing would happen to him to transform him. It had not happened. He was so nervous around women. He could not get past the idea. Each time he thought of marriage, and what that would entail…he was certain he would not get it right. The poor lady would despise him.

That was the crux of the problem. He was a man. He was meant to lead. A wife would look to him for direction. He was meant to set the tone. He did not like to do anything like that. And then, to lead a lady into a bedchamber…the very thought of it sent a chill down his spine. She would not know what she was doing and neither would he!

A lady would look for everything he was not.

The idea had really been hammered home at the queen's

drawing room. Manderbey had left him standing there with the dowager as he confidently strode over to Lady Winsome. Why could he not do that? Why could he not confidently stride over to a lady?

And then, the duke had approached him and informed him that Lady Marchfield had left them high and dry. What a dullard he was to not have instantly offered his carriage. The duke had been forced to come right out and ask him.

He could not even manage to approach Lady Winsome when he already was acquainted with her and she had proved herself a nice person. She was so pretty too. Well, except for that court dress, but that could not be helped. No, the only reason he'd ever talked to her in the first place had been because his great state of alarm over having to dine with the hoi polloi had overridden his fear of women.

If he could not talk to a lady he'd already met, how was he to talk to any lady? And that was only talking! What would come after was terrorizing.

Perhaps it was not too late to go Catholic and become a priest? Or throw himself down a flight of stairs and pretend to be paralyzed? Or maybe pretend at some sort of madness of the mind?

Perhaps he would not have to pretend at madness. He might be quite mad already for all he knew. Was there another lord in England who was frightened of women? They were so mysterious.

His cousin had dragged him to Almack's. He was expected to talk to ladies he'd never set eyes on. He pulled on his neckcloth and wondered if he would faint.

"Lord Landry."

He turned and found Lady Winsome and the duke. "Your Grace, Lady Winsome," he sputtered. He bowed but he did not think it at all well done.

"Goodness, you do not look well," Lady Winsome said. "Are you quite all right?"

Landry felt as if he might weep. It was the first time anybody had asked him if he was all right in years.

"It's nerves, is it, Landry?" the duke said.

"I am afraid so, Your Grace."

"Winny, what do you say about supper with this fellow? Manderbey has been wrestled into escorting Lady Whoever-She-Is. I can arrange it with the patronesses."

"Yes, let's do," Lady Winsome said.

"Would you really?" Landry said. "That is so kind. Really so kind." One of his greatest fears had been the supper. He could dance well enough, his mother had employed a dancing master for years. But the supper would be all talking while his various relations stared at him from their locations round the table, attempting to discern if he made any progress.

"In the meantime," the duke said, pulling a flask from his pocket, "have a swig of this. It will put some spirits into you. Quite literally."

Landry did as he was asked. The brandy burned his throat but he was grateful for it. These people were really so kind!

"Take a deep breath, Lord Landry," Lady Winsome advised. "Whatever happens tonight, you will come out of it alive. At least, so I've been told."

"Chin up, as they say," the duke said.

Lady Winsome and the duke left him as they made their way over to their extended family. They left him in a somewhat better state than they'd found him and for that he would be eternally grateful.

WINSOME HAD BEEN nervous to step through the doors of Almack's, but two things buoyed her. Her dress was marvelous, a midnight-blue silk with an organza overlay of the same color. Madame LaFray had counseled her at length over her coloring.

She'd explained that if Winsome went in for pastels, she'd end up looking insipid. Her blonde hair and fair features must be countered and made to stand on their own through the use of deeper colors. The madame had taken note of Winsome's coloring during her other visits and had known just the thing to set them off. When she'd seen the result of the madame's designs, she agreed. In any case, she would not for the world wish to be seen as insipid.

The second idea that buoyed her was her family. They turned out in force to support her—Felicity and Mr. Stratton, Grace and Lord Dashlend, Patience and Lord Stanford, Serenity and Lord Thorpe, and Verity and Lord Wembly. They were such a crowd and all turned up on her account.

Perhaps even a third thing had buoyed her, though it made her feel nervous too. When they'd entered, Lord Manderbey had stood near the doors and approached them directly. After the greetings, he seemed to be in a rush to explain that the Countess of Westmoreland had committed him to taking Lady Edith into supper. He'd made a point of saying he'd not chosen it himself, which of course was flattering as she thought he was hinting he'd rather have escorted her in.

Lord Manderbey had been roped into it on account of Lady Westmoreland owing some sort of favor to Lady Edith's mother. But, he went on to say that he had requested that he be put down for Lady Winsome's first, as a consolation.

Of course, she would wish the lord was taking her into supper. She really wanted to find out more about the dunning and his comment about playing cards. It seemed those inquiries would need to wait until the dinner on the morrow.

And then, this Lady Edith—why should she be dining with the lord on account of a favor? Was the lady inclined toward him? Or he, her? He'd not sounded inclined, but it was a little puzzling. Winsome Nicolet did not like puzzling. She'd read enough stories where things began as puzzling and rapidly deteriorated. Puzzling was never a good situation. She liked things spelled out as one way or the other.

The duke had led her into the ballroom and they'd encountered a very nervous Lord Landry. The poor fellow! The duke had taken pity on him and had gone off to arrange things with the Countess of Westmoreland. He would request Lord Landry be put down for Winsome's supper. She would do her best to cheer him up.

Now she was surrounded by family and felt as safe as a lamb in a paddock. Of course, all too soon the ball would begin and she would be on her own. She would not allow an opportunity to pass, though, that might give her more information about Lord Manderbey and here was his good friend, Lord Wembly, standing by Verity.

"Lord Wembly," she said, "we saw your friend, Lord Manderbey, at the queen's drawing room yesterday." It was vague, but as good an opening as she could think of.

"Really?" Lord Wembly said. "I wonder what he was doing there—he does not have a sister."

"It is my understanding that his dowager wished to go, and he escorted her there."

Lord Wembly appeared taken aback. "The dowager duchess? She's *here*? In Town?"

"Indeed she is, she will come to dine on the morrow."

"I had not known," Lord Wembly said softly. "Gad, she's decided to put him on a short leash, then."

A short leash? Did that have something to do with the gambling debts that had been hinted at?

"What does that mean, Wembly?" Verity asked. "Why is he to be on a leash at all?"

Winsome silently thanked Verity, as it was just what she wished to know herself.

"As to that, I do not really know the details," Wembly muttered. "It's just, well she can be a strong-willed old girl. Likes to have her way."

What way was it, though? Was the dowager here to rein in

Lord Manderbey's gambling? Or was it something else?

"Oh God, there she is," Lord Wembly said, gazing across the ballroom.

Winsome's eyes followed his. The dowager was just now standing by her father. Goodness, they were both drinking from flasks.

"What is she doing?" Lord Wembly asked.

"As to that," Winsome said, "I believe my father mentioned he would bring brandy in a flask. And the dowager mentioned she might do it too. Canary, I believe she said. Considering the size of her reticule, it seems she has done."

"Drinking at Almack's. That is just what I mean about her!" Lord Wembly said.

"Oh dear," Verity said laughing, "the dowager and our father coming together is bound to cause trouble."

"Can you do something to stop it?" Lord Wembly asked his wife.

This sent Verity into peals of laughter. "No," she said.

The orchestra had been tuning for some time, the conductor putting the musicians through their paces. Now he turned and gave a nod to Lady Westmoreland and the sets began to form.

Lord Manderbey approached and held out his arm.

Winsome laid her gloved hand gently upon it and took a breath. Here she went.

LELAND HAD WISHED to shake the Countess of Westmoreland. He was well aware that the patronesses must have their way, but that had not stopped his irritation over being assigned to take Lady Edith into dine.

As that was the case, he'd lurked near the doors for Lady Winsome's arrival. He'd dropped some hints that his dining companion had not been his first choice and that he'd petitioned for Lady Winsome's first set as a consolation. He thought she'd taken his meaning.

He hoped so, anyway. There would be no end of gentlemen doing their very best to impress her. She had looked very well in that absurd court dress, but now, to see her as a proper lady out for the evening…she was spectacular. Everything about her was elegant, from her hair to her slippers. The shade of the dress was perfection for her coloring—so many ladies who were fair attempted a match with lighter colors but there was something about it that looked almost childish.

Lady Winsome Nicolet looked anything but childish.

Leland led her to the top of a forming set, then was irritated to see that his profligate cousin, St. John, joined as the bottom couple. He had not known St. John was in Town. His cousin was partnered with Lady Edith, who Leland would be forced to take into the dining room. Lady Edith was large and a bit ungainly, but that was not what really put him off about her. She was so forceful in her manner, wishing to bend a person to her opinion. She was almost like his grandmother incarnate.

St. John appeared to ignore Lady Edith entirely, as he was determinedly smiling at Lady Winsome. That, in itself, was irritating. And then, Leland was not even certain how the fellow had afforded to come to Town this season, as he'd so recently bailed him out of a crushing gambling debt. He ought to be at home, keeping his head down and not giving the palace any reason to think he might not be the ideal ambassador to Portugal.

The orchestra struck up a cotillion, led by Lady Westmoreland and the Duke of Bolton.

As they were the top couple, Leland led Lady Winsome through the steps. She was so graceful at it. They returned to their place so the other couples might take their turn.

"I suppose you must be relieved to have done with the queen's drawing room," he said.

"I got out of that dress as soon as I could and will never in my life don such a mountain of fabric again," Lady Winsome said.

Leland smothered his laughter. She really had a unique way of expressing an idea. He also could not help his mind drifting to the idea of Lady Winsome getting out of a dress.

In a much quieter voice, she said, "Why does that fellow opposite keep staring over here in such a manner?"

Leland looked over and found the lady referred to St. John, who was still staring, despite Lady Edith's obvious annoyance over it. "A cousin, I'm afraid. Do not ever agree to play cards with him. His name is St. John, a viscount."

"Oh, Lord St. John. He is on my card for the third," Lady Winsome said. "Though, why do you say one ought not to play cards with the gentleman?"

"Just a jest, not a particularly clever one. It is only that he is one of my more serious money problems," Leland said, not paying very close attention to his words. His thoughts were far more focused on the idea that St. John was on Lady Winsome's card. That, taken with the rude staring, began to prompt an idea. Was St. John planning on making a play for Lady Winsome's dowry?

He would not deserve her. He was not certain who St. John *would* deserve, but certainly not Lady Winsome Nicolet.

"I see," Lady Winsome said. "Do you say, then, that you have a lot of money problems?"

"Beset from all sides, it sometimes seems," Leland said. "People crawling out of the woodwork demanding money."

It would not be out of the realms of possibilities that St. John had decided a dowry was the quickest way to alleviate his money pressures. The man had been informed, in no uncertain terms, that he would not be rescued from gambling debts again in future. Perhaps the rogue thought he might turn to other avenues to secure funds?

It was time for the change and Lady Westmoreland had called a Grand Chain. He faced Lady Winsome and extended his right hand. It was lovely to have her delicate gloved hand in his, though it lasted only a moment. He passed her off clockwise as he made his way counter, and they met again where they'd started. Though, he did not like the idea of St. John touching her hand too. What was that degenerate up to?

"I look forward to the dinner on the morrow," he said, as he could not very well say what he was actually thinking.

"Yes, as to that, you might find us a bit…unusual," Lady Winsome said. "My father does not see the need to do everything…precisely as everybody else does it."

Leland had no doubt of it. The duke was his own man with his own peculiarities. "I have some interesting relations myself," he said, "one of which will be coming with me."

"The dowager," Lady Winsome said. "I am afraid the lady has taken my father's advice regarding bringing a flask."

"Did she?" Leland asked. He should have known to ask why she brought such a large reticule to a ball. "Just as a general comment," Leland said, sensing the perfect opportunity for a warning, "do not believe much of what my grandmother says. She is an inveterate liar, always for her own purpose."

Rather than shock, this caused Lady Winsome to laugh. "My father plays very loose with the truth, though it generally has no particular purpose but for his own amusement."

She then went on to tell him about Captain James Cook Day and the resulting barring from several inns.

The dance ended far too soon and Leland stayed on for conversation as long as he could do before having to seek out his partner for the second dance.

"Until tomorrow, Lady Winsome."

She smiled at him. That brilliant smile. He really could look at it all day.

CHAPTER SIX

I F WINSOME HAD looked for any clarity this night, she had looked in vain.

Lord Manderbey had been a perfect partner on the ballroom floor. He was so nonchalantly confident and she found it very attractive. She found *him* very attractive, all of him. When she'd put her hand in his for the Grand Chain, she'd felt something. Something new. She'd wished to skip over all the niceties of society and simply leap into his arms to try it out.

But then, she could not forget what he'd said. People were crawling out of the woodwork to demand money from him. How could he say it so casually? She must suppose he ought to get credit for not attempting to hide his situation. He seemed to be in the habit of losing a deal of money over cards.

Though, why did he not seem at all chastened by it? One would hope, if a gentleman had made such a mistake, he would be embarrassed. He would seek to rectify it. Lord Manderbey seemed to take it all as a joke. How could she trust her life to such a man? And yet she could not dismiss him from her thoughts.

Her dance with Lord St. John had raised even more questions. She'd got the idea that Lord Manderbey owed him a deal of money and she'd gone fishing for more information. She'd said, "Lord Manderbey made an amusing joke. He said people were coming out of the woodwork, dunning him for money."

Lord St. John had seemed very taken aback and answered. "Is

that what he said? Perhaps he ought to recall that we are family and pay up."

She was being given more and more evidence that underneath that urbane and handsome exterior might be somebody dangerous. She had promised herself that she would pay close attention to clues and run the other direction when it was hinted that she dealt with a less than honorable man. So why was she not inclined to run?

It was confounding. All these years she'd silently scolded the heroines in her novels for not running away when they sensed danger. How could they be so foolish? And here she was, acting just like them. She was going forward pretending she did not see what she saw, she did not know what she knew.

She'd done her best to wash away her pensiveness and be a creditable partner to the other gentlemen Lady Westmoreland had put down on her card. She hoped she'd done all right.

Now, Lord Landry led her through the last paces of the dance before supper and then put out his arm. He seemed to be in better spirits than he had been when he'd arrived. The poor fellow was probably uplifted by the idea that he'd somehow got through it.

He walked her into the dining room and looked about for two chairs together. "Would over there be all right?" he asked.

"Yes, yes," Winsome said. "It is really not necessary to gain approval for all of your decisions, Lord Landry. Take me to whatever chairs you like."

He steered her to the chairs he had mentioned and they sat down. Just down the table on the opposite side, Lord Manderbey sat with Lady Edith. Winsome had been introduced to her during one of the sets—she seemed a straightforward sort of person. Though, just now she seemed to be lecturing Lord Manderbey on some matter.

"Oh dear," Lord Landry said softly. "What should we ask for. I've heard, well it's been mentioned that—"

"It's all terrible," Winsome answered for him. "Ask for tea

and the dry cake, it is the best we will do."

"Yes, that must be right, I thought so myself."

After those two items had arrived, such as they were, Winsome said, "How did you get on this evening, Lord Landry?"

His spirits seemed to perk up at the inquiry. "Not as bad as I thought. Some of it was entirely nerve-wracking, I cannot pretend it was not. What was I to say when Lady Finella asked about my interests? My interests, she wished to know. I like to ride my horse and have a look over my estate, make sure the home farm is in good order, but can that count as an interest? To be on the safe side of things, I said I did not have any."

Winsome bit her lip. Whoever Lord Landry landed with, it was likely not Lady Finella.

"But then," he went on, "I danced with Lady Edith. I told *her* I did not have any interests, as it seemed to be the right answer, and she said, 'Good God man, are you not interested in your crops and herds?' Then I said, 'I am, actually.' Then we talked about crops."

"Gracious, it sounds as if you had a genial meeting of the minds," Winsome said.

"I believe so," Lord Landry said. "We are both to attend a card party on the morrow and I think I will ask about her herds. Does she have sheep? She never had time to say."

Winsome was delighted for Lord Landry. However, there was another topic she'd like to touch on. "Lord Landry, as I think I might call you a friend—"

"A friend! Well yes, I will be your friend."

"Excellent," Winsome said. "I was just wondering, Lord Manderbey said he's got people coming out of the woodwork looking for money and then Lord St. John said that Lord Manderbey ought to remember they were related and pay up."

She watched closely as Lord Landry took in the information. "Ah yes, I understand the money problem has created some tension between them."

Before she could question him further, the duke appeared

behind her chair. "Well Landry, still in one piece, I see."

"Yes, Your Grace," Lord Landry said, "and it is no small miracle."

"I see, well guess what, Winny? The dowager and I have drained our flasks. I'd usually say it is time to go home before I throw mine at your aunt's head but she's not made an appearance. So, I suppose it is just time to go."

With that, they left Lord Landry considering what questions about her herds he might pose to Lady Edith.

LELAND HELD HIS arms up while his valet removed his shirt. What a palaver. The beginning of the ball had been perfection, but then it had all gone downhill from there.

He'd watched St. John dance with Lady Winsome and he'd not liked what he saw. His cousin could be very smooth mannered when he put his mind to it.

Then he'd seen his grandmother and he'd not liked what he saw there either. She was blatantly drinking from a flask at the edges of the ballroom, accompanied by the Duke of Pelham.

Then he'd seen that Landry had taken Lady Winsome into the dining room and he'd not liked what he saw there. Why was Landry to be giving carriage rides from court and taking the lady in to dine just because they'd met at an inn?

And finally, he'd himself taken in Lady Edith. Why the lady grilled him on every subject he mentioned, he did not know. The lady had a lot of opinions. Why was he to justify not keeping pigs at his estate in Hertfordshire? He'd been forced to explain that he was rarely there, as he preferred Torquay, which was not a working farm. She'd not been satisfied with that answer and noted that if he simply hired a pig man he would not need to be on the scene. Then he'd had to go into the details of having a tenant who raised pigs as their sole source of income and he would not like to cut into the fellow's profits. She'd still not appeared wholly satisfied, but there really was nothing else to say. Talking to Lady Edith was like facing a massive wave in a small boat—the encounter could not be stopped and one had better just hold on.

He'd finally extricated himself and then had to give his arm to his grandmother, who almost certainly was in her cups. Just now, she was currently lingering outside his firmly locked door despite having been delivered into the hands of Miss Price when they arrived home.

"I only say," she said from the corridor, "the duke is great fun and Lady Winsome is pretty."

"Ignore her," Leland said to his valet, Richards.

"How am I to get out, though?" Richards whispered, glancing at the door.

"Go out through the wardrobe door to the corridor and then run, she will not be able to catch you. I'll lock it after you go, so she is not able to catch *me*."

"But on the other hand," the dowager said, "I like Lady Edith's homegrown country sense. Is she elegant? Well maybe not, but she's got wide hips! They come in handy for babies."

Richards staggered just the smallest bit to hear Lady Edith's hips mentioned.

"I'll have my best coat on the morrow for the duke's dinner," Leland told him. "The new dark-blue wool."

"Now there is also Lady Finella—do not rule her out!"

"Is there brandy in the other room?" Leland asked.

"Yes, my lord, the decanter is full."

Leland nodded. Once he'd arrived to the house and ascertained how difficult his grandmother planned on being, he'd had a door put in, leading from his bedchamber to a guest room. It had since been redone as a library of sorts and had a large bolt added to the inside of the door leading to the corridor. He would retreat in there to escape this current onslaught of opinions.

"Now I think common sense will tell you," the dowager said,

"that this season is chock full of suitable ladies—pick one!" There was a long pause, then his grandmother said, "Miss Price says I have to be abed now. We will pick up this conversation in the morning."

Leland heard them make their way down the corridor, Miss Price issuing low encouragements and his grandmother repeating, "But it had to be said."

She wished to pick up the conversation in the morning. They certainly would do. Leland was prepared to lecture her severely on several fronts. Drinking at Almack's, presuming to manage him, and loitering at his door in the small hours of the morning. He would conclude with how she was to comport herself at the duke's dinner on the morrow. She was to be circumspect. He would not wish Lady Winsome to turn away from him because he was in possession of a particularly strange relation.

Hopefully, a stern lecture would have more effect than all the stern lectures that had gone before.

He picked up a book and took it into his snug new library. He'd written to Lackington & Allen requesting they send over their most popular gothic novel. It was one of Lady Winsome's interests and would be something in common to mention on the morrow.

Leland poured himself a brandy, threw himself onto the leather sofa he'd had brought in, and looked it over.

Mr. Lackington had sent over a book titled *Gloaming at Glenford Cross*. From the description, it seemed a vicar's daughter disappeared after walking through a dark wood at sunset. The villagers had begun to suspect that the newly arrived inhabitant of Werely Castle might be at the bottom of it as several swore they heard screams at night coming from that direction.

He could not imagine what Lady Winsome saw in it, but he would be prepared to talk about it.

MRS. RIGHT FELT pressed from all sides. Whoever was taunting them inside the house had seemed to redouble their efforts. It was as if she were being mocked for changing the locks and imagining that would end the problem. This morning, there was a half-empty teapot sitting on the servants' hall table. She had touched it and it was cold, so it had been there for some hours. There were reports of things all over the house being moved and it had become hard to tell what was real and what was imagination. Had the duke forgotten he'd left certain papers out? Had Reynolds, the duke's valet, accidently misplaced so many of the duke's neckcloths? What had happened to the silver salt cellar?

Who was doing it? Where were they hiding? Why were they hiding? What was the purpose of it all?

And then, Lady Marchfield was not sticking to her usual habits. She'd not made an appearance at Almack's the night before. Why should she suddenly change what she did? She always attended the opening ball of Almack's, and yet, she did not go. She was up to something, though Mrs. Right could not work out what it might be.

It was true that they had foiled the lady season after season, and that might put a person's back up. But Mrs. Right had not imagined she'd ever do something about it other than hurl a few insults and storm off. Was she doing something more about it?

All this to think about on the day the duke was to host a dinner. The footmen were jumpy and she had to keep reminding them about the details of what must go on the table. They'd set down the everyday napkins instead of the exquisitely embroidered napkins with the duke's crest done by Mrs. Wellform in the Dales. Both Charlie and Thomas knew better, but they were in too much of a state to think clearly. What might they do at the dinner itself? Would they forget which wines went with what course?

Cook was a mere shell of a man at this point, and she dearly hoped he would gather himself together. Breakfast had been a shambles and the duke had wished to know why his fried eggs had appeared to be fried for hours together. The kitchen maids, ever ready to panic over London kidnappers and murderers, had taken their lead from Cook and were usually found in tears, whispering to each other. Mrs. Right had already twice pointed out that potatoes could not peel themselves.

There was also the upstairs to think about. She was still sleeping in Valor's room and getting kicked and punched through the night. The girl was a dear, but she was a veritable boxer when she was asleep. And then there was Sir Galahad to contend with. How such loud noises could emanate from such a little pug, she did not know. She'd barely slept last night.

Mrs. Right straightened her fichu and then she straightened her back. She must put some starch into her staff and lead them forward. Whatever was going on in this house, the duke was to host a dinner and they must all pull together. Somehow.

WINSOME HAD LET Valor try on everything in her jewelry case. Years ago, the duke had allowed them all to choose what pieces of their mother's they liked and as Valor had been very young at the time, she'd gone for the most ridiculous paste. For ages, her favorite had been a rather terrible enameled parrot pin. They'd have to do something about that before Valor made her debut.

Just now, Valor wore Winsome's short string of pearls. "I like pearls," she said. "They're pretty and round. They almost look soft, but they're not. And then, I like that they came from the sea and were never buried under rocks."

That was a lot of reasons to like pearls, Winsome supposed. "You ought to keep that necklace, Val," she said. "You did not really have a fair chance at Mama's jewelry."

Valor admired her reflection in the glass. "It will go splendidly with my hostessing gown."

The hostessing clothes. Winsome had almost managed to

forget about that. And some other things Valor was likely to get up to. "Val, I really do not think it is necessary to make any sort of speech to open the dinner."

"Do not make one, then."

"I mean *you*," Winsome said. "You do not need to make a speech."

"Yes, I do," Valor said, showing Sir Galahad her newly acquired necklace. "I am more clever than you think. When I make a speech, I am showing Papa how great I am as his hostess. He'll never want me to get married. Too much to lose."

So that was the aim.

Mrs. Right bustled into the room. "We'd best get you dressed, Winsome," she said.

Winsome nodded. She had picked out a dress specially for the dinner. It was a dark-green lightweight velvet with a subtle trim of copper-colored silk braid. It was distinctive without being showy and set off her hair in some way.

"You will come to me next, Mrs. Right?" Valor asked the housekeeper. "I have hostessing clothes now."

"Ah yes, the hostessing clothes," Mrs. Right said. "I'll be along shortly, Poppet."

Valor seemed satisfied with that and scooped up Sir Galahad. She trounced out of the room, calling over her shoulder, "Thanks for the pearls, Winny!"

"Have you seen the hostessing clothes?" Winsome asked Mrs. Right.

"I am afraid so. The poor little mite looks eighty if she looks a day. Now, you are not to worry over it. If Lord Manderbey is any sort of stalwart man, he will not fan himself over a younger sister's…whatever it is."

"What about the speech she's determined to make?"

Mrs. Right laid out her dress. "He might fan himself over that, if history is anything to go by, but Thomas and Charlie fill the wine glasses rather full at that moment to smooth it over."

Winsome nodded, though she was not certain how much

wine it would take to erase the memory of one of Valor's speeches.

"Might I ask," Mrs. Right said, "are you settling your mind on Lord Manderbey?"

"Oh, as to that, well, it is early days…" Winsome trailed off. She'd not told anybody but Serenity that it seemed he might be a profligate gambler. Last evening, he'd indicated he had no intention of reforming.

Her father had inquired into her views as they rode in the carriage, returning from Almack's, and she'd been noncommittal. She could not bear for anybody to turn against him.

She should turn against him, or at least turn away and wash her thoughts of him. She could not do it, though. At least, not yet. After all, just because a person had no intention of reforming did not mean they might not change their mind. Certainly, that must be true. Even though it was precisely what her heroines often thought, and it was never true.

Mrs. Right helped her into her dress and did up the buttons. Then she wrestled Winsome's hair into order and pinned her small and restrained diamond tiara securely amidst her curls. She was not exactly supposed to wear a tiara, at least not until she was engaged, but Lady Rose had broken with that tradition last year with no repercussions. Her Papa said that anything she inherited from her mother could be worn at any time, even at breakfast if she wished. In any case, she liked it, so she would wear it.

"You look a picture," Mrs. Right said. "Lord Manderbey will be bowled over by it, I'm sure."

"I am not certain whether I wish him to, or do not wish him to. Is that strange?"

Mrs. Right laughed. "Not according to how any of your sisters went forward. Now, I'd best see to Valor. And her hostessing clothes, the poor misguided little mite."

CHAPTER SEVEN

L ELAND HAD BEEN determined to speak forcefully to his grandmother that morning. It had not been possible though. Miss Price had reported that the dowager was under the weather due to the prior evening's late night. Leland presumed it was not the late hour that had affected her, but the flask of Canary she'd seen fit to bring with her.

Now they were in the carriage, having just set off for Grosvenor Square. He would use that quarter hour to say what must be said.

"You were a spectacle last evening," he said.

"Oh really?" the dowager said. "Nobody dared say a word about it though, did they? I am a dowager duchess and I amused myself with a duke of the realm. Only the queen would dare scold me over it, not those puffed-up patronesses."

Leland decided to drop that particular subject as it seemed he would not get anywhere with it. "I hope you intend to conduct yourself with a modicum of restraint this evening."

The dowager shrugged. "Depends on the quality of the duke's wine, does it not?"

"It certainly does not. Furthermore, I demand you cease attempting to manage my affairs, which I am entirely capable of managing myself."

"Do not be ridiculous," the dowager said. "If you were, I'd be surrounded by grandchildren by now."

"Really, Grandmama, I am issuing a warning. If you do not restrain yourself I will have to pack you up and send you home."

This elicited peals of laughter from the dowager. "Oh that is rich. Manderbey, you have no imagination. Can you not conjure a picture of the dramatic show I would make of it? Drury Lane could not rise to the heights of what I could produce. I suppose I might even throw myself on the pavement and cry that I am an old and decrepit woman abandoned by my kin to starve in the countryside alone."

"Nobody will believe you would starve."

"People will believe anything from an old person lying on the pavement."

She really was irascible. All Leland could do was pray she did not say anything outrageous at the dinner. Then, he really would have to find a way to send her home. He could not go on all season in this manner.

Perhaps his father could send a letter regarding…some emergency. Perhaps the duke could send a letter indicating that the new duchess was not getting the hang of things and required her instruction. The dowager would jump at the chance to boss about her daughter-in-law.

He would write his father about it. If there were anybody who knew how much trouble the dowager could be, it was the duke. Of course, since he did know it, he might not want to have her coming in his direction to trouble his wife.

As they rode along in silence, Leland reviewed the book he'd begun reading last night and had finished this morning over breakfast. The point of reading it was to have a common subject of conversation with Lady Winsome. What on earth was he to say about it though?

It seemed the vicar's daughter who'd walked through the wood at twilight had encountered the mysterious man who had taken over Werely Castle. He'd blown a powder into her face and she'd followed him willingly. Then she was locked in a tower and when she came to her senses all she could think to do was scream out a window at night. There was no explanation for why she did not scream in the daytime, or try to break the lock on the door, or how she survived without food and water. The milliner's swashbuckling son had come to the rescue and they wed. As the church bells rang, the castle collapsed in a heap. No explanation of whether the mysterious man was in it, though it was an accepted fact that it collapsed because he could not marry the vicar's daughter.

What was he to make of that?

The carriage rolled to a stop in front of the duke's house. He had not been to the address since Wembly got married there. He leapt down and assisted his grandmother to the pavement, though he'd rather leave her in the carriage.

Surprisingly, a footman showed them in and announced them. Leland had seen no sign of a butler at Wembly's wedding and had assumed some illness or emergency had caused the absence. It seemed strange that he would still be missing from the scene.

The dowager greeted the duke as if they were fast friends, which he supposed they were after their little adventure last evening. For himself, he was all eyes on Lady Winsome. She had such a refined style. The bottle-green velvet with copper-braid trim was the sort of dress that would stand apart and be found superior. And that was before he considered how it brought out the copper highlights of her hair and her perfectly freckled nose.

"Lord Manderbey," Lady Winsome said. "This is my younger sister, Lady Valor. You may remember her from my sister Verity's wedding."

Leland had hardly noticed anybody else was in the room. He looked about and found a strangely attired girl holding a dog. He did remember her, as she'd given a bizarre speech at the wedding. She was young and yet dressed as if she were a hundred years old. Her dress was a heavy brocade in purple silk and embroidered with gold thread, the sort elderly ladies sometimes favored and everybody else would relegate to curtains. The dress sported a lace fichu with a pearl necklace improbably worn over it.

Lady Valor held up a pug. "Isn't he tremendous?"

"Lady Valor," he said. "Um yes, he does seem so."

She nodded in approval. "I will go and show the dowager. Old people are drawn to me and they always love my dog." She marched off to the duke and his grandmother.

"I feel I should apologize for anything Valor has said or will say," Lady Winsome said.

"Not at all," Leland said, "else I'll have to do the same for my grandmother. Lady Valor's mode of dress, it that a Yorkshire style of some sort?"

The faintest blush spread over Lady Winsome's perfect cheeks. "I'm afraid not. She calls them her hostessing clothes and believes they make her appear older than she is."

Leland snorted. "They do accomplish that."

Other people began to stream into the room. Most of the gentlemen he knew—Stratton, Dashlend, Stanford, Thorpe, and of course Wembly. As for the ladies, he often encountered Lady Felicity and Lady Verity, while the rest he'd met at the wedding.

As they exchanged greetings, one of the footmen reappeared at the door looking as if he had some very bad news to deliver. He was positively pale and whispered, "Lady Marchfield, Your Grace."

All of the sisters seemed to take this announcement very hard, though Leland could not ascertain why. The rest of the family was gathered, why should it be unusual that the duke's sister had arrived?

Perhaps it was the lady's demeanor that set them off. She strode into the room with a look of defiance.

"Lady Misery," the duke said, "what have I done to cause you to darken my door? Not a good time, in any case. I'm hosting a dinner."

"As I am well aware," Lady Marchfield said briskly. She turned to the footman, who was stock-still and staring at her. "Set another place."

The footman fled the room and Leland was not certain if he'd gone to set a place or simply fled.

Lady Marchfield strode across the room. "Winsome, you look very well."

"Aunt," Lady Winsome said with a note of caution in her tone. "We did not know you would come."

"Of course you did not, as I was not invited."

"Yes, but how…"

"How did I know? I think you will discover I know quite a bit more than you would imagine."

Leland could not begin to work out what was happening.

The same footman who had run out of the room ran back into it. "Your Grace," he said, breathless, "we went to set another place and…"

"And?" the duke asked.

"And it was already set," the footman said, steadying himself on the doorframe. The young man pointed at Lady Marchfield. "Somebody knew she was coming!"

The duke turned to his sister. "All right, what's the game, Misery?"

Lady Marchfield put her chin up and said, "I do not play games, as I think you will discover."

Leland looked back and forth between them. He did not know what went on in this family, but he was beginning to wonder why he'd ever bothered to worry about anything his grandmother might say.

WINSOME HARDLY KNEW where to look. Lady Marchfield had inexplicably turned up. She acted so strangely these days. How did she know about the dinner?

And then, were the footmen going mad? What did Charlie mean that a table setting had been added and nobody knew who did it? Certainly Thomas must have done. Or perhaps he'd miscounted in the first place?

The duke interrupted her thoughts. "Well now, I suppose we move this palaver into the dining room. I'll take in the dowager. Manderbey? Take in Winsome. Misery, I do not know who will take you in nor why you are here."

Lady Marchfield, inexplicably, did not look at all perturbed to hear it. "I am quite able to walk into a dining room without assistance."

Lord Manderbey held out his arm. Winsome laid her hand upon it but could not meet his eye. What must he think of all this?

She already knew how the place cards had been set. Her father took the bottom with the dowager to his right. Felicity took the top with Lord Manderbey on her right. Winsome would sit next to Lord Manderbey on his other side. Grace very awkwardly pointed out to their aunt where she was meant to sit, as there was no place card there.

The footmen brought round the wine, but their hands shook and they both stole wary glances at Lady Marchfield.

"Papa?" Valor said loudly.

Winsome pressed her lips together to stop herself from sighing. Loudly. Enough had gone on already, they did not need Valor adding to it with one of her outlandish speeches.

"Quite right," the duke said. "As all my relations know, but for Lady Misery over there who is never invited but decided to turn up anyway, my youngest likes to start us off with some words."

Valor had remained standing at her place. "Welcome to the dowager, who this dinner honors. We are already friends and she thinks my dog is tremendous."

Winsome was well aware of the slight to Lord Manderbey and that it was purposefully done. She glanced at the dowager. The lady's expression was inscrutable, so it was hard to say how she viewed this new friendship she'd suddenly acquired.

"Old people are drawn to me," Valor continued, "everybody knows it."

Winsome dug her nails into her palms under the table. She'd told Valor, repeatedly, to stop pointing out that a person was old. They did not like it!

"The company of women friends, like the dowager and my other very old friend Lady Margaret, is so much better than other kinds of friends. For one thing, they don't sleep in your room and for another, they don't stare at you while you're asleep. Mr. Stratton already admitted he does it but, realistically, I'm pretty sure they all do it."

Valor looked accusingly round the room at her sisters' husbands.

"For heaven's sake, Valor, do sit down," Lady Marchfield said.

"I am trying to convince Winsome not to get married!" Valor said. "She's the last one!" Valor threw herself into her chair, looking entirely disgusted.

"Well now, another rousing speech from my youngest," the duke said.

"I have some words to say too," Lady Marchfield said.

"I knew it," the duke said. "Whatever nonsense you are about to inflict on us, do not carry on with it all through the soup course."

Lady Marchfield, as it seemed was becoming her habit, ignored the duke's barb. Into the air, so it was not entirely clear who she was aiming at, she said, "I have never been one to admit defeat. A person would be exceedingly foolish to imagine I have."

Her eyes drifted to her brother and now it *was* clear who she was aiming at.

The duke laughed and said, "Do not tell me, you have another one of your endless string of hapless butlers waiting in your carriage."

"Mr. Wicket, I believe it is time to introduce yourself," Lady Marchfield said with a smile.

Mr. Wicket? Who was Mr. Wicket? Who was she talking to?

Winsome flinched as the curtains across the windows shifted. A very tall and thin man wearing a severe black suit of clothes emerged from behind them. He had hooded eyes and his sunken cheeks and rail thin physique made Winsome wonder how long he'd been hidden there. The footmen staggered back. Valor ducked under the table. The rest of them stared wide-eyed.

Lord Manderbey leaned toward Winsome. "Who is that?" he whispered.

"I'm afraid it might be the new butler," she whispered back.

"Correct, Lady Winsome," Mr. Wicket said. "Yes, I was able to perfectly comprehend your whispers, my hearing is exceptional, as is my eyesight." Mr. Wicket passed behind the duke and circled the table. The footmen backed out of his way. "Your Grace, Lady Marchfield hired me a month ago. I have been in the house since before your arrival, observing. I am skilled at remaining unseen, having recently served the palace in several clandestine operations. When Lady Marchfield explained what a challenge this household would pose, I knew I was the only man for the job."

"Get out," the duke said.

For some reason, Lady Marchfield did not look particularly alarmed over this directive. She simply nodded approvingly at Mr. Wicket. That gentleman strode to the doors, turned, and said, "Goodbye for now." He then disappeared out the doors to who knew where.

What did he mean, *for now*? Her father had just ordered the man out of the house and he'd said goodbye for now? Did he imagine the duke would change his mind and invite him back in?

Lady Marchfield laid down her napkin. "Well now, I have accomplished my aim here and need not suffer through this dinner." She glanced down at her soup. "I imagine your cook is somewhat rattled by recent events. This does not look up to the usual standards. I trust your diabolical housekeeper is likewise shaken."

Winsome's aunt rose. "Goodnight to you, Dowager, Lord Manderbey. I am sorry you had to witness this family contretemps, but the duke has unfortunately made it necessary."

As she walked to the doors, the duke said, "I warn you, Misery. Take that fool with you, let him be the last, and do not darken my doors with such nonsense again."

Lady Marchfield turned and smiled at her brother. "We'll see," she said.

She shut the doors behind her and was gone.

The dining room was suddenly filled with peals of laughter. The dowager was positively heaving. Catching her breath, she said, "Gracious, that was invigorating. What was it? Is this some sort of new style of a tableau? I've not seen it done before."

Valor slowly emerged from under the table. "Is that what it was, Papa? A tableau?"

The duke sipped his wine and said, "More or less, Val."

"I was never so amused," the dowager said. "Is Lady Marchfield coming back?"

"Not if the fates smile upon me, Duchess."

In a low tone, Lord Manderbey said, "That was not a performance, was it?"

"No," Winsome said.

"I never knew Lady Marchfield to be so…I do not actually know what that was."

Winsome shifted in her seat, searching for just the right sort of vagary that might explain what he'd just witnessed. "There were perhaps some circumstances over the past several seasons that have pushed my aunt too far," Winsome said, hoping Lord Manderbey would not ask what they were.

"Do you suppose that fellow has really left? I could not tell if he meant to leave or to hide behind another pair of curtains," the lord said.

"I do not know," Winsome said. Had he left? Where had he been hiding? The house had been searched top to bottom. He could not have been behind curtains all this time. How would they know if he left or was hiding again?

It was very uncomfortable to imagine that specter of a man lurking in the house somewhere.

"Lady Winsome," Lord Manderbey said, "I was wondering, have you read *Gloaming at Glenford Cross*? I understand it is very popular."

Winsome turned to him in surprise. Of course she had read it. The book was all the rage at this moment. "Have *you* read it?"

"Indeed, yes."

That was a surprise. Had he read it because she'd mentioned her interest in gothic stories? She did not know, but she did understand he'd brought it up to move beyond what they'd all just witnessed and she was grateful for it.

"I did have some questions and would be interested to hear your thoughts," he said.

"I imagine you found the vicar's daughter not very clever," Winsome said. "Really, why the girl did not shout out the window during the day was confounding."

"I will admit that I did wonder about her," Lord Manderbey said.

"They often are like that, ignoring warning signs from all directions and missing vital opportunities." As she said it, she wondered if that was what she was doing. Was she just ignoring warning signs? "I did think the castle collapsing at the end of it was a nice touch, though."

"Yes, but was the mysterious man in it when it collapsed? That was not made clear."

"Oh I imagine he must have been."

They went on speaking together, engrossed in one another and ignoring the rest of the table. Winsome occasionally heard the duke and the dowager laughing over some matter, or Valor attempting to get her attention which she positively ignored, or the gentle hum of husbands and wives talking.

The beginning of the dinner had been hair-raising, but the rest of it was going rather well. She put aside the strange Mr.

Wicket, as certainly he had left the house.

Hopefully.

MRS. RIGHT WAS doing her level best to keep Cook calm and stop the kitchen maids from shrieking.

It had started when Charlie abandoned the dining room and had come flying down the stairs. "Is he here? Did you see him?"

"See who?" Cook had asked, his eyes drifting round the kitchens.

"See *me*," a voice had said behind her.

Mrs. Right had jumped and leapt away from the voice. She turned and found a cadaver of a man in a black suit staring sternly at her.

"Mr. Tobias Wicket, His Grace's butler," the man said. "I have been here all along, observing."

"It was you, creepin' round the house," Cook said, pointing the knife in his hand at the intruder.

The kitchen maids took that moment to clutch and each other and wail.

"Silence!" Mr. Wicket shouted.

They wailed for another minute before they decided to follow that directive.

As the maids settled down to a whimper, Mr. Wicket said, "I will have eyes everywhere, watching everything. You would be well-advised to ensure this household is run impeccably."

Now that Mrs. Right had managed to catch her breath from the fright of this person's sudden arrival, she attempted to take his measure. It did not look as if he ate much and she could not imagine where Lady Marchfield had found him.

What was more worrying was that he'd been here all along. Where had he been hiding? Was that how he meant to go on? How was she to get rid of him?

Mr. Wicket pointed at Cook. "You are going to burn the house down if you don't do something about that oven."

They all turned and indeed, the oven was smoking. Cook wrestled the pan out of it which contained what was now a very well-done roasted beef. Cook looked at it dejectedly. Mrs. Right could only imagine how the duke was viewing what was coming up from the kitchens.

She turned back to Mr. Wicket. Then she looked around the room. Where was he?

"He's gone!" Cook cried. This prompted the kitchen maids to take up their wailing again. Mrs. Right grabbed an apron from a hook on the wall and rolled up her sleeves. Something had to be done about this dinner. She would deal with Mr. Wicket later.

If she could find him.

CHAPTER EIGHT

LELAND SUPPOSED THERE had never been a dinner like it. First, Lady Marchfield turned up, unexpectedly and apparently unwelcome. Then, a butler nobody had known was in the house had emerged from behind a pair of curtains. Between those two unlikely events, Lady Valor made an outrageous speech about men staring at their wives while they slept, naming Stratton as being particularly implicated in the habit.

The dinner itself was odd as well. An overcooked roasted beef had come round, sliced very thin and covered in a sauce. It really seemed as if it had been cooked well past its time and then the sauce was meant to cover that fact. The potatoes looked as if they'd just been thrown into a dish and had not even been composed with a sprinkling of chopped parsley. The rolls were positively black on the bottom. There was the subtle aroma of burning that wafted over it all. The wines, at least, were good.

The footmen were at sixes and sevens. They had run out of the room, only to run back in again a half hour later and say to the duke, "He never left the house and now he's disappeared again."

It seemed as if Mr. Wicket had suddenly appeared in the kitchens, just as suddenly disappeared, and the cook and kitchen maids were in a collapse about it. Which would explain the state of the dinner.

The footmen did not know where Mr. Wicket had disappeared to. They'd found the door to the wine cellar ajar and had bravely gone down with candles to search it, but they'd found nothing. They could not be sure if they themselves had left it ajar when they'd gone to fetch wines for the dinner.

It was beginning to seem as if the duke's new butler was some sort of genie disappearing into thin air. The duke remained remarkably unaffected by the information and only assured his footman that the housekeeper would rid them of the interloper.

The housekeeper? How was she to order the fellow out if the duke could not?

Despite all that, Leland was really enjoying himself. Lady Felicity had been determined to never even glance in his direction, leaving him to speak to Lady Winsome all through the dinner. After they'd thoroughly dissected *Gloaming at Glenford Cross*, and developed several improvements the author might have adopted, their conversation was more wide-ranging.

There were times he had to force himself to concentrate, as he was all but bewitched by the sprinkle of light freckles across her nose. He'd almost lost the thread of the conversation when he suddenly realized she was asking him about his house.

That was a promising sign, he thought.

"My father's estate is in Sussex, but I live mostly at Stonewall Manor in Torquay. There is another farming estate in Hertford-shire that I visit from time to time to keep it going, but it's rather staid. Stonewall is not large and there is in fact very little land. It is just the house, some outbuildings, the stables, and some gardens. However, it sits atop a cliff overlooking the harbor and the views are very good. As well, there is a little tavern in town that is quiet and keeps a good fire in the cozy during the cold months. I often go there to escape my grandmother." He paused, realizing he'd left out an important description. "And, I should probably say, she does live there now, in a little cottage on the grounds. When my grandfather died, she discovered she could not bear to be in the vicinity of the family seat, overruled by her daughter-in-law, so she refused to move into the dower house in Sussex."

"Oh, I see, yes, that must be hard for the dowager. She has ruled the roost for years and now she has to give way."

Leland nodded. "She is not particularly adept at giving way."

"We do not see my own grandmother—my mother's mother. All we know about her is that she is very stern and religious. She sends Christmas gifts every year and they are always very dreary with a scoldy letter coming along with it. I suppose it must be nice to have a grandmother who takes such an interest in your day-to-day life."

Of course, Lady Winsome supposed entirely wrong, but he did not correct her. He would not wish to frighten the lady off with any real description of what it was like to have his grandmother on the premises. The lady had been known to track him down in the tavern when she was bored and wished for his company.

"Well now," the duke said loudly from the other end of the table, "we have suffered through a rather terrible dinner on account of Mr. Wicket haunting the house but I will not blame the kitchens—Lady Misery is renowned for her ability to ruin an evening. Do not despair, though, as we can only go up from here."

Leland supposed there would be cards in the drawing room. Or perhaps there was a music room somewhere and the ladies would play.

"Has anybody warned our guests about what is to come?" the duke asked, looking jovially round the table.

Warned? Why should he be warned about it? Had they not experienced quite a lot already that they might have been warned of? What could possibly be next?

As Leland gazed round the table it was apparent that there were conflicting opinions on what was to come next. The ladies appeared in very good spirits, their husbands very much less so.

"Sorry," Stratton said, shrugging.

"It cannot be helped," Stanford said.

"Just get through it," Wembly advised. "That's what I did."

Good God, it sounded as if he were to go through some sort of trial.

"You can drink port in the drawing room," Thorpe said, "that can be looked at as a positive."

"Fact or Fib!" Lady Valor shouted.

Leland glanced at Lady Winsome with the hopes that she would provide some illumination.

"It is only a drawing room game," she said. "It is ever so much fun."

She said it was fun, but her cheeks said there was something embarrassing about it. They were not just pink but looked positively feverish.

"I do like a game," the dowager said.

"Now that reminds me, duchess," the duke said, "we don't go in for sending the ladies to their tea while the gentlemen sit here with port and cigars. I cannot be bothered with jawing about politics or a horse somebody just bought. We bring the port and brandy into the drawing room. Shall you want either of those? Or perhaps sherry?"

"You know me too well, duke," the dowager said. "Sherry is my preferred glass."

"Charlie, go down to the wine cellar and fetch one of the bottles of sack that just came in from Perry," the duke said.

The footman nodded, though he appeared deeply concerned to be sent down to the cellars. Apparently, finding the door ajar was still on his mind though the place had been searched. It was not particularly illogical. After all, if he were a strange butler hiding out in a house, he supposed the wine cellar would be as good a place to hide as any. One would at least be supplied with good drink to pass the clandestine hours.

The duke rose and led them through to the drawing room. Leland really had no idea what he was to face there, though he was grateful that he'd have a glass of port in his hand while he faced it.

MRS. RIGHT ATTEMPTED to read the expression on Charlie's face. He'd just hurried down from the dining room and into the kitchens. He found her there attempting to help Cook bring order back to his staff of two hysterical kitchen maids. "Has the duke complained about the dinner?" she asked, knowing full well that there had never been a worse dinner sent up to him.

Charlie shook his head. "No, well, he mentioned it was dreadful but he blames it all on Lady Marchfield."

"The duke is a man who sees what is what," Cook said.

"He is very gracious," Mrs. Right said, "but let us not try his goodwill by repeating the experience."

"It would be easier to never repeat the experience if we did not have that lunatic fellow hiding somewhere," Cook pointed out. "Who goes around appearing and disappearing?"

"Mrs. Right," Charlie interrupted, "the duke is sending me down to the cellars to bring up a bottle of the new sack." He stared at her meaningfully and she knew perfectly well what he meant. The wine cellar door had been left ajar. The footmen had searched the place and found nothing, but it was strange.

"I see," Mrs. Right said, "I'd best go down with you. I imagine you boys have not even had the time to open those crates yet."

"We have not. We did not think there was a hurry as he mostly only orders it for Lady Felicity and there are several older bottles still down there."

"Bring the claw hammer so we can get the crate open. If the duke wishes for a bottle from the Perry shipment that is what he will get. We will not wish to disappoint him any further this evening."

Charlie looked most relieved to discover he would not have to descend those dark stairs alone. Mrs. Right took the candelabra from the servants' table, and they made their way down.

She'd not been down in the cellars in an age. Charlie and

Thomas were well able to suggest wine pairings and retrieve them for the duke. It was as cold and damp as she recalled. It was as dark as she remembered, too.

She held the candelabra in front of her, descending the stone stairs into the gloom. "Where did you leave the crates?"

"All the way in the back, I'm afraid. I thought we should put the Perry bottles with the other bottles of sack and the duke does not ask for them as often as the claret and hock."

"Makes sense," Mrs. Right said. She had come down the last step. Rows of shelves holding hundreds of bottles of various shapes and sizes gathered dust in the gloom. She felt a chill go down her back and assured herself it was only the damp of the cellar and not the idea that Mr. Wicket might be down here somewhere.

Mrs. Right led the way, determined not to give away any trepidation she might feel. If the staff were to sense it, they'd fall apart. The crates were just ahead. Mrs. Right peered at the nails that held the lid closed as she did have a small idea that Mr. Wicket might be inside one of them, but everything appeared secure. Charlie began working to pry open the one on top. He popped the last nail and began digging through the hay packing for a bottle. As he did so, Mrs. Right looked warily around her.

Then her eyes scanned the floor. Just to the right of her shoe, there was a folded sheet of paper lying on the floor. At first, she thought it must be a bill of lading, until she squinted and read the first line. *For Mr. Tobias Wicket.*

Charlie fished out a bottle of Mr. Perry's sack. "Got it," he said.

"Excellent, Charlie. Go ahead, I'll bring up the rear, we should not like to leave the duke waiting."

Charlie nodded and proceeded toward the stairs. Mrs. Right swept up the paper and put it in her pocket before following him out.

WINSOME HAD ENTIRELY lost track of her goal as she spoke to Lord Manderbey at table. She was supposed to be discovering if he was deep in debt from gambling. She was supposed to be finding out if he had the sort of temperament that would lead down a very dark path. She was supposed to be discovering if he could be trusted to care for a wife or whether he was on a dowry hunt to solve financial woes. She was supposed to be adding up the cold hard facts and if they ran against him, then she must dismiss him from her thoughts.

What had she done instead? She'd had a very interesting conversation with him about everything in the world but that. She'd been positively entranced when he'd spoken of Torquay— how she would like to see it!

Now, Valor and Grace had pushed the ottoman into the center of the room while Felicity and Mr. Stratton had directed the arranging of the chairs in a circle round it.

Lord Manderbey had led her to a chair and taken the one next to her.

Valor laid the yellow and blue tickets on the ottoman. "The game is simple. We'll ask a question and then if it's a fact you get a yellow ticket and if it's a fib you get blue. Two yellow tickets wins, but a blue cancels a yellow."

"Do not make any attempts to win, Manderbey," the duke said. "It cannot be done."

"This sounds amusing," the dowager said. "Why have I never heard of this?"

"Because they made it up, Your Grace," Lord Thorpe said.

"That's why you cannot win, now or any other day," Lord Dashlend said resignedly.

"No Dashlend, it's only gentlemen who cannot win," Lord Wembly said. "At least, from what I've seen so far. Her Grace might have a very good shot at it."

Thomas had poured the gentlemen their port, and now Charlie hurried in with Mr. Perry's sack for the dowager.

"I go first," Valor said. "One, because I am my papa's hostess, even though Felicity was sitting in the hostess chair at dinner and I don't know why, and two, because I get tired and might say something shocking when I do."

"Now that's a fact," the duke said jovially. "Award yourself a yellow ticket, Val."

Valor took a ticket and showed it to Sir Galahad. As was always the case, the pug was not terribly interested in anything that could not be eaten and only yawned in response. Valor turned her sights on Lord Manderbey, which Winsome had been both expecting and leery of.

"Lord Manderbey," Valor said, "could you really be comfortable with the idea of stealing a sister from another sister who only had one left? Especially if that meant the other sister was to be left all alone?"

The duke snorted. "Very subtle, Val."

Winsome could feel the blood rush to her face. She was not in front of a looking glass, but presumed she was as red as a bowl of cherries. Valor was really too presumptuous! Lord Manderbey was being cornered and it was embarrassing. What happened to the usual question of what did the gentleman first notice?

"I suppose I would sympathize with that sister, but such sympathy could not be the deciding factor," Lord Manderbey said.

Valor rose. "I do not want your sympathy. *Sir*. I cannot talk to sympathy, can I? I cannot walk the hills of the Dales with sympathy, can I? I cannot catch sympathy's eye and make sympathy laugh in church, can I?" This was all said in a tone that might chill a villain's heart. She picked up Sir Galahad and marched from the room.

"Well now, we've seen worst, Manderbey," the duke said. "Several of my sons-in-laws have had blue tickets thrown in their face. Consider yourself to have got off lightly."

"She's a sparky little thing," the dowager said, sipping on her sack.

"Perhaps we should retreat to more usual questions," Verity said. "Lord Manderbey, what was the first thing you noticed about Winsome?"

That was the question Winsome had been fully expecting. She'd always found it so interesting to hear what the gentleman would say when he was asked the same of her sisters. Now that it was herself, well…she did not suppose she was any less red than she'd started.

"Notice?" Lord Manderbey asked.

"Yes, what struck you?" Felicity said.

"I see. I was almost going to reach for some commonplace sort of answer but I will say it as it was—it is the freckles on her nose. I like freckles."

Her freckles? Goodness that was the last thing she imagined he'd say. She did not admire them herself. She was forever going out to the gardens without her bonnet when it was hot and then scolding herself later over it on account of the freckling it produced.

"And the copper tones of her hair," Lord Manderbey added.

Two things. He'd mentioned two things. Winsome did not recall any of her brothers-in-law ever mentioning two things. Her sisters all looked very approving of it.

"Fact," Verity said, handing him a blue ticket.

"Now, I do not think we ought to gang up on Lord Manderbey," Serenity said, "but I do have a question. Lord Manderbey, would you say gambling is an acceptable pastime, even if a great deal of money is spent?"

Winsome stole a glance at him to see his reaction to Serenity's question. It was the answer she really needed to hear the most.

"Do you mean cards?" Lord Manderbey asked.

"Or dice or horseraces or just bets in general," Serenity said.

"I am unfortunate enough to have some personal experience

with the results of excessive gambling. So, perhaps it is not so much acceptable as it is nevertheless commonly done."

What did he mean? He was unfortunate to have personal experience? Did he somehow blame a lack of luck at the tables for excessive losses?

Winsome's heart was slowly sinking. She had hoped against hope that he was not a profligate gambler. Another lady might be fooled into thinking it was no matter, but she knew otherwise! She knew of a real-life case where a lady was fooled and now lived miserably. She knew of an untold number of cases in her novels where money was at the heart of the villainy.

She had promised herself she would not be taken in by a rogue. She had thought all she need do was spot it and had considered some of the ladies in her novels rather stupid for being faced with evidence and ignoring it at their peril.

So why on earth did she have a great desire to ignore all the evidence about Lord Manderbey?

Winsome supposed she'd been foolish to underestimate feelings and how they might work to upend rational thinking.

The dowager picked up two tickets, one yellow and one blue. She held one in each hand. "Manderbey, why do I not have grandchildren yet?"

Lord Manderbey narrowed his eyes at his grandmother. "Because I am not yet wed," he said.

"And that," the dowager said, throwing a yellow ticket at him, "is unfortunately a fact."

The game went on and Winsome was pressed to name what she'd first noticed about Lord Manderbey. She answered that it had been his urbane manner and it was deemed a fact.

Eventually, and after several glasses of sack, the dowager fell to musing on questions and then answering them herself. The questions centered on how long she had to live before seeing grandchildren, wondering how many grandchildren other women her age already had, and speculating that Lord Manderbey would be very sorry if she were to die without them. She awarded herself a yellow ticket for each answer and the duke jovially declared her the winner.

All through it, Winsome fought with her own ideas. Was she to succumb to a rogue? Or was she to stick with what she knew to be true and run in the other direction? Even if the running away would feel like a slog through deep mud, always trying to pull her back.

AFTER MRS. RIGHT had followed Charlie up the stairs from the wine cellar, she'd gone back to the kitchens to establish some sort of order there.

The kitchen maids were reminded that they might sleep together in the same bed if it helped them feel safe, they had a sturdy lock on their bedchamber door, and Mrs. Right would personally search the room before they retired. She then pointed out that no man, not even the disappearing Mr. Wicket, would dare set foot into the women's side of the quarters. Adding in two generous glasses of the servants' supply of sherry had gone a long way toward restoring calm.

Now she hurried into the housekeeper's closet and shut the door. It was good-sized room, actually meant to be the butler's closet. It had a small sofa and two chairs, a small hearth, a desk for writing, drawers filled with the silver of the house, and shelves of carefully wrapped porcelain settings.

As it *was* the butler's closet and as a butler was lurking around somewhere, she peered round the dim room to assure herself that it was uninhabited. It was empty, so she placed her candle on the desk and pulled the note she'd found in the wine cellar from her pocket.

For Mr. Tobias Wicket—

We have been informed that you have resigned your post with His Majesty's government and taken up a position with the

Duke of Pelham's household. We consider this a loss, however we are confident that you hold the security of England as dear as you ever have.

Therefore, in an unofficial role, we ask that you keep your discerning ear to the ground. There is a certain lord who has got himself in rather deep through gambling losses. So deep that we fear he may be vulnerable to bribery or threats from our enemies, particularly if he were to find himself on foreign soil.

As he is of marriageable age, and as the Duke of Pelham appears to have a never-ending supply of eligible daughters who are particularly well funded, we speculate that this individual may make an appearance at the house. He may be looking at every avenue to raise funds and a dowry is as good as any. If that is the case, I am sure you will find opportunities to listen at doors and search overcoat pockets.

We leave you with this hint, so you might better understand the crown's particular interest in this target: TRULOGAP

LC

So Mr. Wicket actually had been some sort of spy. Mrs. Right had considered the possibility that he'd made the whole thing up but that did not seem to be the case.

She could not make heads nor tails of the letter, other than they must be cautious of gentlemen coming into the house. Who, though? And who had sent the letter in the first place. LC...the L could be for Lord...Lord Somebody starting with a C.

She could not work it out. However, ought they not be cautious of gentlemen approaching Winsome at other houses? That might be out of reach for Mr. Wicket, but it was not for Mrs. Right. She would warn Winsome to keep her guard up.

Of course, Mrs. Right reminded herself that Winsome did always have her guard up. Suspicion was in her nature. In any case, as far as she could tell, things were going rather well with Lord Manderbey. If things were to proceed as it looked as if they might, an engagement would stop any unsavory types in their tracks. Nevertheless, she would warn her, just to be on the safe side of things.

Mrs. Right folded the letter and slipped it into her pocket. If only she could work out what a TRULOGAP was.

CHAPTER NINE

Leland found himself rather exhausted from his evening at the duke's house. He'd never been to a dinner so full of unexpected events. An unwelcome aunt, an outrageous younger sister, a butler hiding behind curtains, Fact or Fib…and, of course, his ridiculous grandmother capping the whole thing off.

That particular relation just now sat across from him, swaying with the movement of the carriage. She was doing her best to stare at him intently, though three glasses of sack had made the attitude harder to master than it ought to have been.

"Well? Have you seen enough? Marry the girl," the dowager said. "I won't mind at all finding the duke a relation of mine, he's jolly good fun."

"Perhaps you've had enough fun for one lifetime," he said drily.

"Nonsense. Now be quick about it, I feel the life slowly draining out of me."

Leland did not answer. If she was tired, it was more likely the sack than an infirmity. He would deliver her to Miss Price and give the maid strict instructions to keep her mistress away from his door. He was in no mood to listen to her spouting nonsense while his valet desperately wondered how he could get out of the room without attracting her attention.

He had far too much to think about just now. Aside from all the bizarre happenings, he'd liked spending an extended time with Lady Winsome. She was so interesting! She'd had so many of the same opinions on *Gloaming at Glenford Cross* that he did. She'd not swallowed the narrative whole and simply accepted what the author directed her to. She had questions. Did that not point to a rather insightful mind?

As well, she had seemed very interested to hear of Stonewall Manor and the little tavern in Torquay. He almost got the feeling that she'd like to see it.

Then there were her looks to admire, they really were spectacular. He'd often counseled himself to avoid wedding a lady on account of her looks. Hers would fade, and, such as they were, so would his own. Then what would be left? Nevertheless, her beauty could not be ignored. Not with that dusting of freckles and golden hair he wished to run his fingers through.

And then, she had claimed the first thing she'd noticed about him was his urbane manner. That was rather good, was it not? She'd not hesitated to answer the question either—did that point to her having thought about it prior?

He felt closer to considering marriage than he'd yet done in his life. Though, he would keep that idea under his coat. He would not want his grandmother to get wind of it. Who knew what outrages she might commit if she thought something was in the works.

On the morrow, he intended to leave the house early as she would still be abed, and have his valet send clothes to his club. He would attend Lady Jellerbey's candlelight picnic tomorrow night and he'd already confirmed Lady Winsome would attend too. His grandmother knew nothing about it, and he would not give her the opportunity to insist she go with him. He loved her in his own way, but he'd had quite enough of her recently.

"Here we are, home again," his grandmother said. "Gracious, I am finding the Town invigorating. I wonder why I skipped so many seasons now that I'm here. What do we do on the morrow?"

"Nothing," Leland said. "There is nothing on the calendar for the morrow."

"We ought to go to the theater, then."

"Come on, I'll help you down," Leland said, leaping to the pavement.

"I do not need your help."

"Really?"

"Perhaps just an arm. I am old, after all."

Despite needing "just an arm," the dowager all but fell out of the carriage. He kept her on her feet and walked her inside. Though it was probably petty on his part, he hoped she had quite the pounding head on the morrow.

Mrs. Right had gone above stairs to help Winsome out of her dress. Though, really, she'd been determined to warn her about the letter she'd found.

"Nobody seems to know if Mr. Wicket has left the house or not," Winsome said. "At least, nobody seems positive that he has."

Mrs. Right glanced at the door. "He has not, he's around here somewhere. Lock yourself in when I leave. Just as a precaution, though I do not think he'd have the nerve to stray into the family's private quarters. It's just that…we can never quite pin him down."

Winsome shivered. "I cannot think Valor will sleep a wink."

"She's perfectly fine. One of the housemaids is sitting in her room waiting for me to take charge of her, the little mite will be fast asleep by now. Then I will go to bed and be kicked all night. And not just by Valor either—that dog seems to have his own energetic dreams."

"You will get him out, though? Mr. Wicket, you will make him leave?"

"Oh aye, I'll think of something. Now, I did want to give you a bit of a warning that's nothing to do with our newly acquired butler. I came across some information, vague information but worth passing along all the same. It seems there may be a gentleman out there somewhere who is looking to secure a large dowry on account of gambling debts. Forewarned is forearmed, I always say."

Winsome sank down into a chair. "Exactly what I was afraid of."

"I know it," Mrs. Right said. "All those novels you read have always put you on edge. But I suppose with things seeming to go so well with Lord Manderbey—"

"That's the problem, though," Winsome said. "It's him. He's the one with gambling debts."

"Lord Manderbey? Are you certain?"

"Yes, it is almost certainly so, but Mrs. Right, how did you come upon this vague warning?"

Mrs. Right pulled out the letter and handed it over. She watched Winsome read through it intently.

Winsome handed the letter back. "It's confirmed then," she said. "This is without a doubt about Lord Manderbey. He is being dunned, which I've heard from two people who know him—one a friend and the other a cousin. He shrugs off any idea about debt as if it is of no consequence, and then at Fact or Fib he said he had personal experience with excessive gambling and named it commonplace."

"But are you certain this letter refers to him? I cannot work out what *TRULOGAP* means."

"Oh, I did assume that was the name of a horse he'd bet on. You know how racing horses have all sorts of strange names. It could be a place name, perhaps where the horse was sired. I cannot think what else it could be."

It did indeed make sense. The letter was about gambling and *TRULOGAP* could be a horse's name. Since it was specifically mentioned in the letter, it hinted that this horse had a large part to play in the gambling debts. Perhaps in one of those stupid carriage races the gentlemen were always cooking up. And here she'd been only thinking about cards, but there were endless ways a gentleman could gamble away their money.

"He is after your dowry, then," Mrs. Right said, feeling the anger beginning to boil inside her. As was always the case when one of her girls was in danger or insulted in any way, a fury came over her. The duke said she was a regular herring gull guarding her chicks and would peck out the eyes of anyone attempting to harm them. She preferred to think of herself as a mighty lioness protecting her cubs on the dangerous savannahs of London.

Winsome shrugged as if the situation was no matter, but Mrs. Right could see her eyes were shining. Her girl had been hurt. She'd been hurt by a gambling rogue who had come into this house pretending to be a respectable gentleman. He'd even brought his dowager as a cover of respectability. It was outrageous. It must be answered.

Mrs. Right, being a woman of good sense, did pause for a moment before allowing her outrage to carry her away. As she liked to face the truth head on, she could not avoid reflecting on other seasons when it had seemed that one of her girls had been done wrong.

She'd given away Mr. Stratton's laundry, changed his household's grocery order to exclusively cabbages, and caused a permanent rift with his wine merchant. She'd made Lord Dashlend's hysterical valet believe he was being dismissed, throwing that household topsy-turvy. She'd infested Lord Stanford's house with case moths which had taken specialized assistance to defeat. She'd meddled with the springs on Lord Thorpe's carriage, causing an unfortunate delay to the wedding trip. And then last year, she'd circulated a print that depicted Lord Wembly's pants on fire.

All very unfortunate incidents as it had turned out things had not been what they seemed. Fortunately, those moments really could be considered water under the bridge now. No harm done, as it were. Here, however, she held the proof in her hands. It was incontrovertible.

"I find myself very miserable, Mrs. Right," Winsome said. "Though my head tells me one thing, my heart says something different."

"There now, child," Mrs. Right said soothingly. "Everything will look brighter in the morning, it always does."

Mrs. Right worked to keep a neutral smile of calm on her face. Her thoughts were a different matter. Her thoughts seethed with indignation that one of her precious girls was hurt.

Lord Manderbey must pay for the insult.

LORD LANDRY FELT himself exceedingly bold at this moment of his life. He'd accepted the invitation to Lady Jellerbey's candle-light picnic on his own, with no interference from his relations. Wandering round in dim light seemed almost dangerous, but Lady Edith had assured him she would go and that he ought to go too.

They'd played piquet at the card party they'd both attended and she had pointed out all sorts of things he ought to think and do. He'd never been so relaxed around the mysterious female sex. There was something comforting about her long diatribes where he was only expected to agree. He barely had to hold up his end of the talking.

And then, when his Aunt Agatha had tried to push in, well then he saw Lady Edith's true might. She'd informed the lady that piquet only admitted two players and, furthermore, they were in the midst of a conversation. His aunt, always so pushy and frightening, had positively slinked away! He'd never seen the like of it.

They'd gone on to have a discussion about their herds, which had been very pleasant. Now, he wandered Lady Jellerbey's dim rooms, searching for her distinctive forceful frame. He did not see her, but was suddenly tapped on the shoulder. He jumped and turned to who was sneaking up on him.

"Lord Landry."

It was Lady Winsome, another lady he admired as she was kind and not too frightening. And her father, who he was not certain what to make of.

He bowed. "Lady Winsome. Your Grace."

"Landry," the duke said. "Well met. Entertain my daughter while I search out some claret. I can only abide staggering round in the dark if I have a glass in hand."

The duke went off to locate a sideboard. Lady Winsome said, "I am glad to encounter you, I was hoping to ask you something."

Landry nodded, though he was not very used to anybody hoping to see him or wanting to ask him anything. Then he realized what it must be. "You wonder how I got on with Lady Edith at the card party. It went well. Yes, I think I can claim that—it went well.

"I am very glad to hear it," Lady Winsome said. "Of course I wished to know it. And actually, I had second question too. Have you ever heard of a racing horse name Trulogap?"

Landry wrinkled his brow. "Trulogap? I am not certain. There is something familiar sounding in it, but I cannot place it. There is a Truro-something, but then I suppose that is because the horse hales from Truro. Trulo, though? I suppose I might have, as I said, it does sound familiar."

For some reason, this seemed to disappoint Lady Winsome.

"Though if you'd rather I *hadn't* heard of it…perhaps I never did."

"No, no," she said.

"Lady Winsome. Landry."

Lord St. John had approached. He brought his usual smile and confidence. Where did these fellows find all this confidence they so freely threw about?

"I wonder if I might steal Lady Winsome away for a turn through the rooms? Lady Winsome, you must visit one of Lady

Jellerbey's sideboards—it is the best thing about the candlelight picnic."

Lady Winsome laughed. "So my father says too." Quietly to Landry, she said, "Good luck with Lady E."

Yes, indeed. A little bit of luck would never hurt. In the meantime, he had prepared a list of questions on her views of methods of crop rotations and would be very interested to hear what she would say.

AS WINSOME DRESSED for the evening, she felt as if she were fighting her own nature. It was in her nature to hold suspicion close and follow its hints. She had always prided herself on her logical clear-headedness. While Verity invented fantastical opinions, she based her own on the facts, and only the facts.

Where was Lady Logic now? Despite the evidence piling up that Lord Manderbey was precisely the sort of gentleman she'd been determined to avoid, she did not wish to avoid him. She was driven to discover more about him, some redeeming fact, even though she recognized it was probably a fruitless exercise.

She'd also failed to mention anything she'd discovered to her father. As far as he knew it, Lord Manderbey was an upstanding citizen with nothing running against him. She could not bear to tell the duke, as once she did, that would be that. Her father was exceedingly liberal regarding his daughters' preferences in a husband, but he would not tolerate a man looking to gamble away all his assets.

They'd arrived to Lady Jellerbey's candlelight picnic and encountered Lord Landry. Having a moment alone, she'd gone fishing for more information. Had he ever heard of a horse named Trulogap?

The answer had not been satisfactory. The name sounded familiar but he was not sure. Of course, she was well aware that the only answer that would have been entirely satisfactory would have been: "I am confident there has never in the history of England been a horse of that name and if anybody wrote a letter about it, it is all stuff and nonsense."

Now, Lord St. John escorted her through the rooms. She kept her eye out for Lord Manderbey, even though she ought to have been averting her gaze.

Lord St. John had been prattling on, now he said, "I am likely to be appointed the ambassador to Portugal."

"That sounds a great honor," Winsome said, assuming it was.

"Indeed. Of course, it does raise several questions. The palace prefers an ambassador who is well settled and I remain a bachelor. Lady Winsome, have you ever imagined living abroad, hostessing in a foreign court?"

What in the world was he suggesting? Did she understand him rightly? Was he inquiring into her interest in living in Portugal?

As she did not answer, he went on. "Now naturally, what with Napolean rampaging all over the place, the court is currently being held in Rio de Janeiro, which is not ideal. But then, how long can it last, I wonder? As well, Brazil might be an adventure. I suppose things will move back to Lisbon in not too long a time. It is said that opportunities for mining precious gems are practically falling out of the trees in Brazil. I'm exceedingly interested in it. One might amass a fortune, I am given to understand."

Heavens, Brazil. What an idea. She must stop the notion at once. "I am afraid I would not be very seaworthy, Lord St. John. I prefer my little patch of the world, right here in England."

"I see. But sometimes, when one really thinks about a thing, one might come to a different conclusion."

Winsome did not answer that, as she certainly would not come to a different conclusion. "By the by, Lord St. John, have you ever heard of a racing horse named Trulogap? I believe I might have heard Lord Manderbey mention it, though I cannot quite recall."

Lord St. John's expression spoke of a whirlwind of thoughts running through his mind. "So that's why he's suddenly out of funds, is it?" Lord St. John asked. "Betting on horses?"

"Oh, I really do not know," Winsome said. "I was only attempting to recall where I'd heard the name."

"It all makes sense though. One day free with his money and the next claiming he will not pay out. I should have known." Lord St. John paused, then he said, "Wait a minute. Trulogap. Was that the horse that ran at Doncaster last year? The one everybody bet against because it seemed to have a bit of a limp, but then it turned out his jockey had trained him to display it on command. I did hear a number of gentlemen were ruined and the owner had fled...I had not counted my cousin among the victims though. A rube's mistake."

"Surely not, as I said, I only had a vague recollection of the name." Winsome said. She found she rather regretted asking anything about Trulogap. Every time she inquired into Lord Manderbey, hoping for some shred of redeeming evidence, more damning evidence piled on. A horse with a purported limp had ruined several gentlemen. It seemed Lord Manderbey could be one among them.

"Lady Winsome. St. John."

Winsome spun around. His very voice pulled at her. Deep and confident and everything a man should be. There he was, looking achingly handsome in his perfectly fitted coat and expertly tied neckcloth. He towered over Lord St. John and he was superior in every way. Except for his gambling debts, the fact that he seemed not to take them seriously, and that he was likely on a dowry hunt.

"Speak of the devil," St. John said.

"I'm sorry, what?" Lord Manderbey said, looking through narrowed eyes at his cousin.

"Oh do not mind me," Lord St. John said. "I was just telling Lady Winsome that I am seriously considered for the ambassador to Portugal post. Rio de Janeiro should be an exciting adventure, for a lady willing to take the risk.

Winsome had no idea how Lord St. John had circled back to that preposterous idea.

"Do you say you have plans to wed?" Lord Manderbey asked.

"Only if the lady is agreeable," Lord St. John said. "I had not initially thought of it, but this season has found me quite suddenly struck."

Lord Manderbey looked as if he wished to say something, but perhaps did not wish to say it in front of her. In a low tone, he said, "We should discuss the prudence of that, even with the ambassadorship's stipend."

Lord St. John threw up his nose. "Prudence would not be necessary if family paid what was duly owed."

"I owe you nothing," Lord Manderbey said through gritted teeth.

"Ah! I see, it is acceptable to throw over obligations to family. Well, I hadn't known, but that's Doncaster is it not?" He turned and bowed to Winsome. "Lady Winsome. I will see you soon, I think."

Lord St. John strolled away, leaving her with Lord Manderbey.

"I apologize for my cousin. His temperament is rather unregulated and he often says that which should not be said."

Winsome did not know what to make of that. Lord St. John should have kept Lord Manderbey's secret? Just not mentioned it? Pretended he was not owed a debt?

"You seem a bit pale, Lady Winsome," he said. "Perhaps a glass of wine would restore you?"

"Yes, I suppose it might," Winsome said. She did not really think wine would restore her, but perhaps it would calm her. What was she to do? Everything about him was wrong and all she wanted to do was throw herself into his arms.

CHAPTER TEN

L ELAND LED LADY Winsome to one of the rooms containing a sideboard and poured her a glass of hock. He'd not been at all pleased to find her talking with St. John.

Even less pleased when he'd found his cousin dropping hints about whether the lady might be interested in relocating to the Portuguese court in Brazil. The notion was absurd. Even with the stipend he'd be paid, and that was even if he would be appointed, he could not afford to wed. Nor did he have the sense and maturity to wed, as he'd just mentioned Doncaster and it could be assumed he'd not thought to give up his reckless gambling.

And then for St. John to hint that all his difficulties were somehow his fault? The man was outrageous.

Leland paused his racing thoughts. Of course, St. John could not keep a wife with what he had now, but he could if he got his hands on Lady Winsome's dowry. If he knew his cousin, he'd take hold of any funds he could get his hands on, stupidly determine to increase it at a gaming table, and promptly lose it all.

"Lord St. John was telling me about a horse named Trulogap," Lady Winsome said. She stared at him intently while she said it.

"A horse?" Leland asked, thinking that buying a horse was another thing his cousin could hardly afford.

"Yes, apparently there were gentlemen ruined on account of

betting against him when he was not really lame."

"Would not be the first time, I suppose." Why was St. John telling some story about a lame horse? If he'd lost heavily betting on it, why would he advertise it?

"I just thought, if that were to happen to a gentleman, he might reflect on it and recognize his mistake. Going forward."

Leland laughed. "Or shrug it off and try again another day, more likely."

Lady Winsome looked fairly stricken and he could not imagine why. Certainly, she was not developing ideas about reforming St. John? He understood that ladies sometimes liked to try their hand at it. Lady Melanie had been convinced she could inspire Lord Fartherington to put down the bottle once he found himself happily settled. Then she had discovered she was much mistaken.

But if Lady Winsome were thinking of reforming St. John, that would mean she had an interest in him. Could it be so? He'd been so sure there was something developing between himself and the lady. He remained sure, he could not be mistaken. Why would she ever have an interest in his ne'er-do-well cousin and his improbable plan to sail for Brazil?

"Ah, there is my father, tucked in a corner, just as he likes. I see the dowager agrees with him."

"My grandmother?" Leland asked. How was it possible? She knew nothing of Lady Jellerbey's soiree and he'd steered well clear of the house since early morning to avoid just such a circumstance.

"Oh dear, they have several bottles they've taken off the sideboard and they are heads together. I am afraid my father might bring your grandmother into some mischief."

"Or the other way around," Leland said grimly.

"Lady Winsome, Manderbey, I think you know Lady Edith?"

Leland turned to find Landry escorting Lady Edith. "Of course, yes, from Almack's." He made every effort to be polite, though he was not particularly enthusiastic to encounter Lady Edith. Or Landry for that matter. He wished all these people would take themselves off somewhere.

"Lady Winsome," Lady Edith said, "Lord Landry and I have had an extensive conversation about crop rotations, but I wonder, how do you imagine that might work in a Brazilian climate?"

"Oh, I am sure I do not know."

"But you ought to find it out."

"Why?" Lady Winsome asked.

Leland would like to know just the same. Why should Lady Winsome care to know anything about crop rotations in Brazil? Or crop rotations anywhere?

Lady Edith turned to Lord Landry. "Lord St. John did say the lady was interested in Brazil, did he not? I did not mishear?"

"Yes, yes, he did indeed hint at it," Lord Landry said. "Said he would not be surprised."

"St. John is rather prone to spout nonsense," Leland said.

"Guess what?" the duke said, arriving with the dowager on his arm. "We're going to get tickets to Sir Jonathan's scavenger hunt in two days' time. It's not in the park this year—it's in his garden, at night. Who's ever heard of it?"

"It should be a wonderfully ridiculous palaver," the dowager said. "I'm looking forward to it."

"Grandmama," Leland said, "I did not expect to see you here."

"No doubt," the dowager said. "I noticed you scarpered off early today and did not return. I had to go through your calendar to find out where you'd be."

"My calendar is private."

"Then you should have hid it better," the dowager said.

This struck the duke as rather hilarious and they clinked their glasses together.

Leland sighed. His grandmother was enough to handle in the countryside, but in Town she was far more difficult. With the duke's influence, she was becoming impossible.

"Your Grace, Dowager," he said, "may I present Lady Edith. I believe you already know Lord Landry."

"Ah yes, we know Landry," the duke said, laughing. "Poor fellow always looks shook up."

"I am intending to change that, Your Grace," Lady Edith said.

The duke seemed a bit startled to hear it, as they all were. But for Landry, who seemed delighted.

"Lady Edith really is doing it too," Landry said. "If I say, 'I do not know,' she says 'think about Landry, you probably do know.'"

It seemed there was some sort of budding romance between Landry and Lady Edith and it was just as bizarre as one might imagine from the combination of those two people. Lady Edith was forceful and it appeared that Landry was happy to be forced.

Lady Jellerbey, an energetic lady in general, hurried into the room looking flushed. "Everyone, Lady Lucinda has just had the most marvelous idea. We are to have a Longways country dance running right down the corridor between my rooms. One of my footmen is a fiddler and has gone to fetch his instrument. Hurry now, it will be great fun."

"What say you, Dowager?" the duke said.

"I suppose I am still light enough on my feet," the dowager said.

Leland quietly groaned. It would be a miracle if she *stayed* on her feet. Nevertheless, he could not be unhappy with this development for himself. He would take Lady Winsome away from all these interlopers.

He turned. "Lady Winsome?"

He was unceremoniously pushed aside. St. John said, "Lady Winsome, you did promise me a dance."

She looked surprised to hear it, but St. John led her away before she could absolutely refuse.

"Well, it looks like you are the odd man out, Lord Manderbey," Lady Edith said.

He stared at her, as answering her with his opinion of the events of the last minute would be unconscionably rude.

She held her arm out to Lord Landry and led him toward the

corridor. Leland poured himself a large glass of claret. St. John was on the hunt, though there might be two motives for what he was doing. He might be after Lady Winsome's dowry, or he might have noted Leland's interest in the lady and was attempting to drum up trouble. The trouble would have one goal—get more money out of him for a promise to back away.

Either way, Lady Winsome should be protected from his rogue cousin. Perhaps he would pay St. John a visit on the subject.

Mrs. Right took advantage of the quiet of the house. Valor was long abed, with one of the housemaids sitting in her room to assure her of her safety from the mysterious Mr. Wicket. The duke and Winsome were still out. She'd cleared out the servants' hall early and she'd set the half of a poundcake leftover from dinner on the counter. She was out of patience with that butler forever jumping out from behind doorframes and frightening her staff witless. She was a lioness on the hunt and the poundcake was her bait to lure him in. She was determined to get her claws into her quarry.

She hid in the shadows, waiting.

At first, all was silence. Eventually, her feet began to hurt and she began to think how pleasant it would be to put them up and sip a glass of sherry. She was near giving up for the night, but then, the subtlest of sounds emerged. A low and slow creak. Then a pause. Then another creak. Her prey approached.

She stayed very still as Mr. Wicket took his time assuring himself that the servants' hall was emptied of people for the night.

Then, convinced he was alone, he slithered forward through the gloom in that creepy way that was all his own.

He might be mysterious and a spy for the crown, but he went

for the poundcake like every other man in England would. As he reached for it, Mrs. Right swung the meat cleaver in her hand down into the wood of the table, just inches from his hand.

She was satisfied to hear the shriek that emanated from that individual. "Mr. Wicket," she said in her most threatening tone.

"Mrs. Right. What are you doing? Why are you lurking in the dark? With a large knife?"

"I might ask you the same thing."

"I don't have a knife."

"What are you doing here, though?"

"I'm doing what I was hired to do."

"Which is?"

"Act as the butler, as you well know."

"I know no such thing. You have not acted as a butler, you have acted as a specter. Listen closely, Mr. Wicket, now that I know where you are hiding out, I will tear that wine cellar apart and throw out all your belongings when I find them. Everything you own, out on the street. Unless you care to start telling me exactly what I wish to know."

In the dim moonlight casting a soft haze through the kitchens, Mrs. Right noted Mr. Wicket glancing back at the wine cellar door. "Fine," he said. "What is it you wish to know?"

"Where exactly in the cellar are you holed up? We've looked there before."

Mr. Wicket shrugged. "Lady Marchfield installed me in the house over a month before you arrived. I built a false wall at the back of it. Had your footmen been more astute and perceptive, they might have noticed that the length of the cellar had shrunk by several feet. They might have noticed cement not entirely cured."

"My footmen are not in the habit of suspecting everything they look at. Now why are you here, exactly?"

"That, I cannot tell you."

Mrs. Right picked up the cleaver. "You'd better tell me, else I make your life a living misery. I'll drive you out of that cellar with sulfur smoke like the vermin I suspect you are. I'll see that every scrap of food and drink is securely locked up at night. I'll forever be hiding and jumping out at you with a meat cleaver. You'll slowly wither away from fright and lack of food."

"That seems extreme," Mr. Wicket said, nervously shifting on his feet.

"But I'll do it."

Mr. Wicket sighed. "All right, if you must know. When one spies for the Crown, one may find that one's expenses outpace one's income. Debts are incurred. I suppose it is, after all, a rich man's game, but I did so like it. In any case, the debts piled up and you know how creditors are, they can make things uncomfortable. I saw the advertisement for a butler and I thought it would be an excellent place to lay low. Then, when Lady Marchfield understood my background, she got ideas."

"What ideas?"

"She got ideas that it might be amusing to keep the staff on the back foot. I was to do anything I could do to frighten you all. Above all, I was not to be driven out. She's dangled the settling of all my debts if I can last the season."

"Has she now? Very like her. Well, Mr. Wicket, you will not be going on with your plan. I have a plan of my own."

WINSOME WAS IN the drawing room with Valor, Felicity, and Serenity. Valor had spent the last fruitless quarter hour attempting to force Felicity and Serenity to admit they'd made a grave mistake in getting married.

To her disappointment, Felicity insisted she got on with Mr. Stratton like a house on fire. He was a positive darling to their daughter, even though young Isabelle had inherited her mother's temper and could shake the roof when she was crossed. Then Serenity had gone all moony over Lord Thorpe. Apparently, he saw to her breakfast tray personally each morning and inspected her eggs to ensure they were done properly—fried, with the edges just the smallest bit burnt. He was, according to Serenity, the best man living.

Valor whispered something to Sir Galahad. While Winsome could not work out the words, the tone was most clearly of disgust. It was not clear what Sir Galahad's own opinion was.

The drawing room doors swung open. Thomas hurried through them and shut the doors behind him in the most unaccountable manner.

"Is Mr. Wicket frightening you again, Thomas?" Valor asked. "Mrs. Right has promised she'll get rid of him, but for now we are to pay no attention to him if he pops up somewhere."

"No, Lady Valor. I mean, yes, he is frightening, he could be anywhere! But Lady Winsome, there is a gentleman here. I've kept him in the front hall as I did not know if I ought to let him in. He brings flowers."

Winsome's heart leapt. Had Lord Manderbey brought her flowers? She ought not accept them, though she knew she would. She ought not be happy about it, though she was.

"You did take his name, Thomas?" Felicity asked.

"Lord St. John is what he said."

As fast as Winsome's spirits had risen, they fell. What on earth was St. John doing, coming here and bringing flowers?

"Winsome," Serenity said, "you know how sensitive I am to other people's feelings. I can see you do not particularly like him."

"No, not really."

"Oh let us see him, though," Felicity said. "I would like to hear what he has to say."

Winsome sighed. She was not particularly interested in what he had to say, she'd heard quite enough from him at Lady Jellerbey's candlelight picnic last evening. And then, he was very pushy. She had much rather have danced with Lord Manderbey than Lord St. John but he'd just whisked her away. There had been nothing she could say about it. And then afterward, he seemed to always be hanging around, even when Lord Manderbey clearly wished he would go away. He'd even attempted to see her to her carriage but her father had sent him back inside.

"It might hurt his feelings to be turned away," Serenity said.

"Very well, show him in," Winsome said reluctantly. Though, she was not as worried about his feelings as Serenity was.

Thomas nodded and slipped back out the door.

It was not a moment, before Lord St. John strode in. "Lady Winsome. Ah, Lady Felicity and Lady Thorpe." He looked enquiringly at Valor.

"That is my younger sister, Lord St. John. Lady Valor," Winsome said.

Lord St. John executed a formal and rather deep bow. He was rewarded for the effort by an unblinking stare. "What are those for," Valor asked, motioning toward the pink primroses in his hand.

"Ah, I did suppose Lady Winsome might care for flowers."

"She doesn't."

"Valor. That is enough, I think," Winsome said. "Perhaps you might find Thomas and request a tea tray? Take the flowers with you so he might find a vase for them."

Valor rolled her eyes, which was becoming an unfortunate habit. She slid off the sofa. Patting Sir Galahad, she said, "Do not go anywhere, I will be right back." She all but ripped the flowers from Lord St. John's hand. As she left the room, she said, loudly, "Nobody go anywhere or decide anything."

Winsome motioned to an empty chair and Lord St. John sat down with alacrity. "I see you have a precocious young sister. I do admire precociousness."

Felicity snorted. "We'll see how much you admire it when she gets back."

Not surprisingly, Lord St. John appeared startled to hear it.

"What brings you here, Lord St. John?" Serenity asked. "It is not the household's at-home day."

Winsome noticed the slighted flush across Lord St. John's cheeks. He reached into a coat pocket and brought out a small book. "Actually, I thought Lady Winsome might be interested in this. It's a book about Rio de Janeiro."

"Oh dear," Felicity said, "if it's not a gothic novel set in that far off place, I cannot think she would be."

"Well," Lord St. John said, looking flustered, "it is just that we spoke of Rio de Janeiro last evening."

Winsome refrained from pointing out that *he* spoke about it. She had no thoughts on it whatsoever other than she had no plans to relocate there.

Lord St. John laid it on the table. "I'll leave it, in any case."

The doors flew open and Valor marched through them. "There's another one in the hall. Thomas wants to know if he can come in too."

"Who is it, Valor?" Felicity asked, looking very amused to hear it.

She shrugged as if it did not matter who it was. "The tall one that was at dinner."

CHAPTER ELEVEN

WINSOME SAT UP a bit straighter. Another gentleman had arrived to the house. Or as Valor called him, "the tall one that was at dinner." Lord Manderbey.

"There was a dinner?" Lord St. John said.

Lord Manderbey. He had come. Had he brought flowers too?

"Do tell him to come in," Serenity said.

Rather than go out to the hall, Valor just shouted, "Thomas, Serenity says he can come in."

It must be presumed that this elegant summons reached Lord Manderbey's hearing, as he showed himself in. He was looking very smart in his riding clothes. Winsome thought it odd that he should go visiting in them, but then he did look very good. Very good, indeed. She found herself not even caring that he'd not brought flowers, bringing himself felt quite sufficient.

"Lady Winsome. Lady Felicity. Lady Thorpe. Lady Valor." He paused, staring at Lord St. John. "St. John," he said leadenly.

Charlie came in with the tea tray, which for a moment distracted everyone from the awkwardness between the two lords. Not for long though.

After Winsome passed round the cups, Lord Manderbey seemed to catch a first sight of the little book about Rio de Janeiro. Then his eyes drifted to Lord St. John.

"Yes, I brought it," Lord St. John said, "in case Lady Winsome wished to know more about that foreign locale."

"Why would she." It was posed as a question but it was without the inflection of a question.

"Why wouldn't she?" Lord St. John said. "It is a fascinating place."

"Winsome only reads scary stories," Valor said.

Lord Manderbey nodded. *"Gloaming at Glenford Cross,* for example." As Lord St. John seemed perplexed, Lord Manderbey went on. "We've both read it and had much discussion about it."

"Ah yes, I believe that is just now on my bookshelf."

"No it is not."

Winsome watched their exchanges back and forth. They really seemed to dislike one another. It was a perfect example of how gambling could destroy relationships.

"I stopped by your house just now," Lord Manderbey said to Lord St. John. "I believe we are overdue for a conversation."

"Yes, well I was not there, was I?"

"Obviously not."

"This is boring," Valor said. "Talk about my dog. He's tremendous."

The dog in question was just now laying on his back on the sofa, legs splayed and round stomach pointing to the ceiling, snoring heavily.

Both gentlemen stared at the dog. Winsome guessed they were both searching their minds for something complimentary to say. She suspected they'd be searching for quite some time.

Thomas brought in the flowers, now installed in a crystal vase. He set them on the table and hurried out. Lord Manderbey stared at them.

"Lord St. John was kind enough to bring them," Winsome said.

"How thoughtful," Lord Manderbey said.

Winsome got the feeling he was in some way jealous. It should not mean anything to her, one way or the other. But it did. It was thrilling. She could not help it, it was thrilling to her core.

"Well? My dog?" Valor said.

"He certainly is tremendous," Lord Manderbey said.

"Very tremendous," Lord St. John said.

"It's my understanding that the pug breed is known for their cleverness," Lord Manderbey said. "Have you noticed that attribute?"

Valor, unused to anybody asking her a question in response to one of her demands that her dog be admired, looked very surprised. "He is, rather. He can tell time. He knows when it is time for dinner even when the sun is not out. He just knows—he must be looking at the clock."

"Clever, yes," Lord St. John said.

Lord Manderbey hooked a thumb at Lord St. John. "He's just copying what I say."

Valor narrowed her eyes. "So you don't really believe it?" she said, staring at Lord St. John. "You're just saying it?"

"No, I do believe it!" Lord St. John said, looking as if he were backed into a corner.

Lord Manderbey shrugged. "So he says."

Felicity bit her lip and Winsome knew she was on the verge of laughter. Serenity was wide-eyed, not liking any sort of disagreement. As for Sir Galahad, he remained snoring and had as yet not bothered to display his innate cleverness.

The two gentlemen really were at odds with each other. Bad dealings with money could destroy families and it certainly had seemed to severely damage whatever relationship Lord Manderbey had once had with his cousin. Why did he not see how dangerous it all was?

"I've heard," Valor said, "that when a gentleman, or two gentlemen, turn up when nobody asked them to, they're not supposed to stay longer than fifteen minutes." She then pointedly affixed her gaze to the ormolu clock on the mantle.

"I see," Lord Manderbey said. "Quite right. We should both be going. St. John."

Lord St. John grudgingly got to his feet. "Ladies, a pleasure," he said.

The two gentlemen took their leave and Winsome went to the window while Felicity heaved with laughter and Serenity whispered, "Goodness."

She had hoped to see Lord Manderbey mount his horse, as she imagined it would be quite compelling. Rather, both gentlemen stood with reins in hand arguing with one another. Lord Manderbey, so much taller than Lord St. John, leaned over him threateningly. He poked Lord St. John with his finger as if he'd made a final point, mounted his horse, which did turn out to be compelling, and trotted away.

Winsome sat back. They had seemed near blows. Blows could lead to duels. Lord Manderbey had to be convinced to give up his gambling. He must do, else it lead him into a disaster that could not be recovered from. She could not know precisely how far things had gone, but at least he would not have been able to mortgage his houses. His duke was still living and in control of things. But in future, he could do it and that was, according to the duke, the beginning of the end. Nobody ever recovered from it. There was nothing worse in the world than to be a landless lord.

Lord Manderbey had to give it up! If not for her, then for himself. He would be so angry and disappointed with himself if it went too far and there was no way back. And then, there were those lords who, finding that their errors could not be repaired, did a violence to themselves rather than face it. She must find a way to make him see it.

What other choice was there? Winsome had fooled herself into thinking she ought to walk away. Well, she'd not fooled herself about *that*. She ought to. She'd fooled herself into thinking she could do it. It was becoming more and more apparent that she would not. She could not. There would not be anybody else for her. At Almack's, at Lady Jellerbey's candlelight picnic, everywhere she went, the gentlemen she encountered made not the slightest impression. Most of them were faceless in her memory. She'd seen their faces but could not remember a thing about them.

It was only his face in her mind, all the time.

As she'd finally come to the conclusion that she would not walk away there was only one thing she could do—she must somehow tear Lord Manderbey away from his gambling habits.

How could she do it, though?

MRS. RIGHT HAD overpowered Mr. Wicket through sheer force of will. She'd threatened him with everything she could think of. As he was only in the house to clear his debts via Lady Marchfield's purse, he'd given up the ghost.

Most importantly, he'd given up *being* a ghost.

He remained sleeping in his little hidey-hole in the wine cellar, which Mrs. Right had a look at. The fellow had built the wall almost to where it met the perpendicular wall, leaving only a small space to slip through. As it was deep in the shadows and narrow, one would never spot it unless one knew what was looked for.

Mr. Wicket, being of such a thin build that he looked as if he'd been starved for some months, slipped in easily. Mrs. Right, being of a more comfortable frame, could not get all the way through it. She'd got her head and shoulders through though, and had a look. It was a small compartment of a room with just a mattress and a wood box acting as a side table to hold a candle.

Mrs. Right had offered him a room in the men's quarters but he'd claimed he liked his privacy. It gave him the quiet to think, he said. She had her doubts about that. She rather thought he liked his access to the kitchens at all hours and she would not be surprised if he had helped himself to some of the duke's wines. That was the smallest of her problems though.

Though he retired in the cellar of an evening, he now made his presence in the servants' hall known. Nobody was particularly happy to see him, but they'd been informed that Mr. Wicket was to act at the direction of Mrs. Right for the foreseeable future so they put up with it.

Mrs. Right had decided to put the fellow to good use. He was a spy so he could very well act like one. He was to follow Lord Manderbey and report what he was able to find out. She needed information to know how to proceed in avenging her girl.

Mr. Wicket had just returned from one of these forays and slipped through the servants' entrance.

"Well?" Mrs. Right asked.

Mr. Wicket sat down heavily. "I have been all over the world today, Mrs. Right."

"What did you discover?"

"I will begin at the beginning. First, I was able to make contact with a kitchen maid working in Lord Manderbey's household who was all too happy to be paid for supplying information. Apparently, the dowager has pushed into the house, as she is not usually there. She is determined to see Lord Manderbey wed and has set her sights on two ladies—Lady Winsome and a certain Lady Edith Cullington. The maid says both ladies come with plenty of money. This seems to be of particular concern to the dowager."

Mr. Wicket paused, a faint blush arising on his pale skin.

"What else did she say?" Mrs. Right asked.

"There was some mention of Lady Edith's wide hips being looked upon favorably, regarding children," Mr. Wicket said, staring off into space. He seemed to collect himself by giving his shoulders a little shake. "After that startling conversation, I kept a close eye on the house. Lord Manderbey set off on his horse and I duly followed. When he'd emerged from the house, he carried a velvet case. I was, naturally, interested to know what was in it and where he was going with it."

"Did you find it out?"

"I did. I followed him to Rundell & Bridge, where he went in with the case and came out without it. I was able to lurk near the window of the place and see the jeweler open the case. It was a rather fantastic platinum and diamond necklace. So, now we know."

"Know what?" Mrs. Right asked.

"We know how severe the amount of debt Lord Manderbey carries must be. Do you not see it? A man takes jewelry like that into a shop and leaves without it? He's sold it."

"Sold it," Mrs. Right muttered. "And whose was it? Not his own. It might be his mother's or the dowager's. He's come to such a pass as to steal from his own family."

"It does appear so, Mrs. Right. I have been informed, through a contact in the palace, that such a man might turn up here." He paused, then said, "Though I cannot think where that letter has gone. Very inconvenient, there was a clue I have not yet unraveled. Trulogap. I've only had one idea about it, but it makes no sense."

Mrs. Right did not offer that the letter had gone right into her own pocket. "Trulogap sounds like the name of a horse."

"A horse? Perhaps, but what is the real name? It was a scramble and I have had not much luck unscrambling it yet." Mr. Wicket sighed. "By the by, Lord Manderbey is upstairs at this very moment. He went first to Lord St. John's house but only stood at the door talking to the butler and then left. I thought I would be following him to his club perhaps, but he led me here."

"Don't I know it," Mrs. Right said. "A tea tray was sent for and Lord St. John is up there too. By the by, what is a scramble? Just out of curiosity."

"A mix-up of letters that must be rearranged to show the correct word. The Lord Chamberlain is very fond of them, as inconvenient as they are. I think it makes him feel as if he's in the spy business himself."

"Oh, I see," Mrs. Right said. So Trulogap was not the real word? What was the real word? Mr. Wicket named it a clue—a clue to what? And then, LC stood for the Lord Chamberlain. That was something she'd not guessed.

"Lady Winsome must be warned," Mr. Wicket said.

"She's already been warned," Mrs. Right said, "though it has not seemed to put her off. I must think of some way to turn her from him."

"Why not just go to the duke?" Mr. Wicket asked.

"I will if I have to, but His Grace depends on me to get rid of problems before he is troubled by them. In this particular situation, I believe I may need to take the sort of drastic action he'd rather not know about."

Mr. Wicket appeared leery to hear of drastic action. That did not seem very stalwart for a man who lived in a wine cellar and claimed to be an expert in covert actions.

As for Mrs. Right herself, she was exceedingly stalwart when it came to her girls. There really was nothing she would not dare. This time, she would dare quite a lot. Her girl was at risk of spending a lifetime in misery if she were to go forward with Lord Manderbey. She could not allow that to happen. She *would* not allow that to happen.

LELAND DID NOT find much satisfaction with the day so far. His plan, which had not at all gone to plan, had been to stop at St. John's house, point out to him that he was in no position to wed, further point out to him that Lady Winsome Nicolet was far above his reach, and then continue on to the park to exercise his horse.

The first bump in the road was the dowager insisting that he make a stop to deliver her diamond necklace to Rundell & Bridge. The clasp had broken and apparently it was an emergency that it be fixed and Mr. Rundell was waiting for it to arrive.

He'd done that, then he'd gone to St. John's house. His cousin's butler, who knew him well but perhaps did not know of the current strife between them, had been free with the information that St. John had gone off to Lady Winsome's house. He could feel his blood begin to boil as he rode in that direction.

His blood had not cooled when he noted that St. John had brought flowers and a book on Rio de Janeiro. If he'd had any lingering doubts over what St. John was up to, they were speedily whisked away.

After a rather unsatisfactory visit, Lady Valor had practically thrown both of them from the house. Leland had taken his opportunity to counsel his cousin as they were handed their horses. He'd pointed out two facts. One, even if St. John were to get the Portuguese ambassadorship, he would not be out of the woods financially. Two, Lady Winsome would not be taken in by a gentleman so obviously making a play for her dowry.

St. John had said, "The lady is comely and a duke's daughter and I am a lord, why should I not be interested in pursuing her? It is merely a fortunate happenstance that she comes well-funded. I will get the ambassadorship and I will go to Rio de Janeiro. With funds at my disposal, I will take advantage of the mining for precious gems to be done there."

"So that's the scheme," Leland had said. And what a scheme it was. He wanted to get his hands on Lady Winsome's money so he could roll the dice on mining. A gambler right to the end.

"I hear your derisive tone," St. John said, "though I do wonder at it."

"You wonder at it?" Leland asked, incredulous. "You are near penniless and have not given up your profligate ways—gambling and making purchases you cannot afford. I understand you recently bought a horse, it was very ill-advised, considering."

"Oh ho! Look at you! You are one to be talking about losing money on horses!"

Leland had no idea what he was talking about. Of course, that was nothing new. "I warn you to back away from Lady Winsome. She does not deserve such treatment."

"Well, well," St. John said, "it is fine for you but not for me. That's right, I know what you're up to. Your days of controlling everybody with your money have come to a close, Cousin."

Leland had poked him in the chest and said, "Do as I say. I will not allow you to injure the lady by pulling her into a dangerous situation with a profligate man."

He'd mounted his horse and rode off to the park. St. John had called after him something that sounded like *Trulogap*. He really never understood half of what that man said.

Leland could not say his ride was any more genial than the rest of the day had been. Horses were very astute at picking up on moods and Leland's own mood had put his horse out of sorts—Apollo had enough of the thoroughbred in him to provide for a spirited personality. This day, he made himself difficult to control and did more sidestepping than going forward until Leland could get him going into a canter.

As he flew across the greens of the park, Leland considered that he'd thought he had more time than he likely did. St. John was putting on the pressure and who knew what he might do next. Who knew how Lady Winsome received his cousin's attentions? Especially if he, himself, had not yet made himself clear. The fellow was handsome enough and titled. If one did not know him as Leland did, he might be considered a serious candidate.

Perhaps he ought to make his interest more known, more definite, than he had. He felt there was some sort of unspoken understanding between him and Lady Winsome, but there was the chance that it was in his imagination alone.

He would see the lady at Sir Jonathan's scavenger hunt. That might be the ideal moment to make himself more clear. After all, he did not expect St. John to turn up. Sir Jonathan's annual event was for a charity he sponsored and therefore the price of the tickets was steep for what it was.

Of course, the dowager would be there, encouraged by the duke. However, it sounded as if this year would be held in darkness so perhaps he could slip away from his grandmother. He might keep her away from Lady Winsome before she said anything outrageous. He might keep himself by Lady Winsome's side.

Leland was determined to drop a clear hint of his interest.

LANDRY HAD BOLTED his doors against his relatives. Lady Edith had assured him that he did not need to admit anybody into his house unless he really wished to see them.

The idea had at first struck him as outlandish. He was so used to his aunts and uncles and cousins descending upon him whenever they felt like it. They just barged in and cornered him in his drawing room and listed their demands. They never even bothered to write that they were coming. At home, he spent a good deal of time nervously looking out windows if they hadn't been to see him in a while.

Lady Edith explained that he was a lord with his own estate and nobody could push him around unless he allowed it.

What an idea.

The more he thought about it, though, the more he liked it. The more he liked it, the more he became determined to try it out. It would be enormously pleasant to avoid his relations. He really did not like any of them—they were very pushy.

He'd had a tentative word with his butler to ascertain his views, as that fellow would be the one faced with them all standing on the pavement when they chose to turn up. Could he keep them out?

Marley had been surprisingly enthusiastic about the notion. He'd said, "My lord, nobody you do not wish to see will be admitted to this house by me. I will inform the rest of the staff of the various persons who have made themselves persona non gratis."

The fellow had looked rather gleeful and Landry got the idea that he'd been waiting for just such a directive. It began to seem as if he ought to have barred those terrible people from the house long ago.

Now, they had arrived. Landry pulled the curtain aside just the smallest bit so he could view the proceedings. He felt his heart speed up, as there was always the chance they might push past his butler. What would he do then? He would be questioned mercilessly about why he'd tried to stop them from coming in.

Aunt Agatha led them forward, as always dressed in her black widow's weeds and looking as bad-tempered as ever. Her two lumbering sons stood behind her.

The lady had just been told that she would not be admitted. Really, Marley had taken the thing further than Landry had directed. He did not recall telling his butler to inform her that she would not be admitted "today, or any other day, forevermore."

His aunt shook her cane at Marley, which she was often in the habit of doing. She demanded that he step aside, but he refused to step aside. His cousins offered their own threats, raising their fists and claiming they would push him out of the way if necessary.

Marley stood firm.

And then, in a miracle happening right in front of his eyes, they turned and left.

They left. They were gone. They'd come, and he'd not been forced to see them.

Marley knocked on the drawing room doors and entered. "They have departed, my lord, they will not trouble you again."

"Well done, Marley," Landry said.

"Yes, my lord," Marley said.

"Really well done. I ought to give you more money than I do. Yes, I will arrange that."

Marley appeared pleased. As well he should. As well Lady Edith should, as it had been her idea all along. The lady had such good ideas! He really did like to spend time with Lady Edith.

And then, there had been their conversation last evening. He'd hinted, vaguely he thought, that he was nervous about the idea of getting married. She'd told him he ought not to be. She'd said it was like anything else that was new. One ought to just go forward, step by step, and the proper road would unfold in front of his feet as he went.

He'd never thought of it that way. It began to give him ideas. After all, he did wish for children. He imagined he'd be a terrific father. His own father had been very kind, and he wished to be just the same. It had just always been his terror of women, or rather his terror of measuring up, that had seemed to make the thing impossible. But there was a calm to spending time with Lady Edith. She was so sure of everything and she did not look to him for direction. He was not in charge and it occurred to him that he did not like being in charge.

Now, he began to imagine that it might really be possible to wed. Assuming Lady Edith would have him.

He must just gather the courage to ask. Or maybe she would ask and he would not have to do anything at all.

Chapter Twelve

W INSOME HAD THOUGHT and then thought again about how to save Lord Manderbey from his terrible gambling habit. How could she do it? She had no power to do it. She was just a lady he'd met in Town.

At first, she imagined she might speak to him directly about it. She'd dismissed the idea. It would be so affronting for a lady to lecture a gentleman of her sphere on such a matter. Or any matter. No man would tolerate it. It would damage his dignity.

If she could not speak directly, what could she do?

Mrs. Right laid out her dress and said, "What's on your mind, Poppet? You look very pensive. If it's about Mr. Wicket, pay no mind. That situation is well on its way to being solved."

"No, it is not Mr. Wicket. It is just that, well I know perfectly well I ought to run the other direction from Lord Manderbey—"

"Aye, a gambler is nothing but trouble and heartache. A lifetime of misery."

"But I am not going to. I tried, you see, but I cannot do it. So then I thought, might I be able to help him change the habit of gambling that he's acquired?"

Mrs. Right dropped the dress in her hands. "Change him?"

Winsome nodded. "He is perfect in every other way. It is just this one thing that might be…dangerous."

Mrs. Right hurriedly picked up the dress. "I had not thought of changing him. No, that had never occurred to me."

"But I rather think it could be done. I've just got to think of the right strategy." Winsome paused, examining the housekeeper. "You do not think it could be done."

"Uh, as to that, it is just…well I hadn't really thought."

Winsome had left it at that. She could see very well that Mrs. Right did not hold out much hope that such a thing could be accomplished. She would not give up hope herself though. She was tempted to ask her father, but then she must make him aware of the problem in the first place, which she had not done.

"All right," the duke said, as the carriage barreled along the dark streets to Sir Jonathan's scavenger hunt, "I can see very well that something is on your mind. Out with it."

"On my mind? No, there is nothing on my mind," Winsome said. She did not like to hide anything from her father, but this she must.

"Well now, I cannot know the particulars, but I can guess well enough the subject," the duke said. "It is about Manderbey, one way or another."

Winsome did not answer. Her father was really so attuned to his daughters' feelings, it was very hard to hide anything from him.

"Now listen here, Winny, I have been down this road five times already, always with the same result. One of my daughters becomes convinced things have somehow become hopeless, they never are, and then they discover they never had anything to worry over in the first place."

"Papa, you know very well that I am not prone to wild flights of fancy. I am a very practical person with my feet firmly on the ground." She said it, though it was not entirely true. It used to be true, at least she had thought so.

"I only say, whatever it is, it is likely nonsense."

The carriage had slowed and Winsome was grateful for it. She could not go on lying through omission to her own father. Sooner or later, she would crack like an egg dropped on the pavement. She must just find a way to fix Lord Manderbey's problem before she had to hide it longer.

Sir Jonathan resided in a fine white stone house on Duke Street. They departed the carriage and made their way in, greeting their host in the great hall.

"Everyone is to gather in the ballroom and at precisely nine o'clock I will explain the rules and then everybody may make their way to the garden for the game to begin," Sir Jonathan said. "Duke, you will find several sideboards in the ballroom that I trust you will find up to the mark."

"You read my mind, Sir," the duke said jovially.

The ballroom had filled as it was nearing nine o'clock already.

"Ah, there's that rascally dowager and her grandson," the duke said. "Duchess," he called, leading Winsome toward one of the many sideboards lining the walls of the ballroom.

Winsome took in Lord Manderbey's tall frame standing by his diminutive grandmother. There was nothing for it—whatever bad habit Lord Manderbey had fallen into, he was spectacular.

"Lady Winsome, Duke," he said. "I am glad you found us. Shall we work as a team to solve the clues?"

"Very good notion, Manderbey."

"It's all stuff and nonsense," Lord Manderbey said. "The prize will not be of any significance. But on the other hand, I do like to win when I can."

Winsome suppressed a sigh. He liked to win when he could. There was the ugly head of gambling raised again.

"The competitive spirit of a young gentleman, eh, Duke?" the dowager said.

The duke nodded. To the dowager, he said, "Might I predict that you and I will satisfy ourselves with sipping the glasses we bring out with us for this absurd entertainment?"

The dowager laughed. "Yes, indeed. Let us get started!"

The duke led the lady to the sideboard so they could "get started" as the dowager termed it.

"I hope my grandmother's attempts to keep pace with your father do not end embarrassing," Lord Manderbey said.

"I suppose for one to be embarrassed they must agree to it," Winsome said. "My father says it is caused by caring too much what other people might think."

"I suppose so," Lord Manderbey said. "Perhaps people pick and choose what it is they will find embarrassing."

"I've often wondered about gambling," Winsome said boldly. "There are such stories that go round of gentlemen getting in so deep they flee to the continent."

"Or blow their brains out, which seems faster," Lord Manderbey said. "After all, living penniless in a foreign land, dependent on whatever friends can be dug up, must be a slow kind of death. Everyone will soon tire of propping the fellow up and then he's got nowhere to turn."

Winsome felt frozen where she stood. What was he saying? Was he in any danger of getting in that deep? Did he mean that if he did, he would do a violence to himself? "But I must suppose that a gentleman heading in such a serious direction might pull back. They might give it up before an unrepairable disaster."

Lord Manderbey laughed. "That would be very sensible, but they rarely do. They chase the losses, always believing they can right the ship until the ship positively sinks."

"They could give it up before the ship sinks, though," Winsome said. What was wrong with him? It sounded as if he had no notion of how to save himself. It sounded as if he was powerless against the lure of gambling.

"Lady Winsome."

She turned and found Lord St. John. Why did he have to interrupt at such a moment? "Lord St. John," she said. She'd tried to keep the sullenness out of her tone but was not entirely certain that she had.

The two lords stared at each other in a not very friendly manner and did not even bother to exchange greetings.

"I hope we might travel through the garden together for the scavenger hunt," Lord St. John said.

"I am afraid that will not be possible," Lord Manderbey said.

"The duke has already made arrangements for myself and my dowager to accompany Lady Winsome."

Lord St. John looked at Winsome for confirmation or denial of this claim.

"Indeed, my father did say so," she said.

"More than four would just be a crowd," Lord Manderbey said.

Their host for the evening entered the ballroom at that moment, to the great acclaim of his guests. Sir Jonathan strode to the top of the ballroom and called for everyone's attention.

"Ladies, gentlemen, thank you for attending my little charity event. This year will be different, as I imagine you have already guessed. In the garden, you will find six clues. When you know the answer to a clue, write down the first letter on the slates you will be provided. Once you have all six letters, rearrange them into the word that will solve the puzzle. The first that does so is the victor."

The duke and the dowager returned to Winsome's side. She noticed that they carried glasses filled to the brim. She imagined Lord Manderbey was right about supposing the dowager ought not attempt to keep pace with her father. He was a hearty individual and she was a little sparrow of a lady.

"St. John, what do you do here?" the dowager asked. "I hadn't marked you as a man supporting charities."

"You are mistaken, Your Grace," Lord St. John said, "I often support a worthy cause. I am to be an ambassador, after all."

"Ah, when do you sail?"

This threw Lord St. John on the back foot. "Uh, as to that, I have not been given official notice of the post. At this moment in time."

"Well, fingers crossed, eh?" the duke said. "You'd best go and find your party St. John, this nonsense is set to begin."

Having been thus dismissed, Lord St. John bowed curtly and strode through the crowd. Winsome got the idea that he did not have a party to go to. He'd planned to join their own party. She was not sorry to see him go. In any case, she had more important things to consider. Was Lord Manderbey in actual danger? Had he got himself into such a corner that he might consider the final choice?

It sent a terror through her. She had to save him. Somehow, she had to pull him back from the brink.

They made their way out of the back of the house. Lord Manderbey was handed a slate and graphite. Sir Jonathan's garden was lit up along paths through shrubbery. At various points, such as a fountain or a bench, there were the clues they were meant to unravel.

As people took various paths to begin, the first clue they came upon read: The beginning of an Idea.

"Why is the word 'idea' capitalized like that?" Winsome asked.

"You are right, I had not noticed. It must mean something," Lord Manderbey said.

"The word we're looking for must begin with I," the dowager said. "And that's the last sense you'll get out of me—this Canary is strong!"

Winsome noted Lord Manderbey's sigh as he wrote down I. "Could it be inkling?" she asked.

Lord Manderbey nodded. Then something seemed to come upon him. "Wait a minute," he said, "if the capitalized letter indicates the first letter of the answer to the clue, do we even need the answer? Do not we simply need to have a look at all the clues, write down the capitalized letter, and then see what we have?"

The duke snorted. "Sir Jonathan did not fully think it through."

They hurried down the paths, not bothering to solve the clues but simply writing down the capitalized letters they found. They ended where they started and stared down at the slate.

IWEGSN

"This is what we have to work with," Lord Manderbey said.

Winsome did not know if their strategy was the right one, but even if it were, how were they to divine what the word was?

Lord Manderbey was writing down various combinations, none of which made sense.

Then she had a sudden idea. "Lord Manderbey, have you by chance read *The Laird of Castle Carrigan?*"

Lord Manderbey's brows raised and Winsome remembered that he'd likely only read *Gloaming at Glenford Cross* because she'd mentioned she preferred gothic novels. It was unlikely that he would have made a habit of it.

"What say you, Duke?" the dowager said. "Shall we find our aging bones a bench and leave this to the younger set?"

The duke nodded and they toddled off to look for a seat.

"What are you thinking in regards to the book you mentioned?" Lord Manderbey asked.

"It is probably silly, but in that story, a mysterious note is left in Annabelle's room. She's just arrived as the laird's ward and she cannot make heads or tails of the word on the paper. Then one day, as she has it laid on her dressing table, she sees its reflection in the looking glass. Goodness, I cannot precisely remember what word or phrase she saw, but I *do* remember that something about the reflection helped her escape terrible danger."

Lord Manderbey looked critically at his slate, squinting his eyes as if to see it in a mirror image.

"We passed a ladies' retiring room on our way out," Winsome said. "I imagine you've never been inside one—"

"I have not," Lord Manderbey said laughing.

"I can assure you, they are full of looking glasses. Let me take the slate in and have a look. It's worth a try and I'll be back in a tick."

"It's worth a try I suppose," Lord Manderbey said, handing over the slate.

Winsome took it and hurried into the house. She must be quick in case anybody else had the same idea. She ran down the corridor to where she'd seen Lady Melby exit the room when they'd passed by.

Flinging open the door, she found it blessedly empty. She was a bit surprised that there was no attendant, but perhaps a single gentleman did not employ such people. She held the slate to the looking glass.

It was the same nonsensical string of letters as was on the slate. She sighed, supposing she would not make a very good heroine of one of the books she liked so much. Or perhaps the trick of unscrambling in a looking glass did not actually work. She did not know, but in this case it did not.

Suddenly, she heard the distinct sound of a sliding bolt. She looked around but she was still very much alone. Where had it come from?

No matter. She must return to the garden and inform Lord Manderbey that her idea had not produced a result.

Winsome pulled on the door. Then she pulled again. It was locked.

LORD LANDRY HAD been ginning himself up all night to say the words. The words were in his mind but he could not get them out. How did other gentlemen do it? How did they ask if a lady would wed them? And then, if a person could choke out the words, what next? Would they just stand there, staring until the lady said something? And what if she said yes? What was expected then? Should he say thank you? Or worse, what if she said no? Should he say thank you anyway?

How was it possible that there was not a book written about this?

He had escorted Lady Edith round the garden paths, collecting the clues. He could not say they made much progress, the only clue they'd been able to solve was another word for building, which they thought must be edifice.

He must have looked very white over his nervousness, as twice Lady Edith had inquired if he were sick. He'd denied it, though he felt rather sick. It was only getting worse though, as the more he thought, the more questions occurred to him. If she said yes, was he meant to kiss her? On her face?

Finally, as they were puzzling over a clue that read "the beginning of an Idea," his nerves reached a fever pitch. There was a violent rumbling in his stomach that signaled events to come. He excused himself to visit…well he'd not had to spell out where he was going.

Lady Edith nodded knowingly and speculated that he'd eaten something bad. Not a thing to be ashamed of, as it was a very common thing.

He gratefully grabbed at the excuse and had hurried inside. In truth, his stomach was in a total revolt, as it often did when he was wracked with nerves. He found Sir Jonathan's billiards room and, mercifully, spotted the closed-off curtain that said a chamber pot was within reach.

Landry had shut the billiards room door behind him, hoping there would be no other visitor looking to relieve himself. He found two chamber pots, both blessedly empty. His stomach was in such an attack that he might just fill them both. He ought not have eaten all those greasy potatoes at dinner!

As his insides disgorged, he heard the faint click coming from the direction of the door. He prayed nobody was coming and tried to quiet the ungodly noises emanating from his person. Blessedly, nobody came in. Or perhaps they had and were speedily apprised of the situation. It did not have the scent of roses, after all.

He would stay where he was until his bowels were entirely empty. He did not dare return to Lady Edith and then experience another attack—he might not get back here in time!

How was he ever going to broach the subject of marriage? How was he ever going to ask when just thinking about it sent him into disaster?

Now he'd left Lady Edith on her own while he was very stupidly attached to a chamber pot for the foreseeable future.

LELAND HAD WAITED and waited for Lady Winsome to return. She'd been gone for over a half hour. Of course, it was conceivable that she'd encountered some lady friend and they were engaged in an extended conversation in the ladies' retiring room. He understood women went in for such things, though neither he nor any of his friends had the least idea of what they talked about in there.

He had not known precisely what to do about it. It seemed as if she was gone for an inordinate amount of time. However, he could not insist that she hurry. What was he supposed to do? Knock on the door?

Now, though, the length of time began to seem downright odd. Could something have happened? Could there be something wrong? Perhaps Lady Winsome had been taken ill.

That might make sense. Perhaps she'd suggested checking the slate in the mirror as a way to delicately excuse herself.

He glanced over at the dowager and the duke seated on a bench in the corner of the garden. They seemed to be entertaining themselves well enough.

He strode over. "Grandmama, Lady Winsome went to the ladies' retiring room some time ago. I wonder if you might go and see if she requires any assistance."

"Trying to separate me from my wine, are you?" the dowager asked.

"That would only be an added benefit," he said drily.

"You see the way he speaks to me?" the dowager said, laughing.

"That's a young buck for you," the duke said, equally amused.

"What think you, Duke?" the dowager asked. "Should I go and check on your daughter?"

"Yes, why not? I had not expected any of my other daughters to turn up, but if they have, I can assure you those girls can talk until the sun comes up."

Leland began to think possibly he was overreacting. It was likely that Lady Winsome had encountered a sister and they'd lost track of time.

Still, it would not hurt to check. He had an uneasy feeling he could not quite pin down.

"Hold my wine," the dowager ordered, handing him her glass. "I'll go see what's holding her up in there."

CHAPTER THIRTEEN

L ANDRY SAT ON the chamber pot, his nether region beginning to get sore at this point, mulling over how exactly he was to manage asking Lady Edith the momentous question. He dared not have a repeat of his current circumstances. She was an understanding lady, but no lady should be forced to imagine what had happened in this room.

Perhaps he would pick a day where he ate and drank nothing. Then his nerves could do what they liked but could not cause a disaster of the chamber pot variety.

Yes, certainly, that was what he ought to do. He would starve himself and then just get out the words. If she said yes, he could starve himself on the wedding day. And then maybe other days. He would grow thin, that was only to be expected, but he would manage his condition.

As it usually did, feeling as if he'd found a solution calmed him. There had been no reason to rush into it tonight, after having eaten greasy potatoes. That had been a silly notion. An easily made mistake, as it were. On his next try, he would spend a day surviving on a few sips of ale and nothing else. He would be an empty shell of a man, impervious to any dangers of a revolt in his digestion.

As well, he might write down the question and just hand it to her. Had that been done before? Surely it must have been. Perhaps it might even be preferred, as it supplied the lady with a keepsake. Indeed, what lady would not like to have a memento?

As it had been near a half hour since anything of note had come out of him, Landry felt he might safely return to the garden.

In any case, he'd just heard another sound at the door. Another click. Then, silence. Had he now driven two gentlemen away from the room from the scent of the mess he'd left in the pots?

It would be too humiliating if he were caught at it. There would be jokes going round in the clubs. Sir Howard was still trying to live down something similar that had occurred at Lady Gerard's card party. They were still calling him "Have at It Howard."

He must not let that happen!

Landry hurriedly did up his pants and jogged to the door. Out in the corridor, he noted St. John look out of the ballroom and then pull his head back in, and then Lady Winsome hurrying toward him. She appeared upset or affronted or alarmed.

Good God, had it been Lady Winsome he'd heard at the door? Had she got a whiff of such an abomination? Could he blame it on somebody else?

She even looked a little disheveled. Had her encounter with his unfortunate eruptions caused a discombobulation?

"Lady Winsome," he said hurriedly, "I was going to the billiards room but Lord…Lord, well I forget his name, he was already in there. The point is, somebody else was in there!"

Before Lady Winsome could indicate whether she believed that or not, they came face to face with the dowager. "Lady Winsome," she said, "I was sent to look for you."

"Yes, I was delayed," Lady Winsome said in a tremulous voice.

Landry could not work out why she seemed on the verge of tears. It was true that what was in that billiard room was deeply upsetting, but he'd not thought it could make a person cry. But then, she was a lady and would be more sensitive to such things.

"I was delayed too," Landry nearly shouted. "Somebody else was in the billiard room. I don't know who it was. Just somebody else!" Then he fled lest he be interrogated on the matter.

WINSOME HAD NO idea what had just happened to her. She'd gone into the retiring room to check the string of letters in a looking glass. Then she'd been locked in. She'd banged on the door and called for help but nobody had come.

The oak door was substantial and so well-fitted that she could not even see a strip of light coming from underneath. Nobody could hear her.

As the minutes passed, she began to feel as if she were living inside a gothic novel. Why had she been locked in? Who had done it? Was there some means of escape?

She had searched the room, looking in vain for a secret passage. There usually was one in her books. There was always a way out when the heroine found herself in seemingly impossible circumstances. She combed the room top to bottom and got on hands and knees to peer underneath tables. There was no way out but the door.

Then, just as she was about to give up and just wait for her father to send up the alarm and start a search for her, she'd heard the distinct slide of the bolt. She'd run to the door. It was heavy and it took her several tries to push it open. There was nobody in the corridor.

Somebody had locked her in and then let her out again? Why? What had been the purpose? Had it been a prank of some sort? Was there a mischievous child in the house? Sir Jonathan was unmarried, but that did not mean he did not have relations staying in the house.

The more she considered it, the more it began to make sense. She had allowed her imagination, which was far too influenced by the books she'd read, to think there was something nefarious afoot. That had not been very sensible though. Certainly it had been a childish game. It was the sort of thing Valor would have done but a few short years ago. Or even yesterday. Whoever it was, they'd probably run upstairs in laughing hysterics over it.

She could not say she was laughing quite so hard.

Winsome hurried down the corridor toward the door to the garden. She was nearly bowled over by Lord Landry coming out of another room and babbling about another lord he could not remember the name of who had been in that room.

Then they had both encountered the dowager. Lord Landry, for reasons known only to himself, once again mentioned the mysterious somebody else in the billiards room before fleeing the corridor. She could not imagine who that unknown lord was or what he'd done to Lord Landry, but the fellow was in near hysterics over it.

She hardly knew what to say to the dowager regarding the situation so she'd merely said she had been delayed.

Winsome did not know what the dowager thought about it, but the lady suddenly said, "Lady Winsome, do give me your arm. I find I feel poorly."

"Oh certainly," Winsome said, assisting the lady down the hall. She supposed the effects of trying to keep up with the duke had begun to take their toll.

"Take me to my grandson," the dowager said, "then he can escort me home."

Winsome nodded and suppressed a sigh. Lord Manderbey would leave. This had not been the evening she'd been hoping for. She was supposed to be figuring out how to pull him away from his gambling habit before he went too far. Instead, she'd been trapped in a retiring room, looking for a hidden way out.

They entered the garden and Lord Manderbey strode over to them.

"Manderbey, I an unwell," the dowager said. "Take me home and call for the doctor."

"I see. Yes, of course," he said, taking his grandmother's arm. "Lady Winsome," he said, by way of goodbye.

She made her way over to her father, who still sat on the bench, now holding two glasses of wine. Winsome took one from his hand and drained it. "I've just spent the past half hour locked in a retiring room. What a night."

LELAND HAD THE carriage called and found a chair for his grandmother as they waited. The whole evening was unaccountable. Lady Winsome had disappeared for an extended period. His grandmother had gone off to find her and come back doing poorly. She'd been right as rain before she'd gone back into the house.

He supposed the elderly were prone to sudden attacks and hoped it was not of a serious nature. He suspected the physician would advise her to cut back on the amount of spirits she'd been imbibing over the past days.

The carriage came round, he helped his drooping grandmother into it, and banged on the roof for the coachman to get going.

The horses pulled forward and settled into a trot. His grandmother suddenly sat up straight and said, "I've saved you from humiliation, Manderbey. This will come as a shock, I know, but Lady Winsome has been compromised."

Leland dropped his hat, which had been in his hands. "What?"

"Trust me, things could have gone very badly if I had not discovered it."

"Trust you? I certainly will not blindly trust you. What are you claiming? Specifically?" He did not know what sort of trouble the dowager was trying to drum up, but she no longer looked as if she did poorly. "You do not require a doctor, do you?"

"Of course I don't," the dowager said. "I had to get you away from there in all haste, before you committed yourself to anything. Lady Winsome is not the innocent that she seems."

"Do not be ridiculous," he said.

"Manderbey, I may be old, but I am not blind. I know what I saw."

Leland crossed his arms. "What exactly do you think you saw?"

"As you know, Lady Winsome was missing for an inordinate amount of time. In the ladies' retiring room, you said. Well, let me tell you, that was not where she was found. I discovered her in the corridor, looking very flustered and disheveled, with Lord Landry."

Leland burst out laughing. "Landry?" he asked. "You think Lady Winsome was compromised by *Landry*? He could not seduce a Cyprian he'd already paid."

"That comment was in very bad taste, do not speak to me of Cyprians again, if you please. Now, I know what I saw, Manderbey. The look of guilt on that man's face was unmistakable. He positively fled the scene."

"It's all nonsense."

"It is not nonsense. How does she account for her absence? She simply says she was delayed. By what? Or rather, by who?"

"Even if I believed Lady Winsome capable of what you accuse her of, which I do not, Landry would not be up to such connivances."

"That's why he looked so panicked," the dowager said. "Now, I do like the duke exceedingly so I will not breathe a word of this. I suspect that something kicked it all off. You know how people sympathize with Lord Landry, especially women. I think perhaps she sympathized with him over something and that led to an encounter. Something got out of hand."

"I don't believe it."

"I saw it. Now listen, I do not wish to harm Lady Winsome in any way. The lady has made a mistake, I am sure she feels terrible about it and I would not wish to ruin her future. That future, however, cannot involve this family."

"You will speak of this to nobody, not even Miss Price. I do not wish word of your absurd ideas to travel through the household. Do you understand?"

"I understand. I just hope *you* understand. You must be sensible about this."

They traveled the rest of the way home in silence. What in the world had gone on? He did not believe his grandmother's version of events. That was not the Lady Winsome he knew. It was certainly not Landry. That fellow was terrified of women, not a leering lothario.

Something had gone on, though. Lady Winsome's hair was mussed and her manner was one of unease when she'd returned to the garden. Had she been accosted in some way? Not by Landry, which was ridiculous, but by someone else. Should he have insisted on escorting her inside when she'd gone to check the clue?

But then, it seemed most improbable that a lady would be accosted inside Sir Jonathan's house.

He would have to get to the bottom of it. He would not see Lady Winsome until Lady Darlington's masque in three days' time. Perhaps his first stop must be to see Landry. He had been on the scene and would have better information than his grandmother and her wild speculations.

Whatever had gone on, he could not bring himself to believe the lady had been at all at fault. As well, he could not believe that Landry would be at all capable of attempting a seduction—the fellow could barely attempt a conversation.

So what *had* happened?

THE DAY FOLLOWING Sir Jonathan's scavenger hunt brought rain.

It was the sort of pouring rain that admitted no breaks, the skies had opened and let out a torrent. The streets had been transformed into fast-running, muddy streams and the windows were grayed with foggy mist.

Winsome was perfectly sanguine over the weather. It was the type of day when all sane people stuck to their houses and did not venture out. It suited her mood.

She had fretted long into the night, going back and forth over what had happened at Sir Jonathan's house. One moment, it was some despicable plot she could not unravel. The next moment, it was a child playing at a joke.

Just now, she, Valor, and Mrs. Right were cozy in the drawing room. A fire had been lit to beat back the chill and candles flickered, warming the light in the room. To entertain Valor, Winsome had had written and cut out the letters to Sir Jonathan's clues so she might work to unscramble the word that was the solution. Winsome already knew what it was, as shortly after Lord Manderbey and the dowager had departed, a winner had been announced and the answer given.

"Oh wait," Valor said. "There is an I and an N and a G. ING is the ending of a lot of words. That leaves the E and the S." Valor tapped her chin. "Sewing! It must be sewing!"

Winsome smiled. "That is right, Val. As well, it makes perfect sense, as that is what Sir Jonathan's charity is all about. Young girls are trained to be seamstresses so that they have an independent means of support."

"Because they do not have a kind Papa like we do that will buy all their dresses?"

"Something like that," Winsome said. It was apparent that her youngest sister had not yet reached the age when her eyes were fully open to the world and saw it for what it was. At Valor's age, Winsome had herself thought that everybody in their little village did just what they liked. If a man was a shepherd, it must be because he'd rather spend all his days with sheep than any other thing. It was not until she was older that she began to question why that shepherd would not rather live in a fine house as she did. And then to eventually understand that he could not, even if he wished it.

"Well," Valor said, "I suppose teaching people to sew is a very good idea. They can sew their own hostessing clothes. Should I write Sir Jonathan and describe how I designed my hostessing clothes so he can show them how to do it?"

"No, no that would not be at all necessary, he will already know all about it," Winsome said. Valor's letters were notorious for setting people's backs up and it would hardly be appropriate for him to receive a letter from a girl he'd never laid eyes on, even if he did develop an interest in hostessing clothes.

Mrs. Right suddenly sat up straight. "I've heard the door, I'm sure I have. Who would come out in such weather?"

Winsome smoothed her dress and very much hoped it was Lord Manderbey. They had not had a moment to speak before he'd left Sir Jonathan's to escort the dowager home. She'd said she would be gone for a moment and then had been gone for over a half hour, with no explanation. He must think it so odd.

Of course, the reason for it was even more odd. She'd been locked in the ladies' retiring room. It sounded absurd. It *was* absurd.

The drawing room doors were flung open and a very wet Lady Marchfield strode through it.

Winsome's heart sank. It was not Lord Manderbey. But why on earth would their aunt come out in such weather?

Lady Marchfield gave a withering glance to Mrs. Right. Then she said, "Valor, please take that housekeeper elsewhere. I will have a private word with Winsome."

Both Valor and Mrs. Right looked to Winsome. Mrs. Right said, "I'll stay if you need me to, Poppet."

Winsome had rather not cause some sort of contretemps between her aunt and her dear Mrs. Right, they already were oil and water. In any case, she was all but certain Lady Marchfield had arrived to deliver the same lecture she'd been handing out for years—the household must be regulated and their behavior modified, or they were heading toward disaster. Winsome was well able to stand up to it. She just did not know what could have set her aunt off this time as she'd not seen her all that much this season.

"It's all right," Winsome said. "Mrs. Right, perhaps you could help Valor with her knitting? She's been determined to make Sir Galahad a blanket for his bed, but has not got far with it."

"It's very hard, that's why," Valor said, scooping up the dog in question.

Mrs. Right rose too. "I'll ask Charlie to arrange for a tea tray."

"Not necessary," Lady Marchfield said curtly.

Goodness, the lady was exceedingly out of sorts. She was usually only a regular amount of out of sorts.

The door shut behind Valor and Mrs. Right. Lady Marchfield sat down and took her by the hands. "I pray you will tell me you are engaged."

"Engaged? No, I am not."

"Your father must force him to it, then."

"Force him? Why?" Winsome was mystified. Why on earth would her father attempt to force Lord Manderbey to make a proposal? The duke was in the habit of cajoling and gently pushing forward with his invitations to dine and jocular hints. But he would never go so far. Why would Lady Marchfield think he would? Or that he should?

"*Why* must he be forced to it?" Lady Marchfield said. She sounded as if it were the most absurd question ever asked her. "Winsome, if Lord Landry will not speak, your reputation is tarnished forever. Nobody will have you."

"Lord Landry? What does he have to do with anything? I can assure you, he is quite set on Lady Edith."

"He is set on another lady and behaves in such a manner?" Lady Marchfield said, dropping Winsome's hands. "He is a rake through and through. I would not have believed it of him."

"Lord Landry? A rake? Aunt, that is ridiculous. Please do tell me what this is about. I can hardly understand what you are saying."

"It is not what *I* am saying. It is what society is saying. Everybody is abuzz with the story—Lord Landry and Lady Winsome stole off together at Sir Jonathan's scavenger hunt, were gone for an extended period, and then were discovered, both of them appearing exceedingly disheveled."

Winsome sat back. What a story. She supposed she *had* looked a bit disheveled. She had been on hands and knees all over the retiring room looking for a secret door. Then, when she heard the sound at the door to the corridor, she raced to it with nary a look in the glass.

She had encountered Lord Landry in that corridor, the gentleman being somehow upset over an unknown lord in the billiards room. But how on earth had anybody jumped to the conclusion that something had gone on between them?

The drawing room doors opened and the duke entered the room. "I was informed you had darkened my door again and that you were in high dudgeon. What is it about this time, Misery?"

"I see you have not been to your club, Roland. Else you would have noticed something amiss when the other members turned from you in embarrassment."

"Nonsense, I haven't set anybody's curtains on fire this season. Not yet, though I make no promises."

"Papa," Winsome said, "there is a ludicrous story going round that, oh I can hardly say it—"

"That your daughter has been compromised by Lord Landry," Lady Marchfield said. "They were both missing at Sir Jonathan's scavenger hunt and then discovered disheveled."

The duke took that moment to erupt on laughter. "Landry? Do not be absurd. My daughter has not been compromised by anybody. I know that because if she had I would be the first person told about it and I happen to know precisely where she was during the time in question. Furthermore, Lord Landry could not catch a trout who leapt out of the water, waved to him, and jumped into his net."

Lady Marchfield rose. "I have done your daughter the courtesy of informing her of what is being said. I imagine you will handle it in your usual haphazard and ineffectual manner. I will warn you, though. This is serious and if Winsome does not wed, if an announcement is not made quickly, all will be lost."

Lady Marchfield took her leave.

"Papa, what can this be about? Why would anybody think that I have been compromised? By Lord Landry of all people? Can it be that if a lady is missing for a half hour, suddenly she's done something shameful? Can society really be that pernicious?"

"Now, do not get overly alarmed by this. After all, you know how your Aunt Misery proceeds in life, she's a pole cat forever sticking her nose into other people's henhouses and then sending up an alarm for no reason."

"But if people are saying these things, what should we do?" Winsome paused. "Papa, Lord Manderbey will hear of it. You do not think—"

"That he'd believe it? Not if he is the man I think he is. I will go see Landry. I suspect he's got more information on this confusion. You know what a collection of nerves that fellow is. I would not be surprised if he panicked over some small matter and then blurted out something ridiculous and somebody within hearing misunderstood his meaning." The duke snorted. "Maybe it was the hoi polloi again."

"Oh, Lady Edith! What will she think of it?"

"Winny, calm yourself. Do not allow yourself to imagine we are heading into some kind of disaster when I am sure that is not the case. I will be on my way, and I will send Mrs. Right in to keep company with you. Do not worry, my dear, all will be well."

Winsome curled up on the sofa. She dearly wished her father was right.

Could this terrible rumor have something to do with why she'd been locked in the ladies' retiring room? That had been the cause of her delay in returning to the garden. Could someone have done it deliberately so they might say she'd been missing so long that she must have been compromised?

But then, they would have had to have Lord Landry on hand too. One could not be compromised by oneself. That part did not make sense, as Lord Landry had not mentioned anything about having been locked in for any amount of time. He had said that there was another lord there.

Who was the other lord? Did that signify? Why would someone wish to damage her reputation?

CHAPTER FOURTEEN

LANDRY PACED HIS drawing room. It was extraordinary how things could seem to be going so well and then take a sudden turn down a dark and dangerous alley.

His mishap with the chamber pot at Sir Jonathan's scavenger hunt had not seemed to become public knowledge, though sooner or later somebody would have gone in there and witnessed the devastation. He felt terrible about that, but at least nobody knew who did it.

He'd returned to the garden and to Lady Edith's side and he'd admitted to the greasy potatoes for his discomfort. He'd not made any mention of his nerves being the other ingredient. Lady Edith had been stern in her advice about avoiding them in future. She explained that fried potatoes were notorious for taking a man down.

He had not known! She really did know so many handy pieces of information. And then, he did take comfort in being given a direction on greasy potatoes. He simply would not have them anymore. It was so simple.

The next day, he'd been very sanguine about going to his club. Until he got there. Why were so many gentlemen shaking their heads at him and turning away? He did not know. But, as it was proving uncomfortable and it would be even more uncomfortable to ask them why, he'd gone home.

When he arrived to his house, he discovered the cause of the frowns and turnings away. A letter from his aunt awaited him, and what a letter it was. Her letters were never pleasant, but this one was downright frightening.

Landry—

For shame! Never in my imagination had I thought that you would compromise a lady and cause such talk. This is what happens, I suppose, when you do not take on the advice of your relations. (Or let them in the door to give you that advice.)

I advise you to take on that counsel now. If you have not already done so, you must immediately repair to the Duke of Pelham, gain his approval, and get the banns read. Assuming, of course, he does not run you through on a green for this outrage.

The effrontery of compromising a duke's daughter is not to be borne! You have dragged this family's reputation through the mud and I fully expect that you will drag it back out of the mud and repair this situation. I expect that I will shortly hear of your engagement to Lady Winsome Nicolet. Otherwise, I suggest you leave Town—my boys are very put out about this situation and one old butler will not hold them back from visiting you to express their ire.

Clara Frogbottom

Would she send her sons to break into the house? Was this idea that he had compromised Lady Winsome widely spoken of?

Landry reflected back on his experience upon entering his club and was afraid it *was* all over town. After all, how else would his aunt have heard of it?

Had the duke heard it? Had Manderbey heard about it? Had Lady Winsome herself heard of it? Had Lady Edith heard it?

Aside from his aunt, those four people would be exceedingly angry. He did not like people to be angry with him. Angry people were prone to say terrible things and threaten to do terrible things. He never could stand up against it.

How had such a story got started?

Landry rubbed his chin. He'd been gone for an extended time, had Lady Winsome also been missing for longer than expected too? Could it be that ridiculous? The dowager had encountered them in the corridor, had that lady talked about it? Had she made some speculation about it? It was outrageous if she had, as she must know of Manderbey's interest in Lady Winsome.

But if not her, then who? The only other person he'd even got a glimpse of was St. John—he'd poked his head out of the ballroom, no doubt having repaired there to refill his wine from one of the sideboards.

Landry imagined he probably should not have run away from the dowager like a criminal. Perhaps that had made him look guilty of doing something. He *was* guilty of doing something, but not of compromising a lady. He'd compromised a chamber pot and was only trying to get as far away from the evidence as he could.

It was extraordinary that anybody would imagine he'd compromised a lady. He could barely speak to ladies. How on earth could somebody look at him and see a smooth rogue?

But it seemed that somehow that was what people thought.

He threw down his aunt's letter and hurried out of the drawing room to locate his butler. The fellow could usually be found in the dining room, as he was a stickler for examining every piece of silver for a water spot. The footmen usually hid while he was checking, lest they get blamed for anything found.

As expected, there he was, examining a fork with a quizzing glass. "Marley," Landry said, "you did such a bang-up job keeping my aunt and cousins from entering the house."

"Thank you, my lord."

"Now, I wonder, for the next days, could you keep everybody out of the house? That is, if anybody was to turn up, could you keep them out too?"

"Everybody?" Marley asked.

"Absolutely everybody. There has been an unfortunate circumstance arising and I wish to be incommunicado until things settle."

Marley nodded thoughtfully. "I'll see to it, my lord."

"You really are a good sort of fellow, Marley. I ought to give you another raise."

"Thank you, my lord."

Just then, there was a pounding on the door. Landry whipped round and stared into the great hall in horror. Marley put the fork down and said, "I'll manage it, my lord."

"Good man," Landry whispered as Marley strode past him.

He hid behind the doorframe as his butler answered the door.

"I must see Landry this instant, I do not care if he is busy, it is of the utmost importance."

Landry shuddered. It was Manderbey. He sounded angry. He was such a large man, he could pick him up and throw him across the room if he chose. He'd never done such a thing, but there was always a first time!

"I am sorry, my lord, but Lord Landry fell down the stairs this morning and is currently unconscious," his butler said.

Unconscious? That was good, very good indeed. A person who lay unconscious could not be interrogated or thrown across a room. An unconscious person must be left alone. Marley really was so clever. He ought to give the fellow another raise.

"Does a physician attend him?" Manderbey asked.

"He is on his way as we speak, my lord. He is attended by the housekeeper until that gentleman arrives."

"I see. Bad luck, that. Of course I hope he makes a speedy recovery. Send updates to my house, I would like to keep apprised of the situation and be alerted immediately when he regains consciousness. I really do have something of import that must be discussed between us."

"Of course, my lord."

Landry listened to Manderbey depart and then tiptoed to the windows and peered out. The lord got on his horse looking very annoyed. He wanted to be informed the moment he regained consciousness! He would come back!

Marley returned to the dining room. "He is gone, my lord."

"Yes, yes, very good," Landry said. "Marley, that was an excellent notion about me falling down the stairs and becoming unconscious. I will take to my bed. Let nobody in! Everybody is to know I lay quite unconscious and can see nobody. I cannot answer any questions—I am entirely indisposed!"

"Very good, my lord. Shall I send up a tea tray?"

"Jolly notion, yes, I will lie in bed with tea. And perhaps a drop of laudanum for my nerves."

Landry hurried above stairs and called for his valet. In not many more minutes, he was safe underneath his down covers and there he would stay until he was assured it was safe to come out.

LELAND HAD AN unsuccessful visit to Landry's house. The fellow had somehow managed to fling himself down the stairs with such violence that he was currently unconscious. It was most unfortunate, not only for Landry himself, but for the information Leland was sure he had.

He'd returned home as the weather did not admit for taking his horse to the park and he had no wish to be beset with questions or looks at his club. He was fairly sure that his interest in Lady Winsome had been noted and that this talk about Landry compromising her would be widely known by now. The dowager swore she'd told nobody, but she'd received a note from one of her friends asking about the situation. It made Leland wonder if somebody else had been inside the house and made the same leaps of judgment his grandmother had.

In any case, Apollo had made clear his opinion of the weather. He did not suppose any horse liked to be out in pouring rain, but his own seemed to take a particular offense to it. He kept pulling his head to attempt to look behind him. Leland was sure it was in an effort to catch his eye and let him know he was blamed for the discomfort.

The last thing he had expected upon his return was to find St. John awaiting him. He was there, though, with the dowager in the drawing room. If he were looking for money again, he would be sorely disappointed.

"There he is," the dowager said to Leland. "Well? Did Lord Landry admit his part in this shameful business?"

"Lord Landry is currently unconscious, having somehow fallen down the stairs at his house," Leland said gruffly. "As well, I am quite sure there has been no shameful business."

"Come now, Cousin, you cannot always have your way," St. John said. "The facts will not bend, not even to a marquess."

"If I'd been able to see Landry, I am certain I would have ascertained the facts. As it is, I will be forced to visit the duke's house and speak to Lady Winsome directly. I'd rather not do it, as it must be an affront to the lady to be questioned on such a matter, but unless Landry wakes up sometime soon, I will need to. Something needs to be said to quell these ridiculous rumors."

St. John was shaking his head vigorously. "I just heard at White's that the duke has taken Lady Winsome to some old relation in Kent, leaving the youngest sister to the care of one of the older sisters. Not surprising, what else is one to do with an errant daughter?" St. John paused, then said, "Unless of course he will wish to send her further away. All the way to Brazil with me, perhaps?"

"Do not be absurd," Leland said.

"Well now," the dowager said, "I do like Lady Winsome and wish her settled reasonably. She cannot become a duchess, not after this. If Landry does not come through, then perhaps it is not the worst idea. St. John could certainly use the added infusion of funds and he really ought to have a wife if he is to be an ambassador. There are duties only a hostess can perform."

Leland suppressed the urge to throw both of them from the house. "I have no inclination to participate in these nonsensical speculations. I will get to the truth, and I am certain the truth is that Lady Winsome, and no doubt Landry too, are blameless. The *ton* talks too much and when they run out of truths, they invent things."

He strode out of the room and left the two hens to gossip together. It was frustrating that he could not solve the problem this minute, but with Landry unconscious and Lady Winsome gone to Kent, his hands were tied. All he could do was await Landry's return to the land of the living and Lady Winsome's return to Town.

Assuming she was coming back to Town. If she did not appear at the masque, then he must locate her in Kent.

Though this situation was vexatious in the extreme, it *had* served to solidify his plans. He would see Lady Winsome, secure her, and on no account was she going to Brazil with his idiot cousin.

MRS. RIGHT WAS not precisely certain what she ought to do. When Winsome had cut out letters to the word jumble from the scavenger hunt and Valor had such good luck unraveling it as the word "sewing," the housekeeper had thought that might be just the thing to do with the mysterious hint in Mr. Wicket's letter—Trulogap.

All along, she'd thought it was the name of a horse until Mr. Wicket had said it was a word jumble. She'd tried to unjumble it a few times with no luck.

She'd posed the idea of separate pieces of paper for each letter to Mr. Wicket and he'd written them down and cut them out. They'd spread them across the servants' hall dining table. Then the footmen came in and thought it a good game, Cook had a look, even the housemaids made a show of staring and moving the letters around.

After much false starts, Mr. Wicket had unraveled it.

Trulogap was Portugal.

At first, Mrs. Right had presumed it was not the right word, simply a word that could be made. Mr. Wicket proved it otherwise though, when he'd pointed out that the letter was a warning about a gentleman on a dowry hunt, had specifically mentioned that gentleman might be susceptible to bribes on foreign shores, and Lord St. John was currently empty pockets *and* poised to become the ambassador to…Portugal.

So…she had made a bit of an error there. She'd been certain the letter was about Lord Manderbey and Trulogap was a horse he'd bet on.

That might be easily forgotten, had it not been for what she'd done to avenge her girl. She'd had the idea that she might turn Winsome away from the gentleman completely by submitting a piece for the gossip pages of the newspaper. It read that the banns had been read in Lord Manderbey's home parish, and he was to wed Lady Edith Cullington.

In retrospect, perhaps that had been hasty. A bit quick off the mark, as it were.

The duke had returned from a fruitless visit to Lord Landry. Apparently that fellow was indisposed, having fallen down a flight of stairs and knocked himself out. That was not the really worrying part, though. The duke had come in with the newspaper under his arm, laid it on the table, and Winsome had picked it up.

Mrs. Right had done her best to distract, providing conversation so Winsome might lay the paper down. If that were to happen, she would find a way to get hold of the paper and burn it. What she would do after that, she had not the first idea.

So far, the offending item sat on Winsome's lap.

Whether Lord Manderbey had a gambling problem and got himself in debt or not, Mr. Wicket's letter was not warning about him. Trulogap was not a horse. The man to be guarded against was Lord St. John.

What had she done? If she were successful in driving Winsome away from Lord Manderbey, would it result in her driving her girl *toward* Lord St. John? He'd been to the house, he'd brought flowers.

The duke had left the room with Valor, as she was determined to show her father the improvements she'd made to Sir Galahad's bed. These improvements included several shawls draped over the top of the four poster and the evidence of two rows of knitting that would someday be a blanket.

Mrs. Right relocated herself next to Winsome. "Several things, my dear," she said. "First, that letter I found in the cellar, the one we thought was a warning against Lord Manderbey."

"Oh yes, and that awful horse he must have bet on, Trulogap."

"Yes, that's the one. Well, no surprise really that we would have leapt to that conclusion. However, it seems that Trulogap was a word jumble, just like 'sewing' was last night at the scavenger hunt. We were just an hour ago able to unscramble it and…it spells out Portugal."

"Portugal? The only person who has mentioned Portugal…oh, it is Lord St. John."

"Just so."

"Hm, well that is good news. I am in no danger of succumbing to Lord St. John's charms, whatever they might be, and am certainly not setting off for Brazil. Of course, I suspect Lord Manderbey has got himself in rather deep with gambling, he has said enough to indicate it, but at least he has not lost it all on a horse called Trulogap."

"That is how I see it, yes."

"Mrs. Right, you said there were several things?"

"Oh yes, I did, did I not? Well, as to the other thing, you know how hot I get when I feel like one of my own is in danger—"

"You did not mess with Lord Manderbey's carriage springs as you did with Lord Thorpe?"

"Goodness, you knew that was me, did you?"

"I could not think who else it might have been."

"No, no it was nothing like that."

"Case moths. You sent case moths to his house. Or you changed his grocery order and enraged his wine merchant."

Mrs. Right shook her head.

"Did you convince his valet he was to be let go? Or design an insulting print about him?"

"Not any of those things. You see, Winsome, I had become very afraid that you were not willing to give up Lord Manderbey, despite him being a terrible rogue. I could not help but imagine the disastrous future you would have and how much you would regret it. I had Mr. Wicket follow him and he was seen taking an expensive piece of jewelry into Rundell & Bridge and leaving it there. You see? He sold it."

"Gracious, can things be that bad? It must have been one of the dowager's pieces." Winsome tapped her chin. "I wonder how much the dowager knows about Lord Manderbey's unfortunate gambling problem."

"That I cannot say. Naturally, I was determined to save you from going forward with the idea of trying to change him. If he is willing to sell jewelry, well the problem must be very serious. I was all but forced to take steps."

Winsome looked at her enquiringly. Mrs. Right took the newspaper from her hands and flipped through its pages.

"I might have planted a story on the gossip page that Lord Manderbey was to wed Lady Edith. Ah yes, here it is."

"Oh, Mrs. Right," Winsome said, reading the paragraph the housekeeper had pointed out.

"I know, I know, it was a mistake. Even if Lord Manderbey is a rogue, I should not have done it."

"Or involved Lady Edith. I believe Lord Landry is very set on her and he is not, well he is not a very sturdy character."

"Yes, I did think of that, but then he is unconscious at the moment so will not know of it."

"And Lady Edith? Lord Manderbey?"

"Now I did think about that too. If you are really set on Lord

Manderbey then I suppose I cannot stop you. If that is the case, I thought perhaps we kill two birds with one stone. We could put another piece in refuting the news of the engagement to Lady Edith, and we could hint that the report of it comes from the same person who was just now sending round the false gossip of Lord Landry compromising a lady at Sir Jonathan's scavenger hunt."

"I see," Winsome said. "So it would seem as if there is a villain out there making all sorts of mischief."

"Well it's not wrong, is it? Somebody has sent round that story about you and Lord Landry."

"I am afraid it must have come from the dowager, though. She is the only one that saw us."

"I am doubtful about that. She's a duchess and those sorts like to keep things quiet when one of their own is involved. The dowager would not like Lord Manderbey's name associated with it and he's paid you marked attention."

"I cannot think who else would have said something."

"It could have been anybody in the garden noting that you had been gone for a period of time and then you did say your hair was a bit disheveled."

Winsome nodded sadly. "From crawling round the retiring room looking for a secret passage. Oh, and then Lord Landry did say there was someone else in the billiards room. A lord, though he could not recall his name."

"Well, in any case, somebody has invented the story going round about the scavenger hunt. This ridiculous bit of gossip I put in the newspaper gives us a chance to negate it."

"I suppose it's all we can do," Winsome said. "I was hoping Lord Manderbey might come to the house to inquire about it. Why does he not come? Is it because he would believe such a report?"

"Do not fret over it, my girl," Mrs. Right said. "I will be off to put in the new story." She paused for a moment. "You do not suppose the villain could be Lord St. John? The letter does warn us of him."

"I cannot think so," Winsome said. "If the culprit is the other lord in the billiards room, it could not have been Lord St. John. Lord Landry could not recall the name, but he knows St. John quite well."

"And you are certain you wish to go forward with Lord Manderbey, even though you know about his gambling? Before the season, you did say, repeatedly, that you would not be taken in by a rogue."

"I did say that," Winsome said. "I meant it, too. And yet, I feel there is a lot of good in Lord Manderbey, if only he can get this one difficulty under control. In any case, I tried to talk myself into turning away and was entirely unsuccessful."

Mrs. Right sighed. She saw clearly enough that there was no point in further argument. Of all the duke's girls, Winsome was perhaps the most stubborn in her opinions. The housekeeper also saw clearly, from living in the world longer, that the chances of a rogue reforming himself were slim indeed.

She was very afraid that Winsome would be the one daughter who ended settled unhappily.

CHAPTER FIFTEEN

W INSOME HAD SPENT the past two days waiting for Lord Manderbey to come to the house. He had not come though. She supposed she understood why. First the rumor that she'd been compromised by Lord Landry, that gentleman just now injured and unable to dispute the idea. Then the banns supposedly being read for a wedding between Lord Manderbey and Lady Edith.

He must be very out of sorts. He might even believe that she'd been compromised. And even if he did not, he would not like the gossip. He was to be a duke and would take that seriously. She had learned through observation that other gentlemen were not as freewheeling and freethinking as her father.

It was likely Lord Manderbey would not wish to be associated with such talk.

She supposed she would have her final answer at the masque. Perhaps he would not come. Or worse, he would come and cut her, as if he'd never known her. She did not know if she could bear that. She'd end up in the ladies' retiring room again, wiping her tears and not much caring if somebody locked her in.

Valor lounged on the sofa with Sir Galahad. "I guess you hate him now, so you can't get married," she said, clearly working to keep the glee from her voice.

"I very much doubt I will wed this season," Winsome said morosely.

"Don't worry about it. I bet Lord Manderbey never bothers you again. I bet he just goes away. When he realizes how you feel, he'll just go away."

"Valor, nothing has been said between us. He can have no notion of how I feel."

Valor shrugged. "Maybe he does."

Winsome sat up straighter in her chair. "How?"

Valor put her attention on Sir Galahad and said softly, "I'm knitting my dog a blanket."

"Valor. How would Lord Manderbey know how I feel?"

Her sister looked off into the distance as if she were divining the question. "Well you were mad. At least, it seemed like you were."

"Did you write another letter?" Winsome asked aghast. Valor's letters were atrocious and always caused their own particular trouble.

"Maybe," she muttered.

"But how? Charlie and Thomas have been told not to deliver any more of your letters."

"I disguised my handwriting and put it in the post. I doubt they even looked at it, but if they did I used Papa's seal so they would think it was from him." This was said with a certain amount of pride.

"What did it say? You must tell me exactly what it said. Oh Valor, I already have enough problems, I really did not need this on top of everything else!"

Her sister's eyes welled. She cried, "Well, I can't talk about it now that you're so mad!" She leapt from the sofa and fled the room, Sir Galahad trotting out behind her.

Winsome sat back. The problems were just piling up with no end in sight and Lord Manderbey had not come to the house. Now he was in receipt of a letter from her sister and heaven only knew what Valor had written.

She'd been very much perplexed when her older sisters had run into one thing after another during their own seasons. She was a lot less perplexed now.

LELAND WAS ENTIRELY fed up with the slow passage of time. He'd sent one of his footmen over to Landry's house several times, but the news was always the same—the fellow remained unconscious, the physician was with him night and day, and his condition was very much touch and go.

He could hardly believe that the fellow had managed to injure himself so severely. What had he done? Thrown himself down headfirst? For all that, he wished Landry a speedy recovery. Or at least to wake up for an hour so he could explain what had gone on at the scavenger hunt. Leland was all but convinced that Landry could clear it all up in a moment. If only he were awake.

There had been no news of Lady Winsome returning to Town and he could not be entirely certain if she would return for Lady Darlington's masque. He rather thought she would. The duke was not one to run from a rumor and the best thing a lady who was talked about could do was stare down the talkers. Staying away would seem a confirmation of the tale more than anything.

The masque was in two days' time and it could not come too soon. He would go. If Lady Winsome were there, he would speak to her in private as soon as he saw her. If she were not, he'd have to figure out where in Kent she went and follow her there.

Richards came in with a letter. "This just arrived, my lord. It was sent through the penny post and I believe the seal is from the Duke of Pelham, so I thought you'd want it right away."

She was back. He thought it would be so, though he was surprised she would have written him. He took the letter, and Richards closed the doors behind him.

As he read through it, he felt alarm run through him. She hated him? He was a rogue?

But then he got to the signature and clarity swept in to wash the alarm away. The only person who he'd heard call Lady

Winsome "Winny" was her younger sister, Valor. That little lady was also strongly opposed to her sister leaving the house. According to St. John, that young miss was currently away from the supervision of the duke and staying with a sister. Furthermore, it seemed a bit odd for a lady as sophisticated as Lady Winsome to write such a badly composed letter. Especially with every sentence punctuated with an exclamation as if she was shouting it.

Sir—

You probably already know that I have decided to hate you forever! You know I am right! You are a rogue, Sir, and I have found it out! Do not approach me for any reason! As a gentleman, you have to honor my wishes so do not say anything to me ever again! Stay away!

Lady Winny Nicolet

No, certainly this was some ridiculous gambit of Lady Valor's. She was a bold creature. He pulled a sheet of paper out of the desk and wrote her back.

Lady Winny Nicolet—

I received your recent missive! I do not believe you hate me forever! I do not know you are right! I am not a rogue, madam, and you have not found it out! I will approach you for any and all reasons! As a gentleman, I only have to honor the wishes that I actually believe! I will not stay away!

Manderbey

PS. Very entertaining, Lady Valor

He snorted as he read it through, answering each of her sentences with one of his own, equally hysterical. He would address the letter to Lady Valor and she could read it at her leisure when she returned to her house. He expected it would put some starch into her.

In the meantime, he would see Lady Winsome soon enough, one way or the other. Whatever confusion might be between them, it would be sorted out, they would face the *ton*, and with any luck they would face each other and plan a future.

The dowager bustled in with a newspaper in her hands. "I do not understand how you managed it so quickly, but I am delighted. Hips, that's the ticket."

"What on earth are you talking about?" Leland asked.

"The banns, what else. Lord, you must have hired a fast messenger." The dowager paused. "Unless this was what you planned all along and I have been somehow hoodwinked. And then, why not a special license?"

"What banns?" Leland asked, truly mystified now.

"Do not bother trying to keep it a secret now, it's in the papers." The dowager handed him the newspaper and pointed out a passage.

We hear that Leland Dunmore, Marquess of Manderbey and eldest son of the Duke of Albany is out of the marriage mart for any unmarried ladies interested. The banns between that future duke and Lady Edith Cullington have been read in his home county.

Leland laid the paper down. "What is this nonsense? Who is stirring up such trouble?"

"Trouble? It's just the thing. Mark me, she will produce a goodly amount of children and some of them are bound to be boys. She might not be a stunner, but her reputation is unblemished and she's got the hips for it. Just what is needed."

"Grandmama, this is all nonsense. I have not engaged myself to Lady Edith! And for God's sake, stop talking about that lady's hips."

The dowager pointed at the newspaper laying on the desk. "Says here, you did engage yourself, and I can hardly be blamed for noticing the woman's hips—they are very wide."

As if he did not have enough problems just now. What was

Lady Winsome to think of this? Was she to imagine she'd left Town for a few days and he'd engaged himself elsewhere? Then there was Lady Edith to think of. And Landry too, whenever he woke up.

LANDRY WAS GROWING used to living as an invalid. There was something comfortable in it. Trays came in on the regular with all sorts of things to distract him—eggs and rashers of bacon, rolls and butter, toast, coffee, tea, biscuits, an array of small sandwiches, and then always a very nicely composed dinner of several courses, accompanied by some of his best wines. He was surrounded by books his valet could read to him and Marley brought him the newspapers each morning.

As he was in his repose, Marley was downstairs barring the door against all comers. Manderbey's footman had turned up several times to inquire into his condition. The duke himself had come, which was a terrifying prospect. However, as far as they would know it, Landry was hanging onto life by a thin thread.

At first, the distant conversations being had at the door were alarming and he'd clutched his covers. Sometimes he could hear nearly all of it and sometimes just bits and pieces. After his two brutish cousins turned up though, he put all his faith in Marley. They insisted they would come in and his butler had given them a stern what-for. He'd dressed them up and then he'd dressed them down. What did they mean by it? Had they come to stare at a dying man? Had they no respect for the sanctity of such occasions? Did they think the Lord God would be pleased to see two ghouls harassing a dying man? Were they prepared to face the bishop, who was even now praying over him?

Those two creatures had turned round and left. If Marley could bar the door to them, there was nobody he could not keep out. He was determined to give the fellow another raise.

The days began to have a comforting rhythm to them and Landry began to wonder why he'd not taken to his bed long ago. It was safe and quiet and peaceful. He had everything he needed. He really was finding it a delight.

In the distance, he heard the door knocker, but he did not pull the covers over his head as he had done when he'd first retreated from the world. Whoever it was, Marley would get rid of them.

And then, he heard a familiar voice and his teacup clattered on its saucer. It was Lady Edith. What did she do here? Had she heard he was dying? He would not wish the lady to think so, as he still had a great determination to propose to her at some later date, when it was safe to go out of doors and he'd not eaten any greasy potatoes.

Should he call down to Marley? Send some sort of signal that he was still alive and she could go away? Where were a person's footmen when a person needed them?

Then he heard Marley shouting. Why was he shouting? What was he shouting?

The shouting came closer. "My lady, please do not proceed further!"

His door burst open. Landry clutched the covers around him. She was in his bedchamber—what was he to do?

"There you are," Lady Edith said matter-of-factly. "I suppose you've seen the banns and wonder what it's all about."

Banns? Was she getting married? To someone else? Had he waited too long?

"I can see from your expression that you do not have the first idea of what I'm talking about. Landry, you are surrounded by newspapers, do you not read any of them?"

Landry glanced at the pile that lay beside him. "Oh as to that, I was meaning to get to them. What banns?"

"There is a bit of nonsense in yesterday's paper about my supposed engagement to Lord Manderbey. Can't think who put it in there, my father's hair is practically on fire over it. Says if I do not come up with a real suitor we're going home."

"Oh dear no, I did not see."

"Over and over again this morning," Lady Edith said. *"Edith, if you do not come up with a real suitor we are packing up before the week is out."*

"Before the week is out?"

"So he says," Lady Edith said. *"A real suitor, Edith, or it's all up."*

"A real one, I see, well, it would be terrible to have to go home…"

Landry knew perfectly well that this was his chance. But it was all so untoward and nerve-wracking! He was in his night-clothes in bed!

"My advice, just spit it out, Landry," Lady Edith advised.

"Spit, yes, well, what I wonder is…do you want to get married…to me?" My God, he'd said it. He stared at Lady Edith in horrified fascination.

"Yes, finally. Very good, I am glad that is settled," she said, much to Landry's amazement.

Had it really been so easy? He'd just said it and she said it was settled?

"I can tell my father he can pour water over his head and calm down," Lady Edith went on. "Now, here is my advice to you. Do not speculate far into the future; you don't have the temperament for it. One step at a time, one foot in front of the other. It grows late in the day, so continue your repose, as there are times where a good lay-around is just the thing. On the morrow, get up and get dressed. You must see my father and then we must see Lady Winsome to assure her that all reports of my engagement to Manderbey are nonsense. I will call for you at eleven."

Lady Edith turned on her heel and was followed out the door by a dumbstruck Marley. As they went down the stairs, he heard her say, "Beef tea is what's wanted, it will put some strength back into him."

Landry lay back on his pillows. It was done. He felt a soothing comfort in the idea that Lady Edith had been so sure of the arrangements to be made! He was to rest until tomorrow and he was to have beef tea. She would take him round to her father. She would know what to say to Lady Winsome. She'd probably manage Manderbey too.

And that idea of putting one foot in front of the other was really rather good. It was very true that he did not have the temperament for considering the future—it made him nervous. Now, he was to just not think about it.

He suddenly laughed. His relations held no further power over him. With Marley on one side and Lady Edith on the other, he was invincible. He was safe.

The Earl of Landry had got himself engaged, despite all predictions to the contrary.

Winsome had wished the day to come and also wished for more time to stew in her father's house. She had not left it in some days. All they'd had on the calendar was a card party and the duke had been more than happy to beg off. Now, the day of the masque had arrived.

If there were one thing that did not hang over her head like the Sword of Damocles, it was her costume. She was to go as Cleopatra from her favorite Shakespeare play. She had decided on it long ago, as the dying for love was highly romantic and the dress was so interesting. It was all white, a very fine lawn, with a marvelous wide and stiff circular collar embroidered with gold thread on a blue background. There were matching cuffs of embroidered fabric for her wrists, and a gold-plated belt. She would carry a gilded staff, topped by the head of a serpent. She would wear a half-mask in gold, with a little fashioned gold lotus flower at the top.

In a few hours, she would don her costume, hold her head

high, and walk into Lady Darlington's ballroom to see what she would find there. She was just now in the drawing room pretending to enjoy her tea while secretly looking for her courage.

Thomas hurried in and said, "Lady Winsome, a Lady Edith and Lord Landry have come. Lady Edith says it is vital they see you."

Winsome was indeed startled. The last she'd heard of Lord Landry he'd been bedridden and asleep to the world. He must have made a recovery. And then why should they have come together?

She could guess it had something to do with the report in the newspapers that Lord Manderbey was engaged to Lady Edith. They would have no way to know that she knew it all to be nonsense, as her own Mrs. Right had put it in the newspaper to begin.

"Do show them in and bring up more tea, Thomas," she said. Goodness, she sounded so calm and unperturbed. It was just as she must sound at the masque.

Lady Edith strode in with Lord Landry on her heels. "Lady Winsome, sorry to barge in without so much as a by your leave," Lady Edith said.

"She did think it would be all right, though," Lord Landry said.

"I'm delighted to see you. Do sit. I've sent for a fresh pot of tea."

"Very gracious, I'm sure," Lady Edith said, taking a chair. "Now, I'll fly straight to the point, as I do not like to dilly-dally round a thing. This report of my engagement to Lord Manderbey is rubbish. I am engaged to Lord Landry. We've seen my father and it's all squared."

"You are engaged?" Winsome said to Lord Landry, entirely forgetting to appear shaken by the newspaper's gossip. "That is wonderful news. Really wonderful." She had thought Lord Landry had it in his mind, she just had not known if he could get it done.

"Yes, we're thrilled," Lady Edith answered for her betrothed.

Lord Landry nodded vigorously. Thomas hurried in with a fresh pot and two more cups and saucers.

Winsome picked up the pot and said, "How do you take it, Lady Edith?"

"A dash of milk. Landry will have plenty of milk and liberal sugar."

Lord Landry nodded. "She knows how I take my tea."

Winsome smiled in what she hoped was an approving expression. Lord Landry seemed poised to have every aspect of his life managed for him, and he seemed delighted to have it so.

Lady Edith took her tea and said, "Now that we've got that report in the newspaper cleared up, what are we to do about all the talk going round about that scavenger hunt? I, personally, did not believe it for a minute and was very stern with my father on that point. However, people do like to talk."

Gracious, she was direct.

Lord Landry hooked a thumb toward Lady Edith. "She knew I would never compromise a lady."

Lady Edith snorted. "Goodness no, could you imagine?"

"I do not know where the talk came from, nor what to do about it," Winsome admitted. "It was only the dowager there and I feel less and less confident that she would have invented such a tale. And there is still the question of who locked me into the ladies' retiring room."

"You were locked in?" Lady Edith said. "That, I had not known."

"I had not known it either," Lord Landry said.

"Yes, well, I did not mention it to anybody. My father knows, of course. I just feel that whoever did that might also have started the rumor, though I cannot think why. I do not have any enemies that I'm aware of."

"Most mysterious," Lady Edith said, tapping her chin with her forefinger.

"Lord Landry," Winsome said, "you did mention there was

another lord in the billiards room. Can you not recall his name if you really think on it?"

Lord Landry took that moment to turn several shades of red. "As to that, I might have been mistaken about somebody else being there."

"Mistaken about somebody being there? I do not understand," Winsome said.

Lady Edith looked him over, as if she were sizing him up. "Landry, was it the greasy potatoes?"

He nodded sadly.

Now Winsome was really confused. What did potatoes have to do with anything?

Lady Edith said, "My lord was faced with an untenable situation."

"Yes," Lord Landry said, "I really was."

Seeing the look of confusion on Winsome's face, Lady Edith said, "Lord Landry consumed an ill-advised portion of greasy potatoes that came back to haunt him, in private, if you get my meaning."

Winsome nodded slowly. She supposed she got Lady Edith's meaning. Lord Landry had experienced a stomach complaint?

"As you may know, these things can run very unpleasant," Lady Edith said.

"I was just trying to get away and blame somebody else!" Lord Landry exclaimed.

Winsome pressed her lips together. Now she did see rather more clearly. "So there was no other lord there."

"Nobody," Lord Landry said. "At least nobody I saw. I did think I heard a sound at the door, two times, but I never saw anybody. Oh, except for St. John. He was in the ballroom."

Lord St. John? The lord Mr. Wicket's letter warned about. The lord who had done some ridiculous pressing on the idea of Winsome relocating to Brazil.

Could he have done it? Could he have locked her in and then started that rumor? If he had, it would have been done to ruin her chances with Lord Manderbey. Did he imagine it would increase his own chances?

Could he really be so devious? Or perhaps it was revenge? Lord Manderbey owed him a gambling debt. But would he really go to such lengths to express his ire over not being paid?

And then, Lord Landry had heard a sound at the billiards room door twice—had it been that door being locked and unlocked, as hers had been? Had Lord Landry simply not known because he'd been…indisposed? If St. John had seen Lord Landry go into that room, which she now knew he had, then he likely also saw Winsome enter the retiring room. Perhaps he'd seen the situation and thought how he might use it to his advantage.

"St. John," Lady Edith said. "I do not like that fellow. Smarmy, for one thing. For another, I don't trust him and I've got very good instincts. I look at a person and I know what I'm looking at. He's got to be at the bottom of it."

"St. John, though?" Lord Landry said. "Why would he do it?"

"Perhaps he is angry that Lord Manderbey has not paid his debt to him?" Winsome said. "Perhaps he noted that Lord Manderbey…paid me certain attentions? Perhaps he wished to stir up trouble for that reason?"

"But that cannot be," Lord Landry said. "How could Manderbey owe St. John money when it is always St. John needing money *from* Manderbey?"

Winsome wrinkled her brow. "I do not understand," she said. "I had thought Lord Manderbey had got himself in deep with gambling and Lord St. John was one of his creditors."

"No, no, that cannot be right," Lord Landry said. "Manderbey is forever dunned by his relations. He jokes that they come out of the woodwork, trying to drain him dry. Now, I did think he'd informed all of them that are in the habit of gambling too much that he would no longer fund their debts. Whatever the situation, Manderbey certainly does not owe *them* money."

Dunned by his *relations*? Not dunned by creditors? Was that why Lord Manderbey had laughed it off whenever she'd mentioned gambling? Is that why he'd never seemed embarrassed nor claimed to have any hope of the situation improving? It was never him? It was his relations like Lord St. John?

"So," she said slowly, "Lord Manderbey does not have a gambling problem?"

CHAPTER SIXTEEN

IT WAS SLOWLY sinking into Winsome's mind that she might have been entirely mistaken about Lord Manderbey's proclivity for gambling. "Lord Landry," she said, "you are sure Lord Manderbey has not got himself deep into debt?"

Lord Landry laughed. "Not that I know of," he said. "He's never been keen on cards or dice. He does bet on one of his own horses from time to time in the usual way, but nothing too extravagant, I do not think. Anyway, he's very rich and can afford it, and far too sensible to get into any trouble with it. Why did you think so?"

Winsome swallowed a sigh. She'd thought it because she was the most suspicious lady living and had been determined to root out any evidence of roguishness she could find. She heard something, and then rather than consider all the variations of its meaning, she'd homed in on the worst possible meaning. Lord Manderbey had admitted to being dunned and she'd not bothered to ask why.

"I was misled by my own suspicions," Winsome admitted.

"Did any of those suspicions come from Lord St. John?" Lady Edith asked.

Winsome nodded. "Indeed they did. It seems I was taken in by him. He kept talking about what was owed, so naturally…"

"Ah, I think he meant Manderbey ought to haul him out of trouble every time he got in it because of the family ties," Lord

Landry said.

"I think we might confidently make the leap that Lord St. John is the villain," Lady Edith said. "He will be very lucky if he does not hear about it from me."

"She can give an awful dressing down when she wants to," Lord Landry said gleefully.

"My advice, Lady Winsome, is proceed to the masque this evening and straighten it out with Manderbey. He'll know what ought to be done about St. John. As for society, once you have it fixed with Manderbey they will close their mouths."

"Or she'll make them!" Lord Landry said, pointing at his fiancée.

Just then, Valor came into the room, looking very pale and holding a letter. "Lord Manderbey wrote me back," she whispered.

Lady Edith looked her over. "You correspond with Lord Manderbey? Whatever for?"

Valor appeared supremely uncomfortable at being questioned so directly. Winsome said, "Lady Edith, Lord Landry, this is my younger sister, Lady Valor. She was hoping that I would never leave the house and may have written a letter to Lord Manderbey to drive him off."

"That was bold," Lord Landry pointed out.

"Yes, she can be very bold, unfortunately so," Winsome said. "Val, let me see the letter."

Valor handed over the letter. Winsome scanned it. It was surprisingly shouting, with exclamations on the end of every sentence. As far as she could gather, Valor had written posing as Winsome and claiming to hate him and he must stay away. It was very encouraging that he wrote he did not believe it and would not stay away.

Then at the bottom, in smaller letters, "P.S. Very entertaining, Lady Valor."

He was so clever to at once see it was from Valor and not herself. She suspected using Winny rather than Winsome had given Valor away. As well as the general tone of the letter. Based on the response to it, Winsome guessed it had been ridiculous.

Lady Edith leaned over her shoulder. "He will not stay away. Excellent. Though why is he shouting? I never saw so many exclamations in one bit of writing in my life. Manderbey has never struck me as particularly hysterical."

"He's mocking me," Valor said darkly.

"Chin up, Lady Valor," Lady Edith advised. "If you keep sending out preposterous letters, it will not be the last time that happens to you."

Valor, shocked to her shoes to be so scolded, turned and marched out of the drawing room. She would no doubt track down Sir Galahad and pour out all her condemnations and refutations to him. He would, as always, be in hearty agreement.

Lady Edith and her grateful fiancé took their leave and left Winsome to contemplate Lord Manderbey's letter. It really was very funny and it did make clear he was not planning to go anywhere.

She felt lighter than she had in days. And, as for Lord St. John, he would not get anywhere with his machinations and ought to get on the first possible boat to Brazil. Very much alone.

LELAND HAD STARTED his morning with the newspapers and had almost fallen off his chair over what he read there. There was *another* piece about him.

This one had said that the initial report of banns being read was not true, which he obviously knew. But further, it claimed the writer had particular knowledge that a certain person was deliberately causing all this trouble, including the gossip going round about Lady Winsome being compromised at Sir Jonathan's scavenger hunt.

That, he would really like to know more about. He was certain Landry was the only person who could shed light on it. At a decent hour, he'd set off for Landry's house. Before now, he'd sent footmen and they'd not been admitted. He would demand entry and have a look at the fellow. It seemed impossible that he was still unconscious. These sorts of situations did not stay static. A person either improved or worsened.

Marley had appeared more than a little startled to see him at the door. "My lord, Lord Manderbey."

"Let me in, Marley. I demand to see him whether he is awake or not."

"He's not actually here, my lord."

Leland staggered back. "My god, he died?"

"Died? No, why would he die?" Marley asked.

"Because he was comatose and now he's not here."

"Oh, as to that, I am very sorry to say he never was unconscious, just frightened and hiding in his room. You know how he gets, thought you might wish to throw him across a room. But, it's all come right now. He's engaged to Lady Edith and they've gone off to see the lady's father."

Marley said all that as if it were the most natural thing in the world for a lord to pretend at being unconscious when he wasn't. And then the even more startling news that Landry had somehow got himself engaged. How in the world had that happened?

Pushing off those questions, he said, "I really must speak to him. Has he said anything to you about how this ridiculous rumor that features him as the leading man got started?"

Marley shook his head. "He doesn't know. He was on a chamber pot in Sir Jonathan's billiards room for a half hour, greasy potatoes he says, then he encountered Lady Winsome in the corridor and shortly thereafter your dowager. He did not wish anyone to suspect he'd been the culprit of…whatever was left in the pot. So, he ran away."

It was preposterous, and it sounded very much like something Landry would do. "When do you expect him to return?" Leland asked.

Marley looked at him as if it were an absurd question. "I do not know, my lord. That will be up to Lady Edith. She'll decide."

That also sounded right. He left and mounted Apollo. He took his horse to the park for a gallop as it was a fine day. As he did so, he tried to piece together everything he knew. Who was so bent on making trouble?

He'd thought the rumor that came out of the scavenger hunt had been just one more instance of bored matrons talking about whatever they could think up on scanty evidence. But the announcement of the banns, then the further announcement that somebody was intent on stirring trouble, put it in a different light.

If all of this was not simply coincidental, if it were part of a concerted effort, who was at the bottom of it?

Could it be St. John? Would he go so far? His cousin was irritated that he'd shut off the fountain of funds and had certainly expressed a wish to win Lady Winsome, despite how hopeless that was. Would he take active steps to get his way?

Leland was not certain he would. But then, he was not certain he would not.

He headed for home to get his horse and himself out of the unusually hot weather. He would change clothes and take another of his horses to visit St. John. He'd just come right out and ask him.

He might admit to it, he might deny it. Whichever way he went, Leland could express that it was to come to an end, regardless of who was doing it. He would send a message and that ought to be enough.

Then tonight, he would see Lady Winsome. She must have returned to Town by now. She must have plans to attend the masque.

If she did not, Leland would discover which sister Lady Valor stayed with and demand to know where in Kent Lady Winsome could be found. After that absurd letter she'd sent him, Lady Valor owed him a favor. He hoped it would not be necessary, but he'd shake the information out of her if it came to it.

He would see what happened this evening, and then he would know what to do. With any luck, on the morrow he would not be setting off for Kent, but rather in the duke's study, looking for his approval for the match.

MRS. RIGHT FELT she'd flown a bit too close to the sun recently. She rarely made mistakes, aside from the several times that she'd imagined a gentleman was hurting one of her girls and then in answer to it she'd tried to ruin those men's lives.

Lord Manderbey had seemed just such a rogue and she'd been determined to sway her girl away from him. The housekeeper was older and more seasoned and she knew that excessive gambling could only lead to heartache. How many times had she seen it, even outside of the high and mighty? The man would become gripped with it, always trying to recover what had been lost, and then losing more. He would be deaf to the pleas of his family until there was not a sixpence left to them. She could see how Winsome's life would be destroyed and she wished with all her might that she could save her.

That had led her to take the rather dire step of announcing the banns.

But then Winsome had the idea that she would attempt to correct him in it. She became determined to rehabilitate him. That was even worse! Why did women forever think they were the cure when they always ended up being the casualty?

Still, what she'd understood from that idea was that Winsome would not be turned from the gentleman, despite the obvious risks. Once that girl dug her feet in there was not much anybody could do about it.

Winsome, of all people to connect herself to a rogue! She'd been so determined to avoid danger at all costs. Her head was filled with tales of innocent ladies, taken in by evildoers. She'd gone into the season suspicious and on her guard, lest she be one of the unfortunates. And then she changed her mind about it.

Mrs. Right had been apprised of her girl's steadfastness to the gentleman after it was too late to recall the announcement she'd invented about the banns between Lord Manderbey and Lady Edith. She began to think it was *she* who would be the agent of Winsome's grief. She had not been certain she could fix it.

But then after that ridiculous rumor of Winsome being compromised at the scavenger hunt went round, she'd had an idea. She could blame both circumstances on some villain nobody knew.

It seemed she'd come through it. It seemed Lord Manderbey had come through it too. Valor, that naughty little thing, had managed to get another letter out of the house. She'd posed as Winsome and screamed a bunch of insults of the written variety. Then Lord Manderbey had the temerity to scream back. What a letter he'd sent to her poppet.

Winsome was delighted with it, though Valor was in a stormy frame of mind on account of being poked fun at. Mrs. Right had counseled her that she must not do anything further, lest she was thinking up some plan of revenge. Someday, she promised, Valor would look back and laugh about this circumstance.

Considering the poor mite's expression, that someday would not be this particular day.

She had cheered Valor by letting her in on the plan for this evening. Winsome was to go to the masque and Mrs. Right had sent notes out to all her sisters. They were coming early and in force to escort her and it was a surprise. Valor was much mollified over the news, and then further cheered when she decided she'd better wear her hostessing clothes to greet their guests.

Mrs. Right had nodded gravely. Though Valor would not attend the masque, her hostessing clothes were more suited to it than any other occasion, including hostessing. She might have attended claiming she was an old dowager and nobody would have blinked.

Just now the housekeeper bustled into Winsome's room to help her into her Cleopatra dress. She found Valor in there too, sitting primly on a chair and already dressed in one of those ghastly hostessing dresses. The particular look for this evening was a dull green brocade with a very full skirt and the requisite lace fichu. She'd made some strange attempt at arranging her hair, with the crown pinned and some limp curls hanging down either side.

"How did you get dressed without me?" she asked Valor. Those dresses had at least a thousand buttons running down the back of them.

"Meggy," Valor said, smoothing out her skirt. "She came in to clean out the ash in the fireplace and I had her do my buttons and curl some of my hair. I assured her you would not mind that she stopped her work to do it."

This was all said in a graciously condescending tone so Mrs. Right presumed her little poppet was working hard to sound like the mistress of the house.

Winsome had so far said nothing, but only stared into her looking glass.

Valor pointed at her and said, "I haven't told her anything. I am getting very good at keeping secrets."

Winsome turned. "What secret?"

Mrs. Right sighed. Perhaps the first step in keeping a secret was not announcing you had one. Nevertheless, it was just as well it did not stay secret—Winsome could use some bolstering up just now.

"See? She doesn't know!" Valor said.

"It is not so much a secret as it was to be a surprise," Mrs. Right said. "Every single one of your sisters is coming to the house to escort you to the masque. You will arrive to Lady Darlington's as a regular ladies' army."

"What a splendid idea!"

"I would have thought of it," Valor said, "if somebody told me to think of something."

"Of course you would have," Mrs. Right said soothingly. She turned to Winsome. "Let us get you into this dress."

Winsome nodded. Valor jumped out of her chair. "I heard a carriage stop. I will go downstairs to hostess until you come down, Winny. Take your time, I've ordered champagne for the drawing room."

Valor skipped out of the room. Winsome said, "Since when can Valor order champagne for the drawing room?"

Mrs. Right shrugged. "Since now, I suppose. I imagine she directed Thomas to do it, she's always had that footman wrapped round her finger. Never mind what your imp of a sister gets up to. It is time to dress, Cleopatra, and go find your Antony."

WINSOME WAS VERY much buoyed that her sisters had come. Mrs. Right always knew just what to do to help them all. She would be supported on all sides by five ladies who knew her through and through and would always stand behind her, even if she was wrong.

She'd come downstairs to a full drawing room. The duke was delighted to see all of his daughters together and thought it a very good game to go to the masque in force. He was just now getting a report on his grandchildren from Felicity and Grace, Felicity dressed in a medieval gown and Grace as a milkmaid. The duke himself wore his favored costume—a white domino with red flames painted on the bottom of it that was supposed to represent the two times he'd set a lady's curtains afire. He would not give a toss for the idea that it looked very much like a vicar in a surplice going to the devil.

Valor had indeed managed to get champagne served and everybody seemed very jolly over the idea. She appeared enormously proud and carried round her own half glass of it, though Winsome knew she would not drink it as she thought it tasted terrible and the bubbles itched her nose.

Patience, Verity, and Serenity were dressed as the Fates—the Spinner, the Allotter, and the Inevitable. Each was dressed in similar Greek robes, only their hand-fashioned tiaras indicating which role they took. The Fates surrounded her just now as she told them everything she knew about the gossip going round about her, the newspaper mentions, and Lord Manderbey's hilarious response to Valor's letter.

After they took it all in, Serenity said, "Here is a strange thing, Winny. Thorpe was out all day and I'd not had a chance to tell him I would be coming here and I would see him later at the masque. He would not mind it, I know, so I was not concerned about it. He got home as I was dressing and I informed him of it and he asked if I was certain."

"So he did mind it?" Winsome asked.

"No, of course not, he's too darling to mind it. He wondered over it because while he was out he encountered Lord Manderbey who wished to know if you had returned from Kent. Thorpe said he did not know. Then my dear husband asked me if you *had* gone to Kent and if I was certain you had returned."

"I did not go anywhere," Winsome said.

"That is what I said. But then Thorpe just shrugged it off and said Lord St. John told Lord Manderbey but he must have been mistaken."

St. John. There he was, making trouble again.

"How would Lord St. John make such a mistake though?" Verity asked.

"Perhaps he confused Winny with some other lady?" Patience said.

"No, I am afraid not," Winsome said. "I believe Lord St. John has been at the bottom of it all. He wished to turn me from Lord Manderbey so I suppose that is why he would tell him that I'd left Town. That is why Lord Manderbey did not come to the house, and I fretted terribly about it."

"Is Lord St. John so violently in love with you that he would stoop to such ungentlemanly behavior?" Serenity asked, dabbing at her eyes.

"Would that be a usual thing?" Verity asked.

"That is not it," Winsome said, lest Serenity turn on her eye faucets or Verity wildly speculate on it. "I believe it is all about the money. He was dependent on Lord Manderbey to fix up his gambling debts but that source of funds has dried up. Lord St. John is being considered for the ambassadorship to Portugal, the court currently residing in Rio de Janeiro. He had some notion of making his fortune mining precious gems there."

"Which would take money to get started," Verity said.

"My dowry, to be exact," Winsome said. "He made some very bold hints about how an ambassador ought to be married and how I might like Brazil."

"That devil," Patience said.

Winsome nodded, as indeed it did seem true. What sort of man was Lord St. John that he thought he could lie and connive his way into a dowry? Perhaps he might have got away with it, but Lady Winsome Nicolet had read a few too many novels to have the wool pulled over her eyes in such a manner. She was beginning to think any lady agreeing to set off for Brazil with Lord St. John would be lucky to even come back again. Maybe it would be more convenient to tip her off the side of the ship on the way back. He might stoop to anything that seemed convenient.

"As a general thing," Serenity said, "I do not like to be cruel, but in this case…"

"The point, though," Patience said in her usual toe-tapping manner, "is that it has not worked. Winny will go to the masque and see Lord Manderbey and they will talk and everything will be all right."

Winsome nodded. She had every hope it would be so.

"Well now," the duke called from the other side of the drawing room, "I suppose we'd better get this circus going."

Valor stood at the duke's side, nodding graciously. "Thank you all for coming," she said, holding up her untouched champagne.

Winsome smiled. It was time to go. It was time, finally, to see Lord Manderbey.

CHAPTER SEVENTEEN

L ELAND HAD MEANT to go and see St. John in the late afternoon and then return home to change into his domino.
However, it seemed whenever the dowager was nearby, all plans
must be upended.

The dowager was determined to attend the masque and then
remembered she had nothing to wear to it. Leland had counseled
that nobody would mind it if she wore her regular clothes, but
she became a regular badger about it. She must have something.

Miss Price had named for her several shops that might have
something that would suit. Miss Price had claimed those
shopkeepers would all lock their doors by six.

Time was suddenly of the essence and he was sent halfway
across London to dig something up. The first shop had stared at
him uncomprehendingly and had nothing but bolts of cloth,
ladies' gloves, and hats. The second had gone up into their attics
and, after an interminable time, returned with a moth-eaten
beaver coat and matching hat.

Leland had inquired what his grandmother was meant to
portray dressed in that ensemble. The shopkeeper had shrugged
and said he understood that trackers and hunters in the American
West dressed in such a manner.

So, the dowager was going to the masque as a moth-eaten
pioneer.

It was no surprise to him whatsoever to find the dowager

waiting for him at the door, flanked by the ever-nosy Miss Price. They examined his offering and declared it preposterous. He'd declared back that it was the only thing going and if the two of them had been more organized they would not be in this fix.

Miss Price had sniffed and claimed they could do something with it, before carrying it up the stairs. His grandmother lingered. "I will look a madwoman, but I've got to attend the masque. Important to be on hand, I think."

"I really do not imagine so," Leland said, hoping very much that she would choose to stay home rather than drape herself in moth-eaten beaver fur.

"We've got to broaden the search for a wife," the dowager said. "I found out that Lady Edith is betrothed to Lord Landry, so that's out. Good hips on that one, I still say."

Leland ignored yet another reference to Lady Edith's hips. "I am aware of the engagement and, as you are well aware, it means nothing to me more than good wishes for Landry. I am set on Lady Winsome."

"Un-set yourself! Her reputation is in tatters! First she is compromised by Landry and then that fellow leaves her to face it and instead engages himself to Lady Edith. It is one humiliation after the next."

"None of it is true, though," Leland pointed out.

"I do not think what is true and what is not true matters at this late date. What matters is what people think is true. Now, I am in no way against Lady Winsome. When two people make a mistake of that variety, it is always the woman who will pay the price and I recognize the unfairness of it. That does not change the situation."

"There is no situation."

"Manderbey, do see sense. Now, the best thing for Lady Winsome is to be far away for a long time. Then she might return and it is all forgotten about. Remember? Lady Wilhemena did just that after her indiscretion with Lord Moresby. She went off to the Netherlands for two years. One sees her everywhere now."

"Lady Winsome is not going to the Netherlands, Grandma-ma. I am tiring of this going round in circles."

"Who said anything about the Netherlands?"

"You did."

"Not for Lady Winsome," the dowager said, shaking her head at him as if he were a dolt. "I'm thinking of Brazil. St. John was here this afternoon and he's got the ambassadorship. He has graciously offered to step into this situation and rescue us all."

Leland had his back to his grandmother as he sorted through letters laying on the table in the hall. He whipped round to her. "He offers to graciously step in?"

"Well why not? He likes her well enough and she's got enough money. It will be good for her and good for him. Everybody wins."

"Do not be absurd."

"He is going to pose the question this very night, and if Lady Winsome has a sensible bone in her body she will accept. Furthermore, if you really had a care for the lady you would wish to do right by her. She must take herself out of view for an extended period if she is ever to recover her place in society."

"Richards!" he shouted toward the stairs. "I will be in my domino and off in the next quarter hour. Somebody get a horse saddled."

"Do not tell me you go to see her," the dowager said. "Have some control over yourself."

"I am going to see St. John. And as for control, perhaps look inward, Madam."

Leland took the stairs two at a time. His valet had the domino laying on the bed at the ready and he was quickly changed. The dowager made one last effort to stop him from going to St. John, with the ever-present Miss Price fanning herself as if the sky was falling. He paid them no mind and set off.

He trotted through the dark streets and thought of what he would say to St. John. He'd like to pound him, but would rather not end up on a green over it. He was by far the superior shot and equally skilled with a sword, but St. John could be impetuous and might throw all caution to the wind. If he did, St. John would not survive the encounter.

Unlike what his grandmother thought, Leland was not over-worried that St. John would get anywhere in attempting to press his ridiculous suit. No, it was that St. John was the author of all this trouble, he was sure of it. St. John, for selfish and venal reasons, had damaged a blameless lady's reputation and then would have the unmitigated gall to pretend to rescue her from it.

As if marriage to that man would be a rescue of any sort. St. John was too concerned with his own wellbeing to have a care for a wife. His wants and needs took precedence above all else. Whoever he eventually talked into it would end up miserable. St. John would forever chase the money, whether at cards or the stupid idea he had of mining precious stones.

Perhaps Leland ought to pay him off? He would not like to do it, but his cousin must be got rid of in some manner. First, though, he would ensure that St. John knew he'd been exposed in all his villainy.

He dismounted his horse, handed the reins to a groom, and banged on the door. He was admitted by St. John's rather startled butler who claimed St. John was not at home.

Leland did not have to guess if that were true of not, as St. John had just appeared at the top of the stairs. It seemed he was dressed as an old king. Henry the VIII, no doubt. Very fitting.

"What do you do here, Manderbey?" he asked in a suspicious tone.

"I would have a private word," Leland said.

St. John seemed to debate his response, then he said, "Very well, go into the drawing room. I will attend you after my valet puts the finishing touches on my costume, which is clearly more elaborate than your own."

With that, St. John disappeared down a corridor. Leland supposed he did not have much choice but to wait, as he would get this matter settled.

The butler led him into the drawing room and closed the door. Leland looked around, noting the signs everywhere of a man in financial straits. He'd even sold some paintings, as evidenced by the darker squares of wallpaper that had not had the same exposure to sunlight.

As he stood in the silence, he began to think he heard whispering in the hall. He walked to the window to be certain St. John was not attempting to slip out of the house.

A few minutes later, the butler came back into the room with a tray and a glass of brandy. "My lord, Lord St. John's valet is struggling the smallest bit with Lord St. John's crown. It is too big and he is making adjustments. Lord St. John begs your patience."

His crown, indeed. His cousin was a puffed-up idiot. At least he could be counted on to have decent brandy. St. John's pockets might be empty but his tastes had remained rich.

Leland took the glass and downed it in one gulp. Then he coughed. There was a bitterness underneath the brandy that came as an aftertaste. It was revolting.

He stared at the butler, who stared at him back. "What is in this?" Leland said.

Rather than answer, the butler backed out of the room and closed the door.

As the bitterness settled on his tongue, he understood what it was. Laudanum, and quite a lot of it. If he sipped it, he might have been all right, but he hadn't. He swallowed it all.

He had to get on his horse and get home before the worst effects overwhelmed him. He could take an emetic when he got to his house and might still be all right.

Leland made his way to the door. It was locked. The devil. He could already feel the effects beginning to steal over him. He did not have much time.

He staggered to the window. It was a long drop down to pavement. What were the chances of coming out of that sort of fall without a broken leg or broken head? And where was his horse? The groom had taken his horse somewhere. It would leave him to walk home and he'd never make it.

His head was clouding over rapidly. He staggered to the sofa and the room began to dim.

WINSOME WAS EVER so cheered. She and her sisters had been very merry. The six of them had squeezed into one carriage, leaving the duke to take the other. Valor had made a great show of waving them off in what Winsome supposed was meant to be a dignified manner, though there was nothing much dignified going on inside the carriage.

They had giggled and poked each other and whispered as if they were children again. It was so comforting to be all together!

Felicity said Stratton was terrified of encountering the feminine horde coming in force. He claimed he did not know what it was all about, but it was bound to be something hair-raising.

Grace claimed Dashlend had said nothing about it, but gave himself away. He had a habit of scrunching his brows whenever he was concerned.

Patience explained that Stanford had inquired if the other husbands knew about it. She'd said she thought so and he clearly wished to know more but she'd changed the subject.

Verity said that Wembly had whispered, "Oh, I see."

Serenity mentioned that Thorpe did not give it too much thought, as he was too caught up on whether or not Winsome had actually gone to Kent. In any case, he got a note from Lord Wembly that they were all to meet at White's and then would travel together to meet their wives at the masque.

Patience speculated that their dear husbands were to have some sort of meeting of solidarity at White's, to better withstand whatever their wives were up to.

"I do not see why our husbands should worry we are up to something, just because we all come together in one party,"

Verity said.

Felicity had laughed and said, "We have too often been up to something. And just have a look at us this moment, Verity. All together, we look very formidable. They probably have a right to be worried."

They looked round the carriage at one another and then laughed the rest of the way to Lady Darlington's front door. The Nicolet sisters piled out of the carriage, collected their dear Papa, and made their way inside.

As they made their way into the ballroom, Winsome looked round it. She did not know for certain what Lord Manderbey would wear, but she suspected it would be a simple domino and half mask. There were those gentlemen who would compose elaborate costumes, but that would not suit him. He was elegant and sophisticated; he would hardly arrive as Zeus or a Turkish potentate.

"Does he know that you come as Cleopatra?" Felicity whispered.

"No, I do not believe we ever touched on the subject," Winsome said.

"Well now, here we all are," the duke said jovially, "at the masque that is not a ball. Thank the heavens for good sideboards."

It was true that Lady Darlington's masque was not done in the usual way. There were some violinists providing soft music, but no orchestra. It was held in a ballroom, but there was no dancing. There was no supper, either. Rather, there were sideboards lining the room with all sorts, as well as footmen coming round with small bites of food. Verity had said that their father was so fond of the thin-sliced ham rolls, stuffed with herbed creamed cheese, that he'd been known to take over an entire tray. Verity suspected that the footmen were now well-acquainted with the duke and his habits and they would give him a wide berth.

For entertainment, everybody would drift round talking and

admiring one another's costumes before voting on them, prizes to be announced at the end of the evening. There were small tables placed here and there for those who did not like to be on their feet for hours at a time.

"Ho there, you," the duke called to a footman.

The young man trudged over to the duke, holding a tray of petite ham rolls.

"Might as well leave that with me," the duke said.

"Yes, Your Grace," the footman said with a sigh. Winsome suspected the poor fellow had been warned by Lady Darlington's butler to avoid just such a circumstance.

"He is so tall," Winsome said to Verity and Felicity. "I should be easily able to pick him out but I do not see him."

"I am certain he will come," Felicity said.

"He would not have sent that cheeky letter to Valor if he would not," Verity added.

As she talked to her sisters, Winsome caught sight of an alarming vision. A lady, who she believed was the dowager, had come into the ballroom in some sort of costume, though she was not clear what. She was dressed in an old beaver coat that swept the floor and topped by a too-large beaver hat slipping down her forehead. Very improbably, her slippers were covered in tufts of fur.

Perhaps she came as a beaver? It would be unusual, to be sure, but then Serenity had come to her first masque as a bee so Winsome supposed anything was possible.

The dowager looked round, then her eyes settled on Winsome and her sisters. She shuffled her way over.

Why was she alone? Why did not Lord Manderbey escort her?

"Duke, Lady Winsome, glad you are not hiding yourself away. Not the thing."

"We never hide," the duke said, "nor do we have any reason too."

"Quite right," the dowager said.

"Duchess, I am off to the sideboard to pour a glass," the duke said. "I presume you are not opposed to a glass yourself."

"Very perceptive, Duke, as always. That will be just the thing."

The duke set off for the nearest sideboard.

"I put the blame on Landry," the dowager said.

Winsome was stock still, hardly knowing what to say to that.

Patience jumped to the rescue. "That is a unique costume, Your Grace," she said. "I wonder if Serenity set off the trend of coming as wildlife when she came as a bee two seasons ago."

"Wildlife?" the dowager said.

"Oh, I did think, are you not a beaver?"

"Gracious no, I am an American Pioneer, that's what I'm told anyway. I'm forging my way across the desolate plains in a beaver coat. I no doubt shot the pelts myself and stitched them all together round a campfire, for what reason I cannot say, but that's Americans for you. Now where is St. John? He comes as a medieval king, but I've not seen him."

None of the sisters answered where Lord St. John could be, as none of them wished to see him, least of all Winsome.

"You must chin up, Lady Winsome. This talk *can* be defeated," the dowager said. "Simply retire from view for a good amount of time and then when you return it will all be forgotten. St. John is just the ticket."

What on earth was the dowager attempting to say? Did she mean that she believed the rumors going round? And worse, did she say that Winsome ought to accept Lord St. John's suit?

A feeling came over Winsome upon hearing such ideas. She had enough. She simply had enough of this nonsense.

"Your Grace," she said, "nothing would induce me to engage myself to the 'ticket' you mention. I believe Lord St. John is at the bottom of all these rumors and I believe he's done it for personal gain."

The dowager staggered back and Serenity caught her to stop her from tipping over. "Lady Winsome, you are surely mistaken.

St. John would never invent tales about a lady."

"I think it is you who are mistaken," Winsome said with some determination. "May I inquire why Lord Manderbey did not escort you here?"

The dowager waved her hands. "He had some idea of having words with St. John. I presume they have worked it out between them, they are family after all."

The duke had returned and handed the dowager her glass.

"Papa," Winsome said, "the duchess thinks I ought to hook my carriage to Lord St. John's horses so I might be out of society's view for a few years."

The duke peered at the dowager as if she were deranged, which Winsome very much thought she was. "Duchess, I would not sanction such a match, even if my daughter wished it, which she certainly does not."

"You do not think it a wise arrangement?" the dowager asked, looking exceedingly perplexed.

"Nothing more unwise, in my view."

The dowager appeared pensive. "Gracious, I was certain you'd be for it."

"No offense to any of your relations, but I do not care for the fellow," the duke said.

Just then, the fellow in question, dressed as a preposterously ornate king of old, approached. Lord St. John greeted them all in his jovial manner, though there was not much that was jovial coming back to him.

Winsome felt she was about to lose all control of her temper. Lord Manderbey had gone to see this fool—where was he? Had St. John invented some new tale that kept him away?

"Papa," she said, "perhaps you might take the duchess to our aunt? I am sure Her Grace would like to hear more about the tableau she witnessed at our dinner."

Her father would be as well aware as she was that Lady Marchfield was not in the ballroom. At least, not yet. Even if she were, what the dowager witnessed was not a tableau of any sort—it was her aunt's launching of Mr. Wicket as the new butler. However, the duke was nothing if not perceptive and took up the hint.

"Quite right," he said, holding out his arm. "Duchess?"

The dowager was not left with a choice, though Winsome was certain she would have preferred to stay.

"There was a tableau?" Lord St. John asked. "I hadn't heard about it. Now Lady Winsome I was hoping we might have a moment alone to speak? It is of some urgency, as I have been given the ambassadorship to Portugal. Time is of the essence."

The man was persistent and absurd. Winsome stared at him but did not answer.

Seeing he was not to get a response, Lord St. John hurried on. "What I say is, considering the circumstances, a match would be beneficial to both of us…considering."

Considering. Considering this rogue had put her in her current position to begin. Considering he was a conniving liar. Considering he had put her happiness at risk and she might even now be in danger of losing it.

Winsome said, "What did you say to Lord Manderbey when he came to see you today?"

Lord St. John glanced around him as if Lord Manderbey might be lurking nearby.

"Today? Who said he came to me today?" Lord St. John asked.

"The dowager," Winsome said. "Now, what did you say to drive him away?"

"Say?" he asked.

"Yes, you hear me clearly, my lord, what did you say?" Winsome asked.

"Best to come out with it," Patience said.

Felicity nodded in agreement. "We are like badgers, Lord St. John. You will not slip away from our grip until we've heard the answer to the question we ask you."

"Well I did not say anything, actually," St. John said, eyeing

Winsome's sisters, who were slowly circling round him and cutting off any escape. "I was taken up with the arrangements with my costume."

"He came to your house," Winsome said, "and yet you said nothing?"

CHAPTER EIGHTEEN

WINSOME AND HER sisters had surrounded Lord St. John. She was determined to pry answers out of him and her sisters appeared equally steadfast in the effort. Even Serenity, who would likely prefer to flee and cover her eyes, put a good face on it.

"How is it a gentleman comes to your house and yet you do not have conversation?" Winsome asked. "That does not ring true."

Lord St. John nodded vigorously. "I really did not say anything to him. Except that I was busy."

"Why should we believe you?" Verity asked.

"Believe me? Why would you not?" Lord St. John asked.

"I would not because I believe you to be the author of this terrible rumor about me having been compromised. I believe you are the one that locked me in the ladies' retiring room, then you took advantage of Lord Landry's absence from the party too, and invented a ridiculous story. I believe you did all of that because you were after my dowry. Now I think you've said some new outrage to drive him off, which is why he does not appear."

"Or worse," Verity said.

Winsome turned to Verity. "Worse? Do you think this rogue would have done something to Lord Manderbey?"

"I do not believe we can put anything beyond Lord St. John at this point," Felicity said.

"He has proved himself to be a villain," Grace added. "Who knows what a villain might do."

"Winsome will know better than anybody," Verity pointed out. "From her novels."

"We ought to beat the truth out of him," Patience said, as they all moved closer to him.

"I do not generally approve of violence, but I will avert my eyes," Serenity said.

Winsome leaned close to Lord St. John. "Where is he? What have you done with Lord Manderbey? If you do not tell me this minute, I will make certain that my father involves himself in your life. He will see to it that you are stripped of the ambassadorship, every bit of your villainy will be widely known, and you will be drummed out of society. You will have no chance whatsoever of recovering your finances, which is the only thing you have ever cared for. No mama would allow a daughter within a mile of you so that avenue will be cut off. We will utterly ruin you."

Her sisters closed the circle round Lord St. John tighter. "Ruin you," the sisters all whispered.

"Stop it!" Lord St. John cried. "I don't know what happened to him."

"When did he leave your house?"

The guilt that passed over Lord St. John's features at that moment gave Winsome the idea that Lord Manderbey might not have left the house at all. "What did you do? Have you locked him your cellars? Have you injured him in some way?"

Lord St. John took that moment to break free. He knocked Serenity to the ground and ran from the ballroom.

Patience pulled Serenity to her feet as onlookers stared.

"We must go there," Winsome said. "We must discover if Lord St. John has done something."

"He must have," Verity said. "He was terrified that we wanted to know when the lord left his house."

The duke pushed in and said, "What was that all about? Are

you girls handing out the what-fors to our hapless lothario?"

"Papa," Winsome said, "Lord St. John has done something, but we do not know what. Lord Manderbey went to his house this evening and has not been seen since. Lord St. John refuses to confirm that he spoke to him or if he even left."

"And Papa," Felicity said, "he was very pushy about wanting to talk to Winsome and mentioned what he called 'the circumstances' and hinted she ought to connect herself to him, as he's now ambassador to Portugal."

"My instincts tell me he's done something," Verity said. "This evening was his last try to convince Winsome to wed, and he wished for Lord Manderbey out of the way."

"Agreed," Grace said.

"I do not like to accuse," Serenity said, "but I agree too."

The dowager, who had followed the duke at a bit of a slower pace due to the drag of a heavy beaver coat, arrived to the party. "Why has St. John run out as if his hair is on fire? Lady Winsome, you did not refuse him? I am sorry to say I believe that unwise."

Nobody answered the dowager. The duke said, "Let us depart in all haste. We will get to the bottom of this no matter how many houses we must visit."

They hurried away, leaving the dowager staring after them in her absurd fur coat.

THE WORLD CAME back to Leland by degrees. At first, he dozed and touched wakefulness and dozed again, unconcerned about where he might be or why. Then he got the vague idea that he was on a sofa. It was not like him to fall asleep in his drawing room. He would not like his staff to find him in such a situation. But then, it was really too hard to get up. He could not seem to make his muscles work. He could not keep his eyes open, so he stretched and went back to sleep.

Suddenly, he was shaken awake. St. John leaned over him. "You've got to go, get up, my carriage will take you home."

St. John pulled him up sitting, his butler grabbed underneath his opposite arm.

"What…" Leland said, grasping at wispy ideas and thoughts.

"Come on now," St. John said. "I don't know why you went to sleep in my drawing room but you have to go home."

"Wait…you—"

"I, nothing!" St. John said. "It's not my problem you are indulging in…whatever it is you are indulging in."

"I did not…you…"

He was hauled to his feet and the two men dragged him toward the door. They dropped him in the hall and Leland could hear the butler's heavy breathing in his ear as they picked him up again.

What was St. John doing?

Out on the pavement, the butler got the carriage door open. As they attempted to get him into it, Leland heard the clip-clopping of a carriage coming to a stop and then a rather familiar and lovely voice.

"Lord Manderbey!" Lady Winsome cried.

WINSOME FELT A terror in her heart. It was as if one of her novels had sprung to life. She was certain Lord Manderbey was in danger and now the villain had made his escape from the ballroom. Thank heavens she had her sisters and her father by her side.

They had raced out of Lady Darlington's house, all six of them flying by Lady Marchfield who was just coming in the doors. As was usual for their aunt, she was dressed in something queenly, though Winsome could not pin the costume down to any particular monarch.

As Lady Marchfield caught sight of them looking as if they

were fleeing the evidence of a crime, she cried, "Roland! What have you done this time?"

"Set more curtains on fire," the duke called over his shoulder, knowing his reputation for setting curtains ablaze, accidental or otherwise, irked his sister to the ends of the earth.

Lady Marchfield hurried toward the ballroom, presumably to put out a fire that never was.

They burst through the doors and onto the pavement. Winsome fretted over how long it would take to fetch their carriage. The duke had a better idea. Lady Wilton was just arriving with her friend Lady Layton.

"Lady Wilton," the duke said, "we are in the midst of an emergency and must borrow your carriage."

The lady, startled but the sort who always liked to be in the midst of the action, said, "Of course. Ought I to come with you?"

"No, no," the duke said, pushing past her, "we will be quite the crowd as it is."

That turned out to be very accurate and they only managed it by Serenity sitting on Felicity's lap.

As they barreled toward Lord St. John's house, the coachman having been instructed to make all haste, Winsome wrung her hands. Nothing could happen to Lord Manderbey. If Lord St. John had harmed one single hair on his head, she would wring his neck. Or if she could not manage that, she would ask Mrs. Right to do something terrible to him.

Thankfully, Lord St. John's house was not far off. Winsome leaned out the window as they approached and saw Lord St. John and his butler attempting to force Lord Manderbey into a carriage.

"Papa, he looks hurt and they are kidnapping him!"

"They're trying to hide him," the duke said. "St. John would have guessed we might turn up. Shame I didn't collect my pistol."

"There are six of us and two of them," Winsome said. "We can overpower them."

The rest of her sisters nodded in solidarity. Patience even

pushed up her sleeves to be at the ready.

The carriage skidded to a stop and Winsome leapt out of it. "Lord Manderbey!" she cried.

St. John and his butler froze. Lord Manderbey shook them off and turned.

"Lady Winsome," Lord Manderbey said. He bowed and then promptly dropped to the ground, lifeless.

"What have you done to him?" Winsome said, running to him and pushing St. John out of the way.

"Nothing!" Lord St. John cried, in a voice an octave higher than his usual. "It's not my fault he overindulges!"

The duke took Lord St. John by the coat collar. "And yet, somehow, I believe it *is* your fault. Now listen here, you rogue, I understand you are shortly to be off for Brazil. You are to take yourself out of London tonight. If you do not, you will lose that ambassadorship faster than a strong wind takes a hat."

"But I—"

"There is no further need for conversation. Go inside, pack, get out. This house had better be empty when I return on the morrow."

"Come, my lord," St. John's butler said. "Come inside."

Presumably, the butler did lead St. John back into the house. Winsome did not see it, as she was wholly focused on Lord Manderbey.

He slowly opened his eyes. "Oh, how do you do?" he said to Winsome.

"Are you all right?" she asked, grasping his hand.

"Fine, fine, say, do you want to get married?"

"Hold on, now," the duke said.

"Papa!" Winsome said. Why on earth was he interrupting at such a moment?

"It's a fine sentiment, Manderbey, but it cannot be said in the condition you are currently in. You must say it when you are not under the influence of...whatever you are under the influence of."

"Laudanum, Your Grace," Lord Manderbey said, his head lolling back.

"As I suspected," the duke said. "Winny, we'll take him home and have the physician give him the once over and then I imagine he'll need to sleep it off."

"Winny," Lord Manderbey said, laughing to himself. "You called her Winny. That's how I knew. The letter."

"Yes, Valor's unfortunate letter," Winsome said.

"Cheeky minx," Lord Manderbey said, before his eyes closed entirely.

"All right now, girls, we have one very tall and sturdy gentleman currently incapacitated. Lady Wilton's coachman and the groom can help me get him in the carriage and then we'll all have to find a way to get in too. It will be a tight squeeze."

"I could stand on the running board, Papa," Patience said.

"You'll do no such thing," the duke said. "We'll all pile in somehow."

Winsome vaguely listened to these arrangements. She was far too busy holding Lord Manderbey's hand, watching his eyes slowly open and close as if he were trying to wake up, and thinking of his proposal. It might not have been flowery, but it was very much to the point. He must say it again on the morrow when he was not so…indisposed. She only hoped he'd remember that he'd done it.

Her father moved her gently out of the way so the coachman and footman could assist Lord Manderbey into the carriage. "Come now, my girl, get yourself inside the coach."

Winsome climbed in the carriage, and found Serenity back on Felicity's lap and Patience on Grace's lap.

"See Winsome, we have arranged it all," Grace said. "You sit there and Lord Manderbey can sit between us, and Papa across."

Winsome smiled. Her sisters really were so good. She sat herself down, leaving a space between herself and Felicity. The coachman and groom hauled Lord Manderbey in. There was a bit of a close call as they made to seat him across from Winsome, but

Verity slid over and took up most of the room.

Seeing they would have no luck in that direction, they propped him between Winsome on one side, and Serenity on Felicity's lap on the other. The coachman appeared dubious and did not seem satisfied with the arrangement. "I'm a'feared he's gonna slump over, my lady."

"We'll keep him upright," Serenity said from atop Felicity's lap.

The coachman nodded, though he did not look convinced. "I'll drive all careful-like." He climbed out and the duke climbed in.

Winsome's father looked at the arrangement and suppressed a snort. "They've got you all right and tight, Manderbey."

Lord Manderbey's eyes flickered open. "Right and tight," he murmured. The carriage jerked forward and he slid toward Serenity and Felicity. Felicity and Serenity helpfully pushed him back toward Winsome until his head rested on her shoulder. It was delightful.

The swaying of the carriage caused Lord Manderbey to several times loll over in her direction. Whenever he lolled the other direction, Felicity and Serenity pushed him back toward her.

She was so close she could smell the bergamot soap on his skin, and then him. His own particular scent. She felt the rough wool of his coat on her arm. At one point he leaned so far over that his cheek brushed her own. Winsome felt as if she could ride in the carriage all night long.

All too soon, they reached the square. It was another procedure to get Lord Manderbey out of the carriage, into the house, and up the stairs. It was initially thought that Charlie and Thomas might do it, but they collapsed under the weight of Lord Manderbey as they pulled him out of the coach. The coachman and groom were once more employed and got the lord into a spare room.

That room happened to be next door to Winsome's room as it was the only spare that had not had its linens packed away. She fully intended on listening at the wall when the physician arrived. She must hear that he would recover before she slept a wink.

Mrs. Right had been apprised of the situation but, fortunately, Valor had not. She was already abed and that was just as well. She would not be happy to understand that Lord Manderbey was just now installed only a few doors down the corridor from her.

Lady Wilton's coachman, who had done far more than he would have expected to this night, took her sisters back to the masque to be reunited with their husbands. It was imagined those husbands would be speechless to hear of where they'd gone and what they'd done. As for her sisters, themselves, they were exceedingly jolly and Winsome heard their laughter as the carriage trotted off.

One of the duke's grooms had saddled a horse and rode off to fetch the physician. Winsome had done what she could do, but now she must wait. Her father had sent her to bed.

Mrs. Right had been in to help her out of her dress and braid her hair. The housekeeper had also thought she might bring Winsome a cup of tea, but then changed her mind and brought her a glass of Mr. Perry's sack. Winsome was glad of it, as it would assist in unwinding her very wound nerves.

After Mrs. Right left and shut the door behind her, Winsome dragged a chair to the wall. The Grosvenor Square house was well-built, but not quite as solid as their house in the Dales. There, the stone walls were so thick a person had not a hope of hearing anything on the other side. However, Winsome knew from experience that these walls were not so thick. When she'd been younger, she and Verity used to listen to Felicity and Grace talking about their more grown-up problems and try not to get caught giggling. The night Felicity had talked of her love for Mr. Stratton they'd nearly died of laughter.

Now, she curled up with her glass of sack and leaned her ear close.

She heard Thomas come into Lord Manderbey's room. He said, "The duke has sent nightclothes."

"How are we supposed to get him into them though?" Charlie asked. "He's too heavy to move."

"We've got to try," Thomas said.

"We fell on the pavement trying to get him out of the carriage," Charlie pointed out.

"He's heavier than he looks."

"I know what we'll do, we'll get Mr. Wicket to help. He does little enough around here."

Thomas must have nodded, as she heard the door open and close and footsteps on the stairs. Not too long a time later, she heard footsteps coming back up.

Mr. Wicket said, "What happened to him? What's wrong with him? Did he fall off a horse?"

"He's drugged, is our understanding," Charlie said.

"Was it the French?" Mr. Wicket asked.

"No," Thomas said, "it was the ambassador to Portugal."

"Really?" Mr. Wicket said. "I suppose I've been out of the game too long. I'd no idea Portugal would get up to such a thing."

"Not *from* Portugal," Thomas said. "The English ambassador *to* Portugal."

"Why in the world…" Mr. Wicket said.

"Mr. Wicket?" Charlie said. "Perhaps you could lend a hand?"

That kicked off a lot of grunting and complaining.

"He's like a sack of bricks."

"Even heavier. It's like trying to move the Rock of Gibraltar," Mr. Wicket said.

Winsome supposed it was no easy task to move Lord Manderbey. He was a very tall and vital sort of man.

"I am sorry to say," Mr. Wicket said, "the nightclothes simply cannot be done."

Then Winsome heard rapid footsteps on the stairs and the duke's voice. "This way, Phillips. He's just in there."

"Very good, Your Grace," the physician answered.

Winsome laid her glass of sack on the side table and leaned

closer to the wall. She must know what the physician would say of Lord Manderbey's condition.

"Good God," Phillips said, "what have you done to him?"

"Nothing, Sir," Charlie said.

"Where are his clothes?"

"On the floor, just this moment," Mr. Wicket said.

"We've tried to get him into nightclothes," Thomas said, "but we're having a time of it."

"I'll say," Phillips said.

"We don't think it can be done," Mr. Wicket said.

"Never mind that. We've got to get him up and walking—it's the only way through from an overdosing of laudanum. He's got to stay awake and keep moving."

CHAPTER NINETEEN

W INSOME HAD JUST overheard the doctor claim that Lord
Manderbey must be kept awake and moving. Thank
heavens her father had sent for Philips, else they would have
allowed the lord to go to sleep.

"Won't he get cold if we're making him walk around while
he's not wearing anything?" Thomas asked.

"Probably," Phillips said, "but that will be a help rather than a
hindrance. His being uncomfortable will help keep him con-
scious. Let's get him up but be warned, he's likely to be bad-
tempered about it."

They must have roused Lord Manderbey as he shouted, "Get
off me, you rogues!"

"See what I mean about the temper, very usual. All the way
up, that's the ticket," Phillips said.

"Unhand me!"

"Calm yourself, Manderbey. You are at my house," the duke
said. "I thought you might sleep off your dose of laudanum, but
Phillips said you've got to be up and walking."

"Phillips?" Lord Manderbey said with a note of disdain. "Who
is Phillips?"

"My personal physician."

"Your Grace. It's you," Lord Manderbey said, as if just recog-
nizing him.

"It's me, all right," the duke said. "There now, let's get you
walking."

There was the sound of shuffling. "Excellent," Phillips said. "Let's keep him awake for several hours and then we should be in the clear."

"Who are you?" Lord Manderbey said accusingly.

"Phillips," the physician said with a sigh. To the duke, he said, "Do not expect much sense out of him for now."

"Excuse me," Lord Manderbey said, "you don't make sense! Why am I here?"

"Manderbey," the duke said, "try to concentrate. You are at my house. You've been dosed with laudanum and now you have to walk it off."

"Did Phillips do it?" Lord Manderbey asked.

"No, Phillips did not do it. Now keep walking."

Winsome heard shuffling. Then Lord Manderbey said, "What's his first name?"

This, apparently, was in reference to her father, as Charlie said, "The duke?"

"That fellow right there."

"Um, well, it's Roland," Charlie said, "though I never in my life said it out loud before now."

"Roland," Lord Manderbey said, "I'm going to marry your daughter and I'll have no complaints about it."

Winsome slapped a hand over her mouth. Gracious, she did not know how much laudanum Lord Manderbey had consumed, but it was having some unintended consequences. She counted on her father's good humor to avoid getting offended about it.

"I see," the duke said.

"I said no complaints!"

"My God this is going to be a long night," the duke said.

And so it was a long night. Lord Manderbey had, for two hours, had all sorts of pronouncements to make as he was walked back and forth. He rather routinely forgot who Phillips was and asked him why he was there. He swerved from calling the duke Roland and then duke and then back to Roland again. He even proposed Rolly as a nickname. He at one point was very suspicious about Charlie, for reasons only known to himself. At another point, Mr. Wicket must have stepped out of the shadows and Lord Manderbey had cried, "A specter!"

When informed it was Mr. Wicket, he said, "Don't know why anybody would have a fellow named Wicked in their house."

As the hours passed, he quieted though Winsome could hear them trudging back and forth in the room. His complaints began to be much more centered on reality, namely that he was cold, would like his clothes back, and would like to go to bed. Very suddenly, he said, "Your Grace, have I said anything...odd?"

He sounded much more like himself.

"Odd?" the duke said with a snort.

"I seem to recall, that is, it is a bit hazy."

"Best forgot is how I would look at it," the duke said.

"There now, I think we're out of the woods," Phillips said. "Let's put him to bed and I'll stay for another hour or so to make sure his breathing does not slow after he falls asleep. I can show myself out once I am assured there is no further danger."

Winsome crawled into bed herself. She was exhausted. Happy though. Certainly, Lord Manderbey would say the words at his first opportunity on the morrow.

After all, he'd been very determined to brook no complaints about it from Rolly.

LELAND WOKE IN a strange bed in a strange room with not a stitch of his clothes on. It took him some minutes to piece together what could have happened. Slowly and by degrees it came back to him. He'd gone to St. John's house, and his butler had given him a glass dosed with laudanum.

His memories were more disjointed after that. He recalled Lady Winsome leaning over him as he lay on the pavement, though he was not certain how he'd got there. Then he leaned against her in the carriage and she smelled like roses, then there was some fellow named Phillips telling everybody what to do and making him walk when he wished to be abed.

Leland sat up. Bits and pieces of the walking part of the evening drifted across his mind. Had he called the duke *Roland*?

He was fairly certain he had. He'd asked a footman what the duke's name was and then used it. Why in the world would he address the duke as Roland? He threw off the covers. It was early morning, the sun just coming up. He must find his clothes. He must be dressed. He must be presentable and see the duke at the earliest opportunity. The Duke of Pelham was liberal, but even a liberal duke might be mortally offended by being called by his given name.

And then, what else had he said? Something about not wishing to hear any complaints about his idea to wed Lady Winsome...He would brook no complaints, Roland...Leland had a horrible idea come over him and hoped he'd only imagined it. Had he called the duke Rolly? No, he could not have.

He heard a quiet sound in the hallway. With any luck, it was a footman and he could send the boy to fetch his clothes from wherever they'd been taken. He jumped out of bed and jogged to the door, cracking it open and peering down the corridor.

An earsplitting scream assaulted his ears. He turned and saw Lady Valor standing there. He quickly shut the door and leaned against it.

Then Lady Winsome's voice. "Val! What's happened? Gracious you look white as a sheet—was it a spider? Come into my room before you wake the whole house."

Leland thought it likely that Lady Valor had already woken the whole house. He did not know how the roof had not blown off from that shriek. Of all the people to be in the corridor. What was she doing roaming the house at such an early hour? He'd been under the impression that ladies stayed abed until late morning and had their breakfast brought to them. How could he be expected to have known one of them would be wandering about just after dawn?

He heard a door close and realized that Lady Winsome's room must be the next door to his own. He hoped she'd not heard any of his babbling last night. Or worse, she'd heard him address her father as Roland. Or Rolly, if he'd really done that.

"What's happened, Valor?" Lady Winsome said.

"Winny," Lady Valor said, her voice full of desperation, "that man is here! I just saw him!"

"Yes, Lord Manderbey was ill last evening and Papa brought him here so Phillips could treat him."

"He's here with no shirt on, did you know that? Why is he in there with no shirt on?"

"Oh, as to that, well I believe Thomas or Charlie would have taken all his clothes to Reynolds to be brushed and set in order."

"*All* his clothes? He has no pants on, either?" Lady Valor asked, sounding very disturbed to hear it.

"Never mind it, Val."

"Never mind it? I haven't even said the worst of it," Lady Valor said. "Oh, I don't know how to even say it!"

"Say what?" Lady Winsome asked, her tone full of alarm.

"It's too terrible."

"Valor. Tell me."

"I saw his chest."

"Well I'm sorry for that," Lady Winsome said. "But I'm sure it was just an accident."

"You don't understand," Lady Valor said. "There was hair on it. *Hair*, Winny. Black hair all over it. Not like on your head, but patchy. I never saw anything so bad in my life. It was horrible."

Leland wrapped a sheet around himself and sat on the bed, really not having the first idea of what he should do next.

He heard the sound of a door and then the housekeeper's voice. "What's this now? Thomas said he heard a shriek up here—is it another spider?"

"Mrs. Right," Lady Valor said, "did you know Lord Manderbey has hair on his chest?"

"Not specifically, no."

"It's horrible."

"He was looking out his door as Valor came down the corridor," Lady Winsome said by way of explanation.

"I was just coming for Sir Galahad and I had to see *that*," Lady Valor said. "You would not even believe what it looks like."

"Ah, I see," the housekeeper said. "Well I'd best have Thomas bring his clothes back to him. Reynolds was putting them in order. Now, Poppet, put the whole thing out of your mind."

"Out of my mind!" Lady Valor cried. "I'll never forget it for the rest of my life! I'll have nightmares about it!"

Leland did think nightmares was going a bit far.

"Lower your voice, Val," Lady Winsome said.

"I feel like my eyes are burning!" Lady Valor cried, not lowering her voice one decibel.

Her eyes were burning? Now that definitely was going too far.

"Your eyes are perfectly fine," the housekeeper said. "Forget you ever saw it."

"Why, though?" Lady Valor asked. "Why is he like that? Is there something wrong with him?"

Leland heard the housekeeper sigh. "Valor, men are different. That's all. Some of them have hair on their chest. Perhaps most of them, though I cannot say that for certain."

Lady Valor gasped. "I would positively die if I had that living on me. Winny, you cannot wish to ever see that. I thought Mr. Stratton staring at Felicity while she was sleeping was the worst of it, but it's not. You really could not bear the sight of it, trust me. What I saw will haunt me forever."

Leland found he was beginning to feel a little offended at this point. He understood a lady would be more delicate in her sensibilities, but being haunted forever by the hair on his chest seemed more extreme than it needed to be.

"Go downstairs to have your breakfast, Valor. Toast and eggs will make you feel better," Lady Winsome said.

"Maybe," Lady Valor said. "Mrs. Right, can you check the corridor? I could not bear to see that abomination a second time."

Now he had reached the heights of abomination?

"Valor, I know you just learned that word, but I'm not sure you entirely understand it," Lady Winsome said.

"I understand it, and I've seen it," Lady Valor said.

Leland heard the door open. "It's quite safe," the housekeeper said. "Come now, I'll take you downstairs and then arrange to have Lord Manderbey's clothes returned to him."

"He really needs to cover that up! Be careful when you go out there, Winny, just in case he hasn't," Lady Valor advised.

Leland listened as the sound of footsteps retreated. He looked down at his chest. He had not thought, until this moment, that it would be capable of scarring a person's psyche.

He heard another sound from the direction of Lady Winsome's room. It sounded like a window sash being opened. He tied the sheet around his apparently deeply offensive chest and walked over.

"Lord Manderbey," Lady Winsome called out the window. "Our housekeeper is seeing about your clothes. They should be back with you shortly."

Leland opened the sash to his own window and found Lady Winsome staring back at him. He pulled the sheet a little higher, lest she have the same reaction to the sight as her sister.

"Lady Winsome," he said. "I hope I did not disturb last night."

"I did not find it disturbing, exactly," she said, leaning on the window frame. "More interesting than anything else."

It was clear enough that she heard at least some of what had transpired. "As to that, I seem to remember that I may have addressed your father in an inappropriate manner."

To his surprise, Lady Winsome laughed. "Roland."

"Yes, just so."

"And then Rolly."

"I do not know what came over me."

"Laudanum came over you."

He nodded, a bit distracted by how pretty Lady Winsome looked in the sunshine. The copper strands in her hair sparkled and then there were those freckles dusting her nose. She was dressed in a simple white muslin and looked springtime personified.

"I hope there was nothing else I said that might cause offense."

"Well, let's see," Lady Winsome said, tapping her chin. "Oh, there was mention of brooking no complaints."

Leland did remember that. He said he would wed Lady Winsome and would brook no complaints about it. She did not look offended, which must be a very good sign.

"Ah yes, I did say that. Perhaps when I retrieve my clothes, we might speak in the drawing room so I might say my piece on that subject. In private," he added to make clear his meaning.

Lady Winsome gave him one of her pretty smiles. "This is private."

It was true, it was private, the two rooms looking out the back of the house. Leland had not imagined proposing out of a window while he stood with only a sheet wrapped round him, but why not? There was nothing typical or usual about the duke's household. There was nothing typical or usual about Lady Winsome.

He cleared his throat. "Lady Winsome Nicolet, would you do me the honor of marrying me despite all the problems that have been caused you by my relations? I cannot promise they will not cause trouble in future, but I can promise to hold you above all others, as I am rather stupidly in love with you and expect to remain so for the rest of my life."

She leaned further out the window and smiled. "Yes, I say yes, and I care not for any trouble coming our way."

She had accepted him. It would be the moment to reach for her and kiss her but she was too far away. They stretched out their hands but only managed to brush fingertips.

There was a knock on Leland's door and a footman came in carrying his clothes. "My lord?" he said, clearly surprised to see him hanging out a window and talking to Lady Winsome.

He said, "I'm getting dressed."

Lady Winsome said, "Hurry and I'll meet you in the corridor."

He ducked back in and grabbed his clothes. He did not suppose another sentence had ever exceeded that one—Hurry and I'll meet you in the corridor.

IT WAS DONE, he had said it. Winsome listened to the bangs and shufflings and Manderbey giving Thomas directions.

"My shirt!"

"Yes, my lord."

"Where is my neckcloth?"

"Just here, my lord."

"Well go ahead—knot it."

"My lord, I'd best get Mr. Reynolds for that, he's the duke's valet. I've never tied a knot on a gentleman—I'm not sure how you want it done."

"There is no time, just do your best."

A minute passed by and Winsome supposed Thomas was working on the lord's knot.

"It's awful, but it will have to do. My coat."

"Here it is."

Then, he shouted, "I am dressed."

Winsome ran out to the corridor just in time to throw herself in Manderbey's arms. He swept her up and whispered into her hair, "There you are."

She pulled her head away and gazed up at him. "Here I am," she said.

He kissed her gently, and she ignored Thomas's muttered,

"Oh my God," as he hurried past them. Manderbey pushed her up against the wall and kissed her neck, slowly moving upwards. He tenderly kissed her nose and she recalled he admired her freckles. Then he moved back down and settled on her lips.

Kissing her gently, his forefinger traced the outline of her cheek. "Let us be married in all haste," he said, his voice low. "I'll talk to your father, get a special license, and put the screws on St. George's to get an early date."

Winsome was more than gratified by his eagerness to get to a church.

He suddenly pulled back. "That is, if you wish to proceed speedily."

Winsome laughed. "I cannot wait to get a look at whatever horrified Valor."

This boldness took him entirely by surprise. "My lady."

"Well?" she said, laughing.

"Yes, well," he said, bending over to kiss her once more. He ran his fingers through her hair. "I adore your hair, I adore your nose and the freckles sprinkled across it, I adore your eyes and your lips. Really, there is nothing I do not adore."

Winsome giggled into his neck. "Wait until I make a habit of reading terrible novels to you, then we'll see."

"If it is very terrible, and I hope it will be, I will throw the book over my shoulder and carry you upstairs."

"Then I will seek out the most awful available. They will be positively ghastly and you will have no choice but to carry me upstairs."

"I think you will like my house in Torquay. It is not large—"

"But it has a view of the sea and a cozy little tavern in the town."

"Just so."

"Might we not go there for a wedding trip?" Winsome asked. "We might say we are going somewhere else and slip off there."

"You do not wish to go on some grand tour of some point of interest, swanning around in new dresses and everybody wondering who you are?"

"Not ever. I'd much rather unpack and settle in. It sounds very romantic there."

"If it is not, I will make it so."

Manderbey kissed her again and Winsome supposed she would not mind spending the entire day in that attitude. They might have done it too, if Meggy had not dropped a bucket full of ash on the corridor's carpet from the shock of it when she came upon them.

CHAPTER TWENTY

THE ASH BUCKET Meggy had dropped sent up a cloud of dust in the corridor. The girl shrieked and fled in the other direction, leaving the mess behind.

This recalled both of them to the idea that they were in an open corridor in a house full of people, including the duke. Or Rolly, as he was sometimes called.

While Winsome was assured of her father's good humor, Manderbey thought he might have pushed that good humor rather far the night before and did not wish to push it further by mauling his daughter in his own house.

Manderbey unhanded her and they proceeded down the stairs hand in hand and laughing. The duke was asked for a private word. Winsome could not know what their conversation entailed beyond seeking the necessary approval, though Valor did assure her that she'd given the duke a full and detailed accounting of what she'd been forced to view that morning.

Whether the duke had been equally horrified by the description would never be known. If he was, it did not stop him from accepting Lord Manderbey as his next son-in-law.

A half hour and it was done. The two gentlemen came out of the library to find Winsome pacing the drawing room and Valor sitting arms crossed and glaring at her.

As the duke nodded in her direction to indicate his approval, Winsome had a great wish to fling herself into Manderbey's arms again. She did not do so out of respect for her father, and they went into the breakfast room in a circumspect attitude. There would be time to be far less circumspect in future.

It came as no surprise to anybody that Valor trudged behind them deeply sighing and muttering to herself.

At table, Manderbey seemed to note Valor's absolute disgust for him and his person. He said, "Lady Valor, I feel compelled to compliment you on being a worthy opponent, right from the beginning."

Valor stared at him with rather dead eyes.

"I had a notion, though, that we might call a truce."

"Why?" she said. "All I have left now is my dog. You are taking my last sister away."

"Yes, I did think about that," Manderbey said. "But then I thought if Lady Winsome is going, why not visit where she is going? When we return from the wedding trip we will settle in my house in Torquay. It has a terrific view of the sea. Why not come there for a few months?"

Valor appeared skeptical, though it was the most darling proposal ever made. And then of course, nobody would ever know that they'd been in Torquay all along.

"Do you go walking around there with no shirt on? Because I could not bear to see it a second time," Valor said.

"Not in the corridors, at any rate," Manderbey said.

"Can Sir Galahad come?"

"I would not dream of leaving him behind."

Valor seemed to consider it. Winsome knew her well enough to know she desperately wished to say she would come. But she just as desperately wished to condemn everything about Lord Manderbey.

"I would also point out that my dowager lives there," Manderbey said. "She would find it a real blessing, as everybody knows old people are particularly drawn to you."

This happened to be one of Valor's strong-held beliefs. She was utterly convinced that she had the natural ability to cheer the elderly, despite pointing out to them that they were old, which Winsome was equally convinced they could not like. She could see that Valor wavered at the idea of an old person requiring her beneficial company.

"Val, I really believe it would do the dowager good to have you there," Winsome said.

"Well, I cannot say I am eager to go, especially because of what I saw this morning," Valor said, once more insulting Lord Manderbey for good measure. "But I wouldn't want an old person to suffer because of my own feelings. I am, before anything, charitable and gracious."

Winsome pressed her lips together to stop her laughter. She adored Valor, but the last two descriptives she would have come up with were charitable and gracious.

"There we go, Val," the duke said with a snort, "it's settled. Manderbey will send word that they've returned to Torquay and I'll take you and the dowager there myself. I have an old friend with very good fishing not twenty miles off. Mrs. Right and the boys will have much needed time off in the Dales as the house will be empty. Everybody will be pleased."

It was clear enough that Manderbey had arranged it all when he was behind closed doors with the duke, but Valor did not seem to apprehend it.

"What about Mr. Wicket?" Valor asked. "Where is he to go? He's not to come to the Dales with us, is he?"

"Ah yes, that fellow," the duke said. "I can't think how he's still hanging about the place. I was mightily surprised to see him last evening, as I imagined he must be long gone."

Charlie cleared his throat from the sideboard. The duke turned. "Charlie, if you know something, out with it," he said.

Charlie stood a bit straighter. "Your Grace, Mrs. Right has the situation well in hand. It seems Lady Marchfield is to pay off Mr. Wicket's debts if he can last the season. So he's been living in the wine cellar and keeping out of everyone's way. Then he'll be off."

The duke laughed heartily. "Our Mrs. Right always has a

plan. Lady Misery's head will blow off her shoulders to discover she's spent money on a fellow living in the cellar and doing nothing. Good fun. Can't wait to see what happens next year."

They went on rather jolly after that. Valor, having felt she'd saved her pride and insulted Lord Manderbey to her satisfaction, adopted a much better frame of mind. How long it would last, Winsome could not say. Her younger sister's worst fear was coming to pass—she was to be left alone with no sister by her side. Thank heavens she had Mrs. Right and Sir Galahad to soften the blow.

Lord Manderbey reluctantly took his leave near noon, intending on returning with the dowager for dinner.

He was to go home to bathe and change and then meet the duke at Doctors' Commons to arrange a special license with the archbishop. The solicitors would meet to work out the details of the contract the following day, though the duke was not at all worried about it. Manderbey had apparently assured him of a more than generous jointure and a ridiculous amount of pin money. And after all, the duke remained unaware of the gambling problem that never was.

Though the duke had warned Lord St. John that he would come to his house to ensure he'd gone, he sent Thomas to do it, as he was fully confident the fellow would have hightailed it out of London. It seemed that he had done so, as nobody answered the door and the house appeared closed up. Thomas had even walked down the mews and found the stables deserted. Lord St. John had gone far away and would go even farther still, all the way to Brazil.

As for Winsome, she took herself to the drawing room to fire off notes to her sisters that they must drop everything and come to dinner. She must have them all here. There was too much happiness to not have them here. Even Valor was much mollified once it was suggested to her that she ought to make lists of what must be packed in her trunks for her grand tour of Torquay. Once that was done, Valor began to compose a list of pieces of wise advice she might deliver to the dowager in a gracious and charitable manner. She intended to monitor what that lady ate very closely, as the vicar had once said avoiding rich foods and strong drink was the best way to keep a body in good working order.

LELAND HAD BORROWED one of the duke's horses to make his way home. He'd thought he'd have to send a groom to collect Apollo from St. John's stables, but he was speedily informed that the horse had been returned in the middle of the night. The groom told him that they'd all been dead asleep and woken by a pounding on the door.

The stablemaster had answered the pounding and been exceedingly perturbed that Lord Manderbey's horse was to come home without him. He'd demanded an explanation from the fellow holding the reins. At first he did not get one, but then he'd handed Apollo off to a groom and taken the fellow by his coat's lapels and lifted him up. He may also have hinted that a person failing to explain why he brought a horse without its rider might expect to be severely injured if that person did not give over a full explanation.

St. John's servant ended by explaining that they were packing the house up and leaving that very night and that Lord Manderbey was currently located in the Duke of Pelham's house on Grosvenor Square. The stablemaster had gone to the duke's house himself to check on the veracity of it and discovered it to be true.

Leland presumed his cousin had considered the duke's threats and thought better of taking him on. His ship was to depart Falmouth in a month and St. John would have relocated there.

He handed over the duke's horse to his groom to be returned to Grosvenor Square. Leland could already see the dowager peering out a window, lying in wait. He was ready for her. She could either fall in line or get out. If she wished to make trouble, he would personally put her in a carriage to the estate she'd once ruled. She could be bossed about by her daughter-in-law if that's how she liked it. No amount of threats or histrionics would turn him from it.

Leland proceeded into the house and she met him in the great hall. "Well? What in the world has gone on?" she asked.

He leisurely made his way into the drawing room, flipping through the letters that had been left in the hall for him.

"Manderbey!" the dowager said. "Where were you last evening and why did St. John run away from the masque and why did all those Nicolet girls and the duke chase after him? I demand to know what's happened."

"You demand? Very well, if you are so insistent, though I think you will regret knowing it," he said. "Your favorite grandnephew drugged me to keep me away from the masque, I was entirely incapacitated. He had the idea he would go to Lady Darlington's house and somehow convince Lady Winsome to wed him and set off for Brazil, though never was there a more preposterous idea. The Nicolets came to the rescue and installed me in the duke's house, availing me of their physician's services."

"I bet they'd liked to have you trapped there. The duke made it known he did not favor a match between Lady Winsome and St. John, though it is foolish in my view."

"I see. You have managed to entirely ignore the part where St. John meant to do me harm."

The dowager shrugged. "Was it really harm if he stopped you from taking an unwise step? His methods might be untoward but the end result…"

"The end result has been that I have engaged myself to Lady Winsome Nicolet. I leaned out a window and proposed to her, she accepted, and I gained the duke's sanction. I will go with the duke for a special license this very afternoon. St. John is the author of this rumor about Lady Winsome, which was so ridiculous on its face that nobody with sense could believe it. The idiot has since left Town, lest he be forced to face his villainy and lose the ambassadorship."

"Left Town?" the dowager asked.

He could practically see the wheels turning in her mind, looking for a way to salvage the situation. She would not get it, though. "The end result, Madam, is if you carry on as you have done, I will ship you home to the dower house you are meant to be living in, you can be bossed about by my mother, and I imagine she will be very happy to oblige. Oh, and do not bother with any absurd threats. I will not care if you do throw yourself on the road and shout that you are being abandoned to starve."

"That was dramatic," the dowager said, staggering back and collapsing in a chair. "Well now, if the rumor really is not true, I suppose we can face it down. Yes, I suppose we can."

Leland could see very well that the dowager understood when it was time to make a retreat. He meant for her to make a very full retreat.

"We will dine at the duke's house this evening. You will be delighted over the engagement. Further, you will never, ever, for one moment, cause Lady Winsome a minute's distress. Understood?"

The dowager barely concealed rolling her eyes. "What sort of person do you take me for? Why should I cause anybody distress?"

Why indeed. "Furthermore, you shall stay here, in Town, until you receive word to come to Torquay. The duke and Lady Valor will accompany you there. This evening, we leave for the duke's house at half past seven. Be prepared to be on your best behavior." With that, Leland left his grandmother to contemplate her future.

His own future was assured and his grandmother could do what she liked about hers. Considering how intolerable she would find it to be in the dower house in Sussex while the current duchess reigned supreme in the main house, he thought there was a very good chance she would cease causing him trouble. She was a rather fine old dowager when she was not causing trouble.

THE DINNER THAT evening at the Duke of Pelham's house was jolly, though there were perhaps two people at table who had to put a good face on it.

Valor chose her own particular route. She pointed out her gracious and charitable nature in agreeing to come to Torquay on account of an old person's feelings.

The dowager had taken a moment to understand that *she* was the old person in question. She did not make a fuss about it, though. She had examined her various futures and determined she could on no account live on a property where her daughter-in-law took precedence. Torquay it must be and she had no choice but to fall in line. It would be far easier to stop harassing her grandson than it would be to put up with her daughter-in-law marching around the estate as the new duchess.

Of course, Valor had not entirely given up her earlier strong opinions and made some dark hints about what she'd seen that morning. She stared accusingly at her sister's husbands as if they too were guilty of harboring the same terrible secret, though she did not specify what it was. Those husbands were left to wonder what in the world she had witnessed. They all had a feeling of guilt for somehow having the same secret, though they could not pinpoint what it might be.

Afterward, Fact or Fib was trotted out, and Lord Manderbey was pressed to reveal how he'd made his proposal. The party found themselves surprised that it had been done out a window, not least of all the duke.

The evening came and went and the days came and went. Manderbey always arrived right after breakfast and they decided what to do, mostly based on the weather. If it were fine, they might take their horses to the park. Manderbey got his first look at what a Dales pony could really do on these galloping excursions. It was lucky that the grooms that followed them were the duke's and rode Dales ponies themselves, as Leland did not know how any other grooms would have kept up.

If it rained, they might set off for Lackington & Allen or shopping for wedding clothes, though Manderbey found himself out of his usual milieu in the shops. The haberdasher would find him a chair near the door and he would wait until everything in the shop had been examined and taken or rejected.

He had often marveled at how quickly rumors and gossip spread over London like a settling fog. Now he understood it was not just passed from drawing room to drawing room and club to club. The shops were a hotbed of news. He began to become attuned to when something of note might be said. It seemed always to begin with "One hears the most frightful things, I can hardly bear to repeat them…though," or "I do not like to trade in gossip…however," or "Far be it for me to pass on a story…but."

Manderbey kept a sharp ear out for anything around the rumor of Lady Winsome being compromised at Sir Jonathan's scavenger hunt, but it seemed the engagement of Landry to Lady Edith and his own engagement to Lady Winsome had now made that story too improbable to repeat.

During these shopping excursions, they did not forget about Lady Valor. Winsome bought her no end of ribbons and bits and bobs. At a visit to Rundell & Bridge, Manderbey purchased an elegant emerald ring for Winsome and a pearl ring surrounded by chip diamonds for Valor. She'd not known what to make if it, but Manderbey claimed it was a tradition in his family to make a gift to the youngest in the wedding party. Valor considered it, and then she claimed that since it was a tradition, she must be charitable and gracious and accept it. It had not left her finger since.

When they were not out and about on the town, Winsome and Manderbey made good use of the quiet corners to be found in the Grosvenor Square house. There was a particular nook in the far back of her father's library that might have blushed if it could have done so.

The day of the wedding finally arrived. Manderbey had been as good as his word and wrangled with St. George's to get an early day. Winsome did not know how he'd done it, as that church was always booked months in advance, but she'd begun to see that her fiancé was a very enterprising sort of gentleman. For his part, perhaps an exceedingly generous donation had smoothed the way forward. After all, now that he'd cut off his relations who were squandering funds at a card table, he had plenty to spare.

Leland's father and mother, the Duke and Duchess of Albany had been sent the news of the engagement on the day it was settled. They were happy to receive the announcement. They had not taken the tack of his grandmother and launched endless complaints about his bachelor status, but they had begun to think it was high time he found a wife. He'd found a duke's daughter and they were well-pleased, as nothing more could have been asked for. Much to the dowager's disappointment, they were easily able to make arrangements for the trip.

Leland's grandmother held a real fondness for his father and was delighted to see her son after an extended parting. Her feelings over encountering the current duchess were another matter. She had always found the lady to lack the deference to herself that she felt she deserved.

The battle of polite but cutting words had gone on for years between them, but now the balance of power had shifted. The current duchess had put up with the dowager reigning over her little kingdom for years, but the mantle had been passed. She would now take her revenge in the most dignified manner possible.

This revenge wholly consisted of statements like, "Dear Dowager, do you remember the dreary looks of the main salon? I am very glad to tell you it is all gone—drapes, carpets, furniture, all of it straight into the attics. New and more tasteful furnishings have been brought in."

The dowager would strike back with something like, "My dear, I can hardly claim surprise. We all fondly remember your penchant for doggedly following a fashion, regardless of its sense. Goodness, I can hardly get out of my mind those green-brocade-covered shoes you were so fond of. I believe they even managed to startle the queen at one moment."

The duchess and dowager duchess might have swords out, but the current duchess was rather adoring of Winsome. As a mother is often prone to do, she based most of her opinion of her new daughter-in-law on the effect the lady had on her son's happiness. Further, she'd never particularly cared for her nephew, St. John, who she found a rather oily and smarmy creature.

Once the duke and duchess were apprised of St. John's villainy, the duchess's regard for Winsome rose even higher. As she said, while staring determinedly at the dowager, "When one with bad intentions attempts to pull one down, a lady with the requisite good breeding rises up to meet the challenge and refuses to be defeated."

The duchess's understanding that the dowager had been against the match made her even more firmly in favor of it.

So, in the end and despite her best efforts, it was perhaps due to the dowager that Lady Winsome was welcomed so enthusiastically into the Duke of Albany's family as the new Marchioness of Manderbey.

Lady Marchfield came to the service and the breakfast. As usual, she hardly knew how to comport herself. On the one hand, she must be happy that her niece was so well settled. But on the other, she felt her pride pricked. She had been certain that this time was the moment when her brother's gross mismanagement of his household would lead to disaster. It was not that she wished disaster on Winsome, it was that she would like to be finally proved right.

Lady Marchfield had been rather hopeful when she'd entered

the duke's house, as she knew Mr. Wicket was still on the premises. At least one of her butlers had persevered. She would pay off his debts and it was worth every pound and pence. She could at least hold her head up high on that account. It was a bit distressing that Mr. Wicket did not show himself, but she was informed he was currently bedbound with a terrible cold. She cheered herself by remembering that even if he was abed, he was here. That diabolical housekeeper had not been able to drive him out.

That she would discover later that all Mr. Wicket had done was live in the wine cellar could not take away the satisfaction she felt on the day of the wedding.

Lord Landry and his bride, Lady Edith, made a good showing. They appeared delighted with one another. Lady Edith laid out what Landry was to think and do, and Landry very happily thought it and did it. She'd pointed out that the chicken fricassee that had come round would probably do no favors to his delicate stomach and he seemed grateful to be informed of it. They would go on to raise a family in much the same manner—Lady Edith was their kindly despot and the rest of them her loyal servants. As everybody knows, this arrangement tends to work very well when one person is driven to be in charge and the other has a mortal fear of it.

The only dispute that ever arose between them was when Lady Edith was apprised of just how much Landry was paying his butler after an endless amount of raises for services rendered of the guarding the door variety. She might have got her way and reduced Marley's pay to what it had been before he'd become gatekeeper of the door, but in the end that fellow had protected her husband so she let it be. Marley retired with quite the hefty nest egg.

As was to be expected, all of Winsome's sisters and their respective husbands were in attendance at the nuptials. As was perhaps not expected by some of the party, so were the various children that had so far been produced.

Grace's son Miles was a young gentleman of six years old. He was just at an age where he had a great wish to be manly and did his best with it. His effort ended being a bit of a mixed-bag—at one moment he was gravely inquiring into the duke's stables and the next he was collapsing in laughter over a face Isabelle made at him from across the table.

Isabelle herself was now a young lady of four. She very much had acquired Felicity's temperament and the duke remembered all too well that it had taken his eldest daughter some years to master her temper. Isabelle was still in the midst of it and prone to becoming very red in the face when things did not go her way. The things in question tended to center on desserts and going to bed. Mr. Stratton remained shaken that she'd once told him she was going to run off and become a pirate, because nobody ever made a pirate go to bed. He'd foolishly inquired if he would be missed. In a very dark tone, she'd said, "Pirates miss nobody."

Patience's daughter, Lily, had just turned two and proved herself impossible at table. She wished to be on her chair, then under the table, then wandering off to find Sir Galahad, then weeping over a piece of chicken on her plate and demanding to know who put it there. She was finally sent down to the servants' hall with Mrs. Right to cry about chicken down there.

All in all, it was a very jolly Nicolet party.

CHAPTER TWENTY-ONE

T HE MARQUESS AND his new bride set off in the early afternoon to much cheering on the pavement. They were married, and they were on their way. As far as anybody knew it, they were on their way to Cornwall, having borrowed a friend's estate there. Nobody but the servants at Torquay knew they were going there directly.

Their plan was to stop for the night at Stanwell. There was a charming inn located in that town and, in any case, it would not be wise to carry on beyond sunset. Hounslow Heath was nearby and teeming with highwaymen. Manderbey might be confident of his ability to outpace, or if necessary outshoot, a thief on horseback, but he would not risk it in a carriage, especially not one carrying his new bride.

From Stanwell, they would make the trip in easy stages.

Winsome was delighted, as she'd never traveled south of London. She was also appreciative of the idea that there would be no innkeeper encountered who had suffered at the hands of her father's jests. There would be no celebration of Captain Cook Day, or requests for brocabbage pie or Grassington Hambac, only to be informed the duke had made the whole thing up. Those harassed innkeepers were all safely tucked away in the north.

The carriage made its way out of London and Manderbey closed the curtains and pulled her toward him, sliding her along the leather seat until she was in his arms.

"Marchioness," he said.

Winsome giggled at the thought. It seemed highly absurd that she was to be a duchess someday. Especially given how she'd carried on, imagining all sorts of things and almost missing her chance.

"I have to admit something to you," she said.

He wrapped his arms more tightly round her. "Is it not always the way? A man weds and then discovers his bride harbors a terrible secret. Out with it, my love. I am certain I can stand up to it."

"It is only a little bit terrible. I had thought, for some time actually, that you were an inveterate gambler and deep in debt."

"Did you really?" Manderbey said, laughing.

Winsome nodded.

"I'm rather surprised you said yes, then."

"Well, I had at first thought I must turn from you. I did come into the season determined not to be taken in by a rogue and it was looking like you were one."

"I am a bit shaken to discover what was going on behind the scenes."

"You ought not be, though," Winsome said. "I decided I could not give you up, therefore I must save you from your worst instincts. I was very firm about it. You were to be rehabilitated."

Manderbey roared with laughter. "I had no idea. Now that I think of it, though, you did bring up gambling several times."

"I am glad I was wrong, I did get swept up in all the ideas I'd read about in my novels. However, I would have been prepared to face it if I was not mistaken."

"I'm glad you were wrong too. I would never place my marchioness in such a position."

"I know that now."

"Come closer, you suspicious little minx."

And so they spent a lovely few hours rumbling along the roads in each other's arms.

The Falcon and Fox was a charming coaching inn and Manderbey had made prior arrangements with the innkeeper to have the best suite of rooms. He'd been asked if he wished to secure a private dining room, but he'd declined and indicated they would dine in their rooms. Alone. The waiter was to bring up what had been ordered and then get out and not come back.

Winsome had smiled at these arrangements and they'd both impatiently waited for the trays to come up. The rooms had a lovely view of the gardens, but they saw none of it.

After the doors were shut behind the waiters, Winsome took her moment to see what precisely had stunned Valor. She undid his neckcloth and stood on a chair to pull his shirt over his head.

She laughed and said, "What in the world was Valor so shocked over?"

"I cannot say, but I pray I do not shock *you*."

"Oh I doubt it," she said, jumping into his arms.

And Manderbey did discover there was not much that would shock his bride. After all, she had five married sisters—she'd heard every detail of what might go on. She was lovely, he was intensely handsome, they were wildly in love. Those ingredients tended to make for a natural and passionate coming together.

Later, they pulled the trays onto the bed and had a picnic of sorts, toasting each other, he with his claret and she with her sack. They fell asleep in each other's arms and found the day so delightful that they repeated it at each inn they stopped at.

The innkeepers at these inns might have been scandalized that the couple arrived, ordered trays, threw the waiters from their rooms as soon as the trays were delivered, ordered them not to come back, and then were not seen until the following morning. However, they'd all had their share of newly married couples and their bordering-on-rude habits. Turning a blind eye and pretending nothing at all had been noticed was the order of the day if one wished to own an inn.

★

As Winsome and Manderbey made their way to Torquay, St. John cooled his heels in Falmouth, waiting for the *Romulus* to set sail for Rio de Janeiro. There, he encountered Mr. Wellcurd and his daughter. Wellcurd was a tradesman from Birmingham with some sort of concern or other. St. John found both father and daughter impressed with his title and the idea that he was the new ambassador to Portugal. He also found Wellcurd the master of a very generous table and as he was short of funds this very moment, he allowed the fellow to fill him with food and drink. As he found out more about Mr. Wellcurd, he was very glad he did.

He could not recall precisely how the man had got all his money to begin, but Mr. Wellcurd was on his way to Rio de Janeiro to oversee his various investments in the mines he owned there. This was, of course, of great interest to St. John and he began to wonder if it would be too outrageous to wed the daughter of a tradesman. After all, the fellow did not have any sons. If he were to wed the daughter, when Wellcurd kicked off, the mines and all the rest of his worldly goods would fall to St. John. If there was one thing of benefit to a tradesman, it was they did not make a habit of engaging in entails. And then to think, all the work of finding a likely spot, buying the land, and digging the mine had been done for him. It was rather ideal.

Mr. Wellcurd was a boastful and rather irritating individual but according to him, the riches that were to be had in Brazil were astounding. Diamonds, emeralds, and topaz as far as the eye could see. And, though he was exceedingly uncouth, when they returned to England, Wellcurd could be left behind in Birmingham from whence he came. Nobody in St. John's sphere need ever set eyes on the man.

As for the daughter, she was pretty in the usual way, though there was not much going on between her ears. She laughed too loud, which must be a habit dropped. Her manners were middling and must be improved. Her mode of dress spoke too loudly, all too-bright colors, rather like her temperament. And yet, she did have that one irresistible attraction—the precious gem mines that would one day be his.

The thing was settled in a rather unorthodox manner. Once aboard ship and being in close quarters and St. John having his own stateroom, he did meddle a step too far with Miss Wellcurd.

That might not have made his decision for him. However, Mr. Wellcurd had discovered it and insisted they wed, else he'd pitch St. John over the side of the ship on a dark and moonless night. Considering Mr. Wellcurd's general outlook on life, St. John did not doubt he'd do it.

After sixty days at sea, they reached Rio de Janeiro. St. John had not had a clear idea of what he expected, but he was soon disabused of his more fanciful notions. It was deadly hot, the heat exacerbated by the water that seemed to hang in the air. The court was stuffy and boring, and nobody much cared to be impressed that he was the ambassador from England. It seemed the Portuguese ambassador did business with the English Crown directly and nobody was inclined to include him in any negotiations.

Things went downhill from there when it was discovered he must wed in a Catholic church. He'd needed a dispensation from one of their absurd bishops to be allowed, which struck him as the height of stupidity. It rankled that he was viewed as some sort of heathen for not vowing his allegiance to Rome.

He went through with it, all along keeping his eyes on the goal—mines brimming with precious gems. He'd acquired a rather tedious bride and he was well sick of her loud laughter before they'd even got out of the church, but she was his ticket to untold riches.

Finally the day arrived when he and Wellcurd were to set off on a journey to see the mines. They began on horseback, and in the beginning he did enjoy the silence away from his bride's raucous laughter. He was surprised to discover on that first night, though, that there was no inn to retire to. In England, there was always an inn somewhere nearby. Here, it seemed a tent was all that was on offer.

After three days of traveling forward and camping overnight, they reached a river and boarded a boat with a local guide. From there, they spent ten days drifting down sluggish tributaries and St. John thought he would go mad over the slow progress. The heat was unbearable and the one time he'd dipped his hand into the river he yanked it out again with a fish attached to it. The boatman had to club it on the head to get it to dislodge its terrible teeth. Coming as no surprise to anyone, a festering wound was the result.

Just as he was primed to suggest they get out and walk, as it might be speedier, they merged onto the main channel of the river. Rather than go too slow, now they went too fast. The boatman explained in Portuguese that "there were rains."

How much could it possibly rain?

He wished he'd never asked that question as he soon found out. It was not an English rain, as there did not seem to be separate raindrops. It was a solid blanket of water and did not let up for days. Each hour that passed seemed to enrage the river further until it was a maelstrom of swirling eddies and tree trunks that had been recently ripped up from their roots flying by their boat. They were tossed in the most offensive manner possible, and St. John really could not say how they came out of it alive.

He'd thought that must be the worst of it, but Wellcurd had failed to mention that the last five days of the journey must be done on foot through the jungle.

St. John realized that very first night that the jungle was not meant for man to be wandering round in. He was aware that there were peoples who lived somewhere in it, but he could not for the life of him figure out how or why. The sounds at night were terrifying and he was haunted by the distant shrieks of unknown animals. And then, was a jaguar silently watching them until all were asleep? Would he be dragged off in the middle of the night, never to be heard from again?

During the day, one had to examine every move lest one step on a deadly snake, of which there were many varieties. Crossing deep streams was problematic, what with the electric eels, caimans, and the previously met piranhas. The guide, in some effort to cheer them up, told them that the streams they were crossing were probably too shallow for bull sharks to bother with. Sharks in the jungle. Apparently, there were even frogs lurking about who could take down a man if one were so unlucky as to even touch their skin.

It felt as if the whole place was one murderous lunatic out to kill him. Despite his worry over dying, eventually he felt his spirits rise. Wellcurd told him they were mere hours from the glorious mines.

And then they arrived. St. John had sunk to the jungle floor. There was an encampment with a few desultory men lounging around, and a foreman with a very downtrodden look about him. There were several deep holes in the ground but St. John did not see the sparkle of emeralds, diamonds, and topaz.

Over the years, that mine would produce a handful of emeralds, just enough to keep paying the men to keep digging. St. John returned to England with a hand that never did work properly after the piranha had got hold of it, and a wife who would harass him with her loud laugh for the rest of his days.

While St. John was busy ruining his life in Brazil, Mr. Wicket left the confines of Grosvenor Square. His debts were now paid and he returned to his lodging. The Crown was eager to reengage his services, and he was eager to get back to doing what he did best.

However, the past years had taught him some hard-won lessons. Through intense bargaining, he negotiated a much more suitable rate of pay. It was such that he saved up and bought himself a house in Cheapside. He would eventually marry a lady who, despite his cadaver-like appearance, found his career quite dashing. A knock on the door in the middle of the night or a sudden trip of some weeks duration only served to send her romantic imagination soaring. She did not know particularly what her husband got up to during these forays, but she liked to imagine he was saving the Crown at every turn.

Mostly, he was just slinking around and listening, as he always had done. Though, he did not wish to disabuse his lady of her grand ideas. One time, he'd had a nasty fall while getting out of a carriage and developed quite the lump on his forehead. If his dear wife wished to imagine he'd been in a deadly fisticuffs, who was he to say he hadn't?

He on occasion spotted one of the Nicolets while they were in Town. However, they never spotted *him*.

Winsome and Manderbey had a lovely time making their way to Torquay. Before they left Stanwell, they'd stopped in a little bookshop and sought out the most dreadful gothic novel the proprietor had for sale.

The man had never had anybody come in to ask for his worst book, but he was happy to oblige. He'd been trying to unload *The Awful Happenstances of Grimwood Hall* by an idiot of a fellow named Richard Roydon for quite some time. Each time he came close, the would-be buyer read the description and put it back on the shelf. Why would they not? The duchess was down the well, then not down the well, then in a cave, then inexplicably down the well again. This sort of pap might play in London, but the ladies of his own town would not be caught reading such drivel.

Manderbey was delighted with it, as it was so badly written that it gave him the opportunity to throw it over his shoulder and leap at his bride before they got further than a page or two. *The Awful Happenstances of Grimwood Hall* became an institution of sorts in their marriage. Over the years, even inquiring into where it was would set something off between them.

The house at Torquay was everything Winsome had imagined. It sat just above the town on a hill and overlooked the harbor. She and Manderbey speedily settled into their preferred routine—rising early in the morning for breakfast on the veranda overlooking the sea, long walks along the wharf, stops at Manderbey's favored tavern where they happily shocked the men inside by commandeering the cozy, leisurely dinners, and long evenings alone with the sea breeze blowing through their bedchamber.

Eventually, though, they could not avoid rejoining the wider world. Word was sent to both the duke and the dowager that the couple had reached Torquay.

Mrs. Right and the staff would return to the Dales to spend their time however they liked. The duke would escort the dowager and Valor to Torquay before continuing on to his friend's estate for trout fishing.

The dowager found traveling with the duke not as amusing as she might have imagined. His Grace mostly slept and she was left with Lady Valor and that girl's dog as her company. This might not have been the worst thing to happen, but Lady Valor had some kind of diabolical determination to talk about how old the dowager was and what she ought to do about it at every turn.

The dowager was informed that she was drawn to Lady Valor because she was old, though in fact she was not drawn to her at all. She was continually counseled on aspects of her old age, much of it seeming to come from the girl's local vicar and centering on the benefits of a lace fichu and avoiding rich dishes and strong drink. If the little miss imagined the dowager would give up her wine, she was very much mistaken.

In between these diatribes, Lady Valor darkly hinted about something she'd seen on Manderbey's person, though she would never spell out what it was. The closest the dowager got to any sort of explanation was "I can still see it in my mind like it was yesterday." Her rude little dog punctuated these wide-ranging pronouncements with eruptions of the gaseous variety, some of them so overpowering that they managed to wake the duke from his slumbers.

At least the evenings at the various inns where they stopped were more entertaining. Every day was Captain Cook Day and the duke had composed a poem about it. The dowager could not say how amusing the innkeepers found it upon discovering the duke had made the whole thing up, but it did pass the time.

After endless days of prattling advice from the youngest Nicolet, the dowager was delighted to see Torquay. She hurried into her cottage and slammed the door.

Her peace was not to last though, as Lady Valor marched over every morning to take her out for a constitutional in the garden, holding her arm as if she were in danger of falling over. In the evenings, she would return again and walk the dowager over to the main house for dinner and heavily sigh if her plate contained things that were not recommended. The dowager was left in the uncomfortable situation of feeling as if she'd somehow acquired a governess.

This went on for several months until the duke blessedly returned and took his youngest daughter home with him. The dowager spent several days recovering from the experience.

Once she did recover, the dowager might have imagined that she would hold great sway over her grandson's wife, but that was not to be. Winsome was a firm believer in the idea that one must begin as one means to go on and she reined in the dowager's ideas. The new marchioness was the most stubborn of the Nicolets and she was steadfast in her protection of her new family. She understood that someday there would be children, and she must be the setter of tone and the arbiter of habits, not the dowager.

There were some initial skirmishes out of view of Manderbey, but Winsome was easily able to stand up to them. She was also in agreement with her husband. The dowager could behave or return home. The last time the dowager had claimed that if they tried to send her away she would throw herself on the ground and say she was being starved and ignored, Winsome had said, "Well, I do not know who would believe you if you did, but try it out if you like. Also, if you insist on keeping up with all these complaints, I will take up the guitar and play it at all hours."

This did give the dowager pause, as she very well knew she had no intention of throwing herself on the ground, the servants would not for a moment believe she was starved and ignored, and she had a real aversion to the guitar.

Through Winsome's steadfastness and well-placed threats, peace was established, as even the most crotchety dowager does not continue to wage a war that cannot be won.

In any case, it was discovered that the dowager was much more agreeable when she respected the might of her opponent. Over time, she and Winsome became great friends and fell into the habit of taking their tea together in the afternoons and reading terrible novels together.

The dowager, being nothing if not determined, hung on to life long enough to see a great-grandchild on the ground. In two years' time, Winsome would bring into the world a jolly little boy and his great-grandmother spent the last of her days being entertained by his wide-ranging moods and small accomplishments.

For now, all the Nicolets carried on with the lives they had established. Due to Valor not yet being old enough to be introduced to society, the duke was given a long-needed reprieve from his endless effort to launch his slew of daughters out of his house. He and his youngest, along with the intrepid Mrs. Right, retreated to the Dales to wait out the seasons.

In four years' time, they would descend upon London once more. Nobody involved in it could deny there was a lingering trepidation over the idea of Valor's turn, least of all Valor herself.

The End.

About the Author

By the time I was eleven, my Irish Nana and I had formed a book club of sorts. On a timetable only known to herself, Nana would grab her blackthorn walking stick and steam down to the local Woolworth's. There, she would buy the latest Barbara Cartland romance, hurry home to read it accompanied by viciously strong wine, (Wild Irish Rose, if you're wondering) and then pass the book on to me. Though I was not particularly interested in real boys yet, I was *very* interested in the gentlemen in those stories—daring, bold, and often enraging and unaccountable. After my Barbara Cartland phase, I went on to Georgette Heyer, Jane Austen and so many other gifted authors blessed with the ability to bring the Georgian and Regency eras to life.

I would like nothing more than to time travel back to the Regency (and time travel back to my twenties as long as we're going somewhere) to take my chances at a ball. Who would take the first? Who would escort me into supper? What sort of meaningful looks would be exchanged? I would hope, having made the trip, to encounter a gentleman who would give me a very hard time. He ought to be vexatious in the extreme, and *worth* every vexation, to make the journey worthwhile.

I most likely won't be able to work out the time travel gambit, so I will content myself with writing stories of adventure and romance in my beloved time period. There are lives to be created, marvelous gowns to wear, jewels to don, instant attractions that inevitably come with a difficulty, and hearts to break before putting them back together again. In traditional Regency fashion, my stories are clean—the action happens in a drawing room, rather than a bedroom.

As I muse over what will happen next to my H and h, and

wish I were there with them, I will occasionally remind myself that it's also nice to have a microwave, Netflix, cheese popcorn, and steaming hot showers.

Come see me on Facebook! @KateArcherAuthor